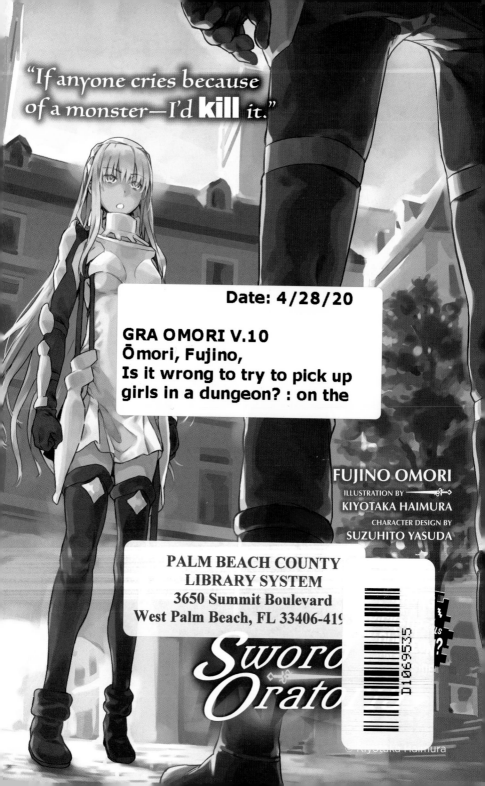

"If anyone cries because of a monster—I'd **kill** it."

FUJINO OMORI

ILLUSTRATION BY
KIYOTAKA HAIMURA

CHARACTER DESIGN BY
SUZUHITO YASUDA

Sword Orato

© Kiyotaka Haimura

CONTENTS

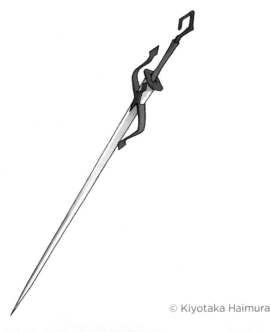

© Kiyotaka Haimura

ANAKITY AUTUMN:
A catgirl and member of *Loki Familia*. Everyone calls her "Aki."

"She's really taken with you..."

LENA TULLY:
An Amazonian girl and a former member of *Ishtar Familia*. Only has eyes for Bete.

"*Loki Familia* has way too many cuties and hotties! Bete is gonna get seduced!"

© Kiyotaka Haimura

RIVERIA LJOS ALF:
The vice-captain of *Loki Familia*. Elf.
The strongest magic user in all of Orario.

As for
me...
As Deimne,
that's the
one thing I
cannot do.

GARETH LANDROCK:
A veteran dwarf soldier and the
oldest member of *Loki Familia*.

VOLUME 10

FUJINO OMORI

ILLUSTRATION BY
KIYOTAKA HAIMURA

CHARACTER DESIGN BY
SUZUHITO YASUDA

NEW YORK

IS IT WRONG TO TRY TO PICK UP GIRLS IN A DUNGEON?
ON THE SIDE: SWORD ORATORIA, Volume 10
FUJINO OMORI

Translation by Dale DeLucia
Cover art by Kiyotaka Haimura

This book is a work of fiction. Names, characters, places, and incidents are the product of the author's imagination or are used fictitiously. Any resemblance to actual events, locales, or persons, living or dead, is coincidental.

DUNGEON NI DEAI WO MOTOMERU NO WA MACHIGATTEIRUDAROUKA GAIDEN SWORD ORATORIA vol. 10
Copyright © 2018 Fujino Omori
Illustration copyright © 2018 Kiyotaka Haimura
Original Character Design © Suzuhito Yasuda
All rights reserved.
Original Japanese edition published in 2018 by SB Creative Corp.
This English edition is published by arrangement with SB Creative Corp., Tokyo, in care of Tuttle-Mori Agency, Inc., Tokyo.

English translation © 2019 by Yen Press, LLC

Yen Press, LLC supports the right to free expression and the value of copyright. The purpose of copyright is to encourage writers and artists to produce the creative works that enrich our culture.

The scanning, uploading, and distribution of this book without permission is a theft of the author's intellectual property. If you would like permission to use material from the book (other than for review purposes), please contact the publisher. Thank you for your support of the author's rights.

Yen On
150 West 30th Street, 19th Floor
New York, NY 10001

Visit us at yenpress.com
facebook.com/yenpress
twitter.com/yenpress
yenpress.tumblr.com
instagram.com/yenpress

First Yen On Edition: November 2019

Yen On is an imprint of Yen Press, LLC.
The Yen On name and logo are trademarks of Yen Press, LLC.

The publisher is not responsible for websites (or their content) that are not owned by the publisher.

Library of Congress Cataloging-in-Publication Data

Names: Ōmori, Fujino, author. | Haimura, Kiyotaka, 1973– illustrator. | Yasuda, Suzuhito, designer.
Title: Is it wrong to try to pick up girls in a dungeon? on the side: sword oratoria / story by Fujino Omori; illustration by Kiyotaka Haimura; original design by Suzuhito Yasuda.
Other titles: Danjon ni deai wo motomeru no wa machigatteirudarouka gaiden sword oratoria. English.
Description: New York, NY: Yen On, 2016– | Series: Is it wrong to try to pick up girls in a dungeon? on the side: sword oratoria
Identifiers: LCCN 2016023729 | ISBN 9780316315333 (v. 1 : pbk.) | ISBN 9780316318167 (v. 2 : pbk.) | ISBN 9780316318181 (v. 3 : pbk.) | ISBN 9780316318228 (v. 4 : pbk.) | ISBN 9780316442503 (v. 5 : pbk.) | ISBN 9780316442527 (v. 6 : pbk.) | ISBN 9781975302863 (v. 7 : pbk.) | ISBN 9781975327798 (v. 8 : pbk.) | ISBN 9781975327811 (v. 9 : pbk.) | ISBN 9781975331719 (v. 10 : pbk.)
Subjects: CYAC: Fantasy.
Classification: LCC PZ7.1.O54 Isg 2016 | DDC [Fic]—dc23
LC record available at https://lccn.loc.gov/2016023729

ISBNs: 978-1-9753-3171-9 (paperback)
978-1-9753-3172-6 (ebook)

1 3 5 7 9 10 8 6 4 2

LSC-C

Printed in the United States of America

VOLUME 10

FUJINO OMORI

ILLUSTRATION BY **KIYOTAKA HAIMURA**
CHARACTER DESIGN BY **SUZUHITO YASUDA**

The Monologue of a Certain Girl

Гэта казка іншага сям'і.

маналог дзяўчыны

What would you call this feeling?

It might have originated as sadness or rage—or maybe even despair.

But it couldn't be encapsulated by any of these.

It was a sharper agony than being sliced by a sword, a deeper throb than being cleaved by an ax, a more painful sensation than being pierced by claws and fangs.

Its impact tore through her heart and left behind a bloody mess.

She felt a profound sense of loss—as though her very existence had been rejected. Just as she thought her heart had been stripped of everything, a tornado of jumbled and incomprehensible words rushed in to fill the void.

No…Get away from that.

I need you to stay by my side. Please don't leave me.

Don't show me this scene.

That is savage, despicable, something that should be abandoned. A detestable, loathsome thing.

Don't hold it close. Don't take its hand. Don't embrace it.

You can't show mercy to a plunderer, especially the guiltiest despoiler of this world.

Do you know its name? Do you understand what it means?

Its name is monster.

What would you call this feeling?

I'm not sure.

Should I call you a liar? Give you hell and say I won't forgive you? Tearfully beg you to stop?

Hey. I want to ask you—over there looking at me like you're about to cry:

Was I wrong to think we understood each other? Was it all an illusion? What are you doing? Why are you over there?
  Why are you protecting that monster?!
  You're cruel! Heartless! Inhuman!
  You're a traitor!

Her heart screeched out in pain without end. She couldn't keep the sword in front of her from trembling, and blood trickled from her ragged body like red tears.

Her limbs started to freeze up, as if a cold winter day had descended upon her and enveloped her in its memory.

She realized that she'd lost something irreplaceable and been left all alone. And that's when she opened her mouth, threatening to say the words that she vowed would never cross her lips again.

"Someone, please—"

CHAPTER
1

OMEN

Гэта казка іншага сям'і.

Аднаактовы ў лагеры

"We still haven't managed to find the key..." someone let out in hushed tones, but it echoed through the office awfully loudly.

The hands of the grandfather clock marked the evening hour in the corner of a room in the home of *Loki Familia*, Twilight Manor. As if to announce oncoming nightfall, the sky started to turn a faint crimson beyond the window.

The others in the room—Riveria, Gareth, and Loki—met Finn's comment with silence. The "key" in question was a certain magic item: Daedalus's Orb, a jewel with the ability to open the doors of the man-made labyrinth, Knossos.

Loki Familia was tracking the whereabouts of that orb using any means necessary.

"Tiona and the others have been looking, but nothing's come of it yet."

"We've found entrances to Knossos outside the city and inside the Dungeon. We're closing in, but...the enemy's holed up, as we expected. After Bete killed Valletta, they won't come out until the time is ripe."

The remnants of the underground force of Evils and the creatures under the control of the corrupted spirits were hiding in Knossos—waiting for a chance to fulfill their ultimate objective of destroying Orario. And their goal wasn't nonsense or a deluded hope, especially now that they were using demi-spirits. Orario was in danger, clear and present.

To stop the enemy and attack the impregnable labyrinth, *Loki Familia* needed the key to the orichalcum doors.

"I thought I was on the right track, but...that sex addict of a goddess plays dumb whenever I try to talk to her. She won't hand over any damn information," added Loki in a voice steeped in disgust from her perch on the edge of a desk.

This was fresh on her mind, since *Freya Familia* had just wiped out *Ishtar Familia*, which had been connected to the Evils' Remnants. And with the intel Bete had gotten from the former *Ishtar Familia* member Lena Tully, they knew Ishtar had been in the possession of a key, but she'd already been sent back from whence she came.

Loki sensed Freya was the one holding the "key"—literally and figuratively.

"...There's no time."

The conversation came to a halt, followed by a brief period of silence.

Finn spoke up solemnly. "Internal conflict...Well, that might not be the right way to put it. But if Loki's right that *Freya Familia* has the key, we have no choice but to weigh all our options."

Riveria's and Gareth's faces became grim.

Their captain wasn't ruling out the possibility of a struggle—aka a *somewhat* forceful transaction backed by more aggressive methods—if negotiations fell through.

It went without saying that the Labyrinth City itself would incur serious damage if the two familias at the top of Orario took an actively hostile stance with each other. And it was hard enough for the members of both groups to interact when they operated under the whims and desires of the two patron goddesses. This whole situation highlighted the pitfalls of the entire system of deity-led familias to begin with.

Finn planted both hands on the desk, narrowing his blue eyes, which seemed very much like the surface of a lake. He opened his mouth, ready to give out instructions.

"Captain! I'm coming in!" Raul barged into the room without knocking.

He was terribly out of breath, wincing when he noticed he'd stumbled into an obviously tense conversation. The gazes of everyone in the room shifted to him, and he gulped uncomfortably when he realized he'd done it again.

"Did something happen, Raul?"

"Um, uh...I was ordered to keep you updated as we get new info...! Though it's got nothing to do with Knossos..."

It's fine—just tell me, Finn urged with his eyes.

Raul flinched before glancing out the window at the cityscape. "We just got word that there was a disturbance on the west side of town—"

"A humanoid monster...?" Aiz parroted back.

"Yeah, yeah. It showed up yesterday in the western quarter," replied Tiona with dramatic flair, spreading her arms as she walked next to Aiz.

Beside Tiona, Tione frowned in annoyance.

The morning sun poured in through a row of windows.

After finishing her daily practice of swinging her sword, Aiz happened to run into the Amazonian sisters in a narrow hall of the manor. The two of them explained the uproar that had taken *Loki Familia* by storm the day before.

"And it's not an oversized monster...?"

"Apparently not. According to the lower-tier adventurers, it was like a harpy or a siren. I bet it's not related to the incident that happened during the Monsterphilia." Tione shook her head.

Aiz was basically asking if it was a man-eating flower, and Tione confirmed that this event was most likely unrelated to the monsters running free in the underground waterways in Knossos—the same monsters they had dealt with during the Monsterphilia incident.

Aiz cocked her head.

It was possible the witnesses had misidentified a beast-headed monster with a humanlike body—like a kobold, for example—for a humanoid. Humanoid monsters appeared only as high as the nineteenth floor, and it was difficult to imagine they could make their way up that many floors without being noticed by adventurers.

And first and foremost, it was a huge deal for monsters to appear aboveground in Orario, which was protected by Babel and its giant city walls. Aside from the Monsterphilia, bringing beasts out of the labyrinth was strictly prohibited. It was common sense that anyone caught breaking that rule would be harshly punished by the Guild.

"It caused a big fuss yesterday. A bunch of Guild workers are investigating things right now, apparently."

According to the reports, the alleged humanoid monster appeared in the middle of a street where regular folk were going about their day. If that was the case, it would certainly be major news. There was no doubt such an incident would cause the peaceful street corner to fall into chaos.

"...Does Finn know about it?" Aiz asked.

"Yep. The captain said he'd like people with free time to try to gather some information without drawing too much attention. I think he's got something in mind," Tione answered.

Finn must have had some thoughts about the incident if the lower-tier adventurers in the familia were already gossiping about it this much.

The appearance of humanoid monsters...If they're guessing it's a harpy or a siren, then it's gotta be a winged species...

And the monster might have concealed itself somewhere in the city, leaving the civilians in a state of perpetual fear. It was unbearable to imagine.

Aiz lifted her head and gazed at the ceiling, telling herself to drop the mental image and approach the situation as an adventurer residing in the city.

"And if someone runs across it?"

"Well, Finn's instructions were 'it's better to capture it alive,'" started Tiona, weaving her fingers at the back of her head.

Tione finished. "And 'dispose of it if it looks like it might hurt someone.'"

Aiz let her golden hair be tousled by a breeze as she touched her trusted sword Desperate hanging at her waist.

"Got it." She nodded after clearing her mind of all thoughts.

"A date with Bete Loga! A date with Bete Looooga! Hey! Hey! Wanna hold my hand?" chirped a girl with brown skin, grinning from ear to ear as she walked beside him.

Instead of taking her hand, Bete elbowed Lena Tully in the temple without saying a word. By this point, he'd gotten used to making these sudden jabs.

"Huh?! Why do I see stars?! Why am I seeing a starry night instead of Bete Loga?!"

"Humor me and tell me what the hell you're doing here."

"I've been staking out *Loki Familia*'s manor, duh! Ack! More stars!"

"Piss off."

The Amazonian girl yelped in pain, clutching the side of her throbbing head and writhing on the ground—paying no mind to the fact that her underwear was on full display. Some passing demi-humans shot her annoyed looks.

Bete kept walking briskly without even a sidelong glance at the broken girl letting out incomprehensible screeches.

"She's really taken to you…"

"Knock it off. Keep that shit to yourself," Bete snapped at Anakity, the catgirl looking at him in exasperation.

Even though they were both animal people, this pairing was extremely unusual, even by *Loki Familia* standards.

"Whaaat?! Split up, you two! Spliiiiiiiiit!" Lena jumped to her feet and pounced between the two of them, yanking them apart with her hands. "Gimme a breeeeeeak! Ugh! *Loki Familia* has way too many cuties and hotties! Bete is gonna get seduced! I'm so worried!"

"You out of your mind?"

"Don't worry. I'd rather anyone but him."

The two of them tromped forward, completely disregarding Lena and leaving her by herself in their tracks.

With a big gasp, she scurried after them.

"Is this where the monster showed up?"

"Yeah, seems like it."

They'd been heading to the northwest section of the city and now stood in one narrow alley among many. It wasn't a main road by any means.

Following Gareth's instructions, Bete and Anakity, chosen for the simple reason that they could follow its scent with their noses, were tracking the humanoid monster.

The most recent sighting of the monster was the previous evening. The Guild had concluded their investigation, but that didn't mean there weren't any more hints or clues.

"Who cares about that monster? It's not like it's got anything to do with the key."

"You don't know that. We have to gather as much info as possible. Am I wrong?" Anakity chided Bete lightly.

"Ha! What you're really saying is that we can't do nothin' else."

...Hmm? What's this? Their banter makes it seem like they're partners in crime who don't get along but have clearly spent years together...! Okay, in all seriousness, is the catgirl my rival...?! What is thiiiis?!

Bete was in an obviously sour mood because it seemed like they had run out of options, and he kept taking it out on others by snapping at them. Anakity was busy trying to placate him. But Lena misinterpreted their entire exchange, and this filled her with unease about their relationship. Her solution was to cling to him more aggressively.

Brushing away Lena's advances with one hand, Bete halted in front of a side alley.

"It disappeared here. An elven girl took the monster away while the locals were throwing stones at it."

"An elven brat?"

"At first, the monster was wearing a robe to conceal its body, but then people say it spread its wings while attacking a kid."

"Somethin' doesn't add up..." Bete furrowed his brow as Anakity gave him a quick rundown.

The two of them started sniffing and immediately picked up on a suspicious scent—the presence of something inhuman. It'd gone undetected by the humans in the Guild and other adventurers, but it couldn't slip past the noses of animal people, whose senses had been sharpened by leveling up repeatedly.

They switched locations, leaving the road to follow the scent down a dimly lit backstreet.

"Tch. They used a damn item to cover their tracks."

"Seems like it…"

"Huh? What? There's no way a monster can use items…With this and our last convo, doesn't that mean someone is sheltering it?"

"How the hell am I supposed to know?" Bete answered Lena, whose head popped out from behind him in surprise.

He was moving on instinct, heading for the seventh district in the city after putting together Anakity's explanation and a hunch he had.

"…Huh. What's with this decrepit old church?"

They passed by the remnants of a building-turned-mountain-of-rubble that looked as though it'd been blasted apart by magic. They could just barely make out a deserted chapel from the crumbling ruins of what used to be a proper stone building.

"…Oh yeah, I think I heard a rumor about some familia using a chapel as their home."

"Which one?"

"Hmmmm…Oh, it's no use! I can't remember their name, even though my brain's chock-full of gray matter…!"

"Go to hell," Bete spat, scanning the debris as Lena crossed her arms and groaned as she racked her brain.

A broken statue of a goddess rolled up to his feet.

"Ikelos Familia?" Lefiya responded quizzically.

It'd been three days since the initial reports of a humanoid monster appearing aboveground.

Lefiya was in a back alley in the city's northern district, diagonally across from a chienthrope girl with light-brown skin.

"Yeah. We only found out recently how shady that familia seems," clarified Lulune Louie, the thief of *Hermes Familia*, leaning against the wall as she nodded.

Lulune had apparently come by the home of *Loki Familia* in the morning, leaving the guard at the gate with a letter stating that she wanted to share some information at a certain meeting place. In addition, she had chosen Lefiya specifically because the elf could move more stealthily than most first-tier adventurers, especially reckless ones like Bete.

At the end of the dimly lit alley, they could see storefronts and feet shuffle forward on the bright road. The reason Lulune had chosen the back alley for their secret meeting as opposed to a tavern or someplace else was because she was unbelievably busy.

Lefiya had struggled to find the right alley for their little rendezvous, but even with that delay, the thief hadn't betrayed expectations when she showed up later than her, exhaustion plain on her face as she'd apologized repeatedly.

"They're the ones handling the smuggling in Meren, which is what the Evils' Remnants were using to raise money."

"Erg!"

"And their main business was smuggling monsters…exporting them at top dollar to royals and aristocrats with odd taste. We have proof of it," Lulune revealed.

Lefiya let out an audible gasp before opening the parchment scroll handed to her and scanning the contents.

Ikelos Familia, a Dungeon-crawling familia established in Orario over twenty years ago. But around the same time they reached the deep levels, all records of them clearing floors disappeared—along with the familia itself. Their name stopped appearing in the circles of the usual adventurers, to the point where Lefiya hadn't recognized it at all. With a rank of B, they were undoubtedly one of the more powerful familias.

"…Ngh! 'In the past, *Ikelos Familia* has been suspected by the Guild of being a member of the Evils!'" Lefiya recited off the parchment with wide eyes.

Loki Familia, *Dionysus Familia*, and *Hermes Familia* had formed a united front to chase down the underground forces of the monstrous creatures and the remnants of the Evils. It was almost certain that *Ikelos Familia* was to be considered a part of the enemy forces.

Lefiya looked up after staring fixedly at the name of the familia on the investigation report. They were the ones who'd captured monsters in the Dungeon, smuggled them outside the city, and sold them. She couldn't shake her shock and disgust at those charges, but she was more preoccupied by the circumstances that had brought it all to light.

"This could be a stretch, but I wonder if the humanoid monster appearing in town is related to *Ikelos Familia*..."

Like, maybe one of the monsters escaped when they were trying to smuggle it and made it to the outside world, thought Lefiya, connecting current events with the findings in the report.

"Nah, that's got nothing to do with them."

"Come again?"

"Well, it's not totally unrelated, but they weren't the ones to blame. We don't need to worry about that angle, at the very least."

"B-but...another one of them might show up..."

"That won't happen, either."

Lulune flatly rejected the possibility, leaving Lefiya visibly confused.

She was caught up on one thing: Lulune was making it sound as if she had a firm grasp on the truth behind the incident with the humanoid monster—which meant, by extension, that *Hermes Familia* knew as well.

"Anyway, we're pouring all our resources into tracking *Ikelos Familia*. If you happen to run across anyone in it...or Ikelos himself, we'd appreciate you letting us know," added Lulune with a look of pure exhaustion.

One look at her face made it clear she was too tired to notice Lefiya's surprise. The elf nodded noncommittally.

The chienthrope thief started to grumble. "Honestly, Hermes should have told Loki to her face about something this important, but...at the moment, he's spread a bit thin."

"Really? Lord Hermes? That's hard to imagine..."

"On the surface, he's got his characteristic fake smile plastered on his face, but...he's definitely on edge. It's gotten bad enough that Asfi is doing as he says without complaining."

Lefiya hadn't interacted with Hermes more than a handful of times, but she remembered him as an easygoing, charming god and found it tough to imagine him in such a state.

The thief shrugged. "...Hey, I guess you're not going to tell me anything about the harvest you reaped from Daedalus Street, right?"

"Um...To tell you the truth, our goddess asked us not to say anything...Not until she knows what Lord Hermes is hiding." Lefiya evaded the question.

Loki Familia hadn't shared their intel with *Hermes Familia* about the hidden base of their enemy—Knossos—or that they'd found it while searching the Labyrinth District. They didn't plan to do so until Hermes put his own cards on the table. He kept lurking behind the scenes by himself, and Loki intended to withhold information about Knossos as a bargaining chip—or as the gods called it, a "give and take."

At the same time, Loki wanted to learn from Hermes what Ouranos's true motives were, since he was connected to the Guild.

"No, it's fine. That's perfectly reasonable," Lulune replied, holding up her hands to politely stop Lefiya, who was struggling to explain her position.

After all, we're the ones not acting in good faith, Lulune thought, choosing not to push the matter about Knossos further, as though embodying the neutral stance of her own familia. Lulune just wanted to make sure they both understood the obligations they were under.

"I know we should exchange information instead of haggling—I mean, we formed an alliance and all...but we're dealing with a messy situation."

And this mess is far out of our control, Lulune implied as she glibly scratched her head and took on an exasperated look, which was uncharacteristic of her. The fact that she was even letting Lefiya hear her rant was due to her fatigue, no doubt.

"We can't talk about what we know now. If you find it suspicious and refuse to give us more intel, then it can't be helped. Well, I guess it can, but...I wouldn't expect you to despite all the circumstances."

I really want to tell you. I'd like to just get it out in the open. But I can't say it, no matter what, Lulune silently communicated through her bearing.

That feeling from earlier made its way back into Lefiya's mind—this time with more force. *It's something they can't discuss, even though it's about something that's tripping us both up...What could it be?*

"For now, could you let Loki know about *Ikelos Familia* for us?...I'm sorry that everything's so half-baked."

"I-it's fine...Um, please don't push yourself too hard, okay?" Lefiya added.

Lulune smiled wryly as she peeled herself from the wall and waved, disappearing down the dim alley, away from the main road.

Lefiya turned in the other direction and stepped out into the street, where the sun beat down on the pavement.

Enclosed by stone walls and ceiling, the room had a single magic-stone lamp for lighting and no windows. It was clearly underground, and the air was cool to the touch, chilly, even. Lining the walls were wooden shelves filled with countless bottles of wine for safekeeping.

"..." Dionysus poured himself some wine, filling a glass set atop a small, round table.

Located in an underground room in the home of *Dionysus Familia* was Dionysus's prided wine cellar, built by a god known as a wine snob. There were bottles and casks scattered around the room. If Loki ever saw the number of famous labels and their fine craftsmanship, she'd call it a wealth of riches without a doubt.

But Dionysus didn't even allow his followers to enter the wine cellar. Except for one person.

The wine glug-glug-glugged, filling the room with its soft burbles. Then he took a seat and drained the glass in a single swig.

The fact that Dionysus downed it in one go without letting the fragrant red wine roll across his palate, without even tasting it, had to mean he was trying to drown his worries in alcohol.

"...Lord Dionysus, you're drinking too much," admonished Filvis the elf, standing at attention by his side.

The god poured himself another glass, ignoring her warning.

"If I don't drink, then I can't go on...Right?" he asked, hanging his head.

Filvis chose not to open her mouth, saying nothing, and Dionysus held the glass up to the light fixed on the ceiling.

"The situation remains at a standstill. We've failed to find any clues. There's been no progress. I've sent Loki and her children on a wild-goose chase with nothing to show for it..."

"..."

"I'm a buffoon, an imbecile...Yet, there's nothing to do but continue moving forward." He continued his soliloquy, trying to convince himself.

He gazed into the reflection on the glass mirroring his eyes of the same color.

"That's right. I'm Dionysus...I'll humiliate myself and work with Loki to get my vengeance...Yes, vengeance for my children."

It was a side of Dionysus he would never allow Loki or the rest—or even his own familia—to see. It was a side that only Filvis knew, and even she softly averted her eyes, as if she was witnessing something she shouldn't.

"...Let's go. Loki is calling us."

Downing the last of the wine, Dionysus got to his feet, betraying no vestiges of his previous mood and assuming a sweet mask of calm composure—and a strong will glinting in the back of his eyes.

He retrieved his coat from the elf and departed the underground room.

"One of Hermes's children contacted mine, saying somethin' about *Ikelos Familia* bein' fishy."

"Ikelos, huh...Another annoying god takes the stage."

On the lawn of Twilight Manor, a few shrubs and richly colored flowers bathed in the afternoon sun. Loki had invited Dionysus and Filvis to her home and, while they sat at a table, was wrapping up a recap of the intel Lefiya had brought back.

Loki impolitely shifted back and forth in her chair, making it creak loudly.

"If I remember correctly, Ikelos is—"

"Yeah, suspected of bein' part of the Evils. Ikelos is the quintessential god who's starved for entertainment…A guy who goes overboard to kill his boredom."

Lefiya was standing off to the side behind Loki, opposite Filvis, who stood on Dionysus's side. The two followers smiled as their eyes met while the gods continued their discussion.

"Their home has been an empty shell for a long time now, apparently. They definitely moved to a different hideout."

"It seems that way."

"…I bet he's hiding on Daedalus Street…In Knossos, I'm sure."

"…"

"I wouldn't be surprised if they've got their hands on a key. If we tell Hermes about Knossos, he'll probably find them in no time, knowing that shrewd dandy," proposed Loki.

"I'm against it," Dionysus replied firmly, his glass-colored eyes not wavering in the slightest as he looked directly at her.

Loki cracked open one of her eyes. "I think we're past the point where we can be picky about our methods…We don't have many leads to go on."

"I've said it before, Loki. Hermes is Ouranos's lapdog. As long as that old god is lurking in the shadows behind him, I won't trust him. If he can't tell us what he's really up to, I've got no intention of sitting down at the bargaining table with him."

Dionysus was unyielding in his resolution. After all, he'd been suspicious of the Guild, of Orario's creator god, Ouranos, even before he interacted with Loki.

As for Loki, she suspected Ouranos was hiding something. But… she simply couldn't imagine how he could be connected to the plan to destroy Orario, especially if she trusted the gut reaction she felt after talking to Ouranos at Guild Headquarters.

Loki could sense Lefiya was feeling vexed by something behind her and pushed toward the crux of the issue.

"Aren't you bein' a bit too stubborn?"

"…"

"Why do you have a grudge against Ouranos? It's weird. You got any real basis for it?" Loki probed.

Dionysus opened his mouth. Filvis watched with a concerned look but knew better than to interrupt a conversation between gods.

"Let's see, when did it start...? The moment I first felt put off by the elder god," he started, focusing his gaze up as if to search through his memories, staring into the sky spreading beyond the tall barriers surrounding the manor.

"It started...when we were still in the heavens...I can't even remember what it was anymore...Hmm, what was it?"

He wasn't lying or telling the truth—merely airing out a question.

His eyes grew unfocused as he became engrossed in reminiscing about the past. As it approached sunset, the sky cast a crimson glow, and across from him, Loki looked on in silence.

Most hadn't realized that the humanoid monster was the opportunity that *Loki Familia* had been waiting for. It signaled the end of the merciless progression of time. It was the move that would send waves rippling through the current gridlock.

It would set everything in motion.

The prum hero felt a faint ache in his thumb.

The goddess of jests intended to use the uproar as a foothold.

The girl with golden hair and golden eyes renewed her determination to exterminate the monsters.

And five days after the news of the humanoid monster broke, it was time.

CHAPTER 2

SOMEONE NAMED FOOL

Гэта казка іншага сям'і.

Яго імя дурань

There wasn't a single cloud in the sky on that day—clear and blue above the city. The weather was perfect.

The residents of Orario believed this to be yet another one of those boringly peaceful days as they wiped the sweat off their brows. The sounds of their footsteps joined together in a ballad, playing the harmony of life in the city. The early-summer breeze was nowhere to be found, and the sun beat down on the city as if to reassert that the summer had just begun. The stone pavement absorbed its rays and gave rise to a heat haze.

Aiz was working up a light sweat as she made her way to Central Park.

I've gotta get to the eighteenth floor and seek out information one more time...

As *Loki Familia* continued to sniff out more clues, Aiz oversaw the Dungeon. Until the previous day, her main mission had been the discovery and elimination of plants—pantries filled with man-eating flowers, whose existence came to light during an incident on the twenty-fourth floor. The goal was to cut off the stream of income funding Knossos, which had been through the smuggling and sale of monsters out of the Dungeon.

In previous days, she'd inspected the pantries of every floor down to the thirtieth. Finn had judged the risk involved in illegally moving things below that level too high for them to establish plants there. Accompanied by an elite squad, Aiz had cleared any and all plants left in the Dungeon.

Now that she'd been freed from this dangerous battle mission, she planned to stretch her legs by heading to the Under Resort.

It was already clear that Knossos was connected to the Dungeon. They had confirmed it the other day when they found an entrance on the eastern edge of the eighteenth floor, and she intended to gather information at Rivira after she rested.

I'm curious about this humanoid beast…with wings.

She noticed several residents whispering to one another and made out the word *monster*. Over the course of a few days, the initial frenzy seemed to die down, though the report of a monster had to be unsettling to the average civilian. There were a few bards with bad taste, singing merrily at bars about the chaos, which was fine and all. But she suspected this was the source of unfounded rumors of the monster appearing night after night and attacking city folk.

This incident was relatively small in comparison to the Monster-philia, but fear and anxiety hung in the air of the city.

Everyone is scared of the monsters…which makes sense…since these people aren't adventurers.

It meant they didn't have the means of fighting back—and there were far more defenseless people than those capable of keeping them away.

In their eyes, monsters were fear made manifest, violence in material form. They couldn't be allowed to take root in human residences, or else their fangs would draw blood, their claws would deliver wounds, and their roars would inspire screams of terror.

As she stepped into Babel, Aiz wondered if there was a way to ease their fears.

I had a late start. By now, the other adventurers should be…

She headed one floor underground in the white tower leading to the Dungeon, descending the silver staircase into the big hole and feeling as though she were being observed by the painting of blue sky on the ceiling. It was long past rush hour, and there weren't many people around.

As she was making her descent with two or three other adventurers going solo, Aiz stopped dead in her tracks.

Bell?

There was a single person coming up the stairs in front of her.

She recognized that wavy white hair and lithe body. They belonged to a boy she knew, a rookie who'd become a bit of a celebrity overnight, the talk of the town.

But Aiz couldn't be sure that it was Bell Cranell at first.

With downcast eyes and a hunched-over posture, he looked dejected—no, he was downright dismal, as if he'd fallen into a bottomless bog. Even Aiz could read his mood, which was saying something.

There was none of his usual nervousness, or earnestness, or bashful little smile.

Aiz could tell that something was wrong, and it tugged on her heartstrings. Of course, she didn't show it on her emotionless face, but she was rattled.

"Ah…" He finally noticed her, lifting his face to look at her blankly.

"Miss Aiz…" Bell mumbled, as if entranced by her eyes.

The two of them had stopped in place—one looking down, the other up. Passing adventurers gawked at them on their way by.

Bell took his time picking his words. Aiz stayed silent.

"Are you…headed into the Dungeon…?"

"Yes…"

"…Um, Miss Aiz…"

"…"

"Do you…um…Right now…" he mumbled incomprehensibly, speaking haltingly as his attention drifted to his feet.

It was as if he couldn't get a handle on his feelings.

Aiz realized that she'd started talking to him. "Let's go."

"What…?"

"Let's go somewhere we can be alone…" she continued, extending her hand.

Bell's eyes snapped open wide. He considered the thin fingers stretched out in front of him before nervously placing his hand in hers. He had on the expression of a lost child abandoned in an unfamiliar part of town.

Aiz called off her plans for the afternoon and left Babel.

To find a quiet place, they advanced past Central Park, ignoring the gazes of the city folk gawking at the pair of top-tier adventurers.

Through his hand, Aiz could make out a mix of emotions—that he was feeling slightly flustered about holding hands, and pathetic, and that he couldn't let go.

Aiz pretended not to notice.

They cut through a number of roads before stopping in an empty area surrounded by houses.

"…Um, sorry. For, you know, taking up your time."

"It's fine…"

There was no one else around, save for the two of them. Bell let go of her hand and looked at her head-on. His eyes drifted downward again, but he stopped himself, gazing directly into Aiz's golden eyes.

"…"

"…"

How long has it been since we've looked at each other this closely? Aiz thought in the back of her mind. There was a nostalgic quality to him for some reason.

His white hair and rubellite eyes did remind her of a white rabbit. But he was visibly distressed, a departure from his usual vibrancy and emotiveness—which was enough to cover her own share of emotions, too. It made her sad to see him in this state.

Anguish. Conflict. Indecision. She could almost see these feelings ooze out of his eyes, begging her for support.

Is something wrong…? Aiz asked internally—not that he could answer.

I want to get rid of the source of your worries, she thought, in the same way as she wished to eliminate the monsters and soothe the general public.

"…What's wrong?"

What happened? Why do you look lost? Aiz pleaded, as if knocking on the door to his heart, asking him to let her inside. And Bell clutched his right hand to his chest, grasping at his wavering heart.

"Miss Aiz…"

"…"

He gulped, taking his time to spill it out. "If monsters had a reason to live…If they had feelings like you and me…what would you do?"

Upon hearing the question behind his gaze, Aiz was met with one emotion: bewilderment.

What are you talking about? she asked in all honesty.

What a meaningless question, a pointless hypothetical.

But his eyes bored into her earnestly, and Aiz found herself pursing her lips—considering the meaning behind his question, coming to grips with it in her own way, while avoiding an answer.

"..."

She was thinking:

Let's say a monster could smile, like a human.

Or be consumed by worry, like a human.

Or shed tears, like a human.

Could I still swing my sword?

Time passed by them in silence. The trees let streams of sunlight through their branches and onto the street, and their shadows transformed as the breeze shifted its leaves. The infernal summer wind swept between the two adventurers.

Aiz thought, and thought, and thought. And at the end, she was left with a totally simple answer.

"If monsters hurt someone...No, that's not it." Aiz paused, shaking her head before continuing.

"If anyone cries because of a monster—I'd *kill it*."

She left no traces of doubt in her answer.

"Ngh?!" Bell was trembling, at a loss for words, broken.

Out of all his emotions, one bubbled to the surface. It was a look of *despair*.

But Aiz's gaze didn't waver in the slightest, piercing straight through Bell as he turned pale, confused by the look in his eyes. She asked through eye contact: *Wouldn't you?*

A tremor ran through Bell.

Wave after wave of emotions came and went from his face, like his life were flashing before his eyes—or as if he was questioning the state of the world. He was standing between Aiz and *something* with a despondent look, as if he were caught in a paradox.

As for Aiz, she was no longer plagued by confusion, staring straight back at him, questioning him.

But there was something that sounded like…shattering glass, as if she were hearing their two paths snapping in opposite directions.

"I—" A drop of sweat ran down his narrow chin, and Bell started to loosen his frozen mouth.

Clang! Clang!!

A bell rang out from a tower, breaking the moment between them.

""Hgn?!"" Aiz and Bell both snapped their heads up.

This sounded different from when the clock struck noon, and it continued to ring louder and louder—as if expressing its suspicions of this tranquil state. No one would believe there was peace on earth upon hearing this sound. As gonging filled the sky and canceled out all other noise in the city, birds batted their wings and took flight.

It wasn't from the eastern bell tower but from the northwest.

"Guild Headquarters is in that direction…Is this a warning bell?" Aiz asked.

Bell snapped out of it.

The great bell tower maintained by the Guild would be rung for a citywide warning—an emergency announcement.

Aiz's eyes widened in silence.

"Is this the great bell of the Guild?!"

At that same time, Lefiya's elven ears perked up and she stopped in her tracks in the street along with all the other people around her.

"—*Emergency alert! Emergency alert! All familias based in Orario are to follow the Guild's instructions!*" boomed a loudspeaker system carved from magical stones.

The thumping of panicked footsteps blended with the reverberations of the bell shaking the air.

"*The Guild will issue a mission!*"

"Raul!"

"A mission...? For all the familias?!"

It seemed that the broadcaster couldn't even hide their unease. Anakity and Raul and every other member of *Loki Familia* around the city froze in place, hit with an ominous premonition.

"*The monsters equipped with armor and weapons* have destroyed Rivira on the eighteenth floor!! We've confirmed large numbers of them on the move!!" screeched the Guild employee, voice turning into an urgent scream as they informed the adventurers.

"Armed monsters?"

"B-Bete Loga, isn't a mass migration of monsters, like, superbad? What if they break through Babel...?!"

"Tch...What the hell is going on?!" Bete asked no one in particular, ignoring the questions of the Amazonian girl tagging along with him to reexamine a deserted building in the restored area of the red-light district.

"*The Guild is ordering the immediate deployment of all adventurers to exterminate—What? R-really?...U-understood.*"

The situation was in flux, breaking into chaos.

"Do I hear panic in the broadcaster's voice?"

"Did something happen?"

Tiona and Tione had leaped to higher ground, observing the stirring city from above.

"*All citizens, including adventurers, are hereby* **forbidden** *to enter the Dungeon!! The Guild will contact familias directly. Please stand by at your respective homes!! I repeat—*" The announcement crackled, recovering its pace and forceful tone as it emphasized the urgency of the situation.

"A change in orders, huh."

"I bet the Guild's confused, too. They can't even keep their plans straight. That, or..."

"There's a big guy *buttin' in*. One or the other."

Riveria, Gareth, and Loki were listening intently out the manor's open window, quick in their attempts to piece together their next moves based on the incoming announcement.

"Is this fanfare marking the destruction of Orario or a gospel to guide us?…Which will it be?"

The blue eyes of the prum leader narrowed as he listened to the destruction of life as they knew it.

Orario transformed into a city of upheaval—the destruction of Rivira, followed by a great migration of monsters.

If the monsters emerged aboveground, it would obliterate the entire concept of safety, which was the pride of the Labyrinth City. The town had fallen into calamity, starting with the wise people who foretold danger and the merchants with a good nose for trouble. The unrest spread from the main streets to the smaller roads to the plazas. In some parts of the city, they could hear a chain reaction of screams and shouts when the populace realized the gravity of it all.

Lefiya, Bete, Tiona, and Tione witnessed peace in the city start to cave in real time.

And there was nowhere more chaotic than Guild Headquarters.

They were overwhelmed by the refugees from Rivira on the eighteenth floor. Incoherent bellows flew back and forth in the offices. According to the escapees, a swarm of armed monsters of varying species descended on Rivira, coming up from the floor below and passing through the Central Tree, stamping out the upperclass adventurers and conquering their base in the Dungeon in no time.

If their reports were true, the armed monsters were subspecies with potential incomparable to their normal counterparts. The Guild members turned pale when they saw the brutal wounds of the adventurers and finally faced reality.

In front of the Pantheon was full-on pandemonium as adventurers and citizens crowded Guild Headquarters, demanding some sort of explanation.

Aiz and Bell felt the urgency of the situation as they slipped through the crowd straight to Guild Headquarters.

The gods were the only ones not in disarray.

There were a few who were concerned, or anxious, or worried, but they were in the minority. The overwhelming majority of them could not conceal their excitement, on the edge of their seats for the adventure and stimulus to come.

In this unprecedented situation, the Guild immediately announced a mission: *Ganesha Familia* was to form a punitive expeditionary force and head for the eighteenth floor.

And every other familia was ordered to remain on standby.

"Standby? What kind of bullshit is that?!" scoffed Bete in a gruff voice that resounded in the parlor of Twilight Manor.

The principal members of *Loki Familia* followed the Guild's broadcast, trudging home and gathering in the parlor. The secondary forces were patrolling the neighborhood to pacify the civilians under the command of Alicia and Cruz and in concert with the other familias.

"It'd be faster to send us in to clean up the mess!! No use in leaving it to Ganesha's guys!"

"Zip it, Bete!!…Do we really have to wait around? The broadcaster seemed confused, too."

Next to Bete as he roared in frustration, Tiona frowned, rattled by the unusual situation.

"But Rivira has been destroyed how many times now? Why's everyone freaking out?"

"Yeah, it's an overreaction to issue a mission to the entire city… Are the monsters with weapons and armor really a big deal?"

"I've seen the bulletin board at the Guild saying something about monsters carrying adventurers' weapons…" Aiz chimed in to Tiona and Tione's conversation.

After all, there had been fake reports of armed monsters among adventurers before. In fact, they were a dime a dozen. But seeing that this situation had escalated, the trio was thinking that maybe these beasts were a threat—maybe they were strong enough to break out aboveground. The misgivings were clear on all three of their faces.

"They're a strange species using actual adventurers' armor, not just nature weapons. It's obvious they're exceptional. I bet they're enchanted. En masse, at that," observed Riveria from her place near the wall.

"All the more reason we should be down there."

"Cool it, Bete. These ain't yer regular ol' Irregulars...Well, *regular* in air quotes. But yeah, it seems fishy." Gareth chided Bete for pouncing on Riveria's explanation.

But the dwarf was furrowing his brow, sensing the intentions of someone—or something—behind the current state of affairs. Despite the situation, the Guild had not yet shared all their information with each familia.

It could be that they hadn't yet gathered enough information to go public, but it seemed too passive.

It was almost as if...

"...It feels like they're trying to hide something," Gareth murmured, as though talking to himself.

"Well, whatever's going on," Finn added, slicing through the discussion from his chair, "it's not going to end if things keep going like this...That's just my hunch, though," he asserted, licking his thumb.

A smile even spread across his face.

"Yeah, bein' out of the loop annoys me, but...I'm with Finn," noted Loki from the table, slightly opening her vermilion eyes. "It ain't gonna end with this. And it'll keep Orario rumblin' as it goes."

The goddess's proclamation brought on a moment of silence. Everyone watched the corners of their patron's lips curl up.

The one to break the silence was Lefiya, who'd been quiet until then.

"U-um...Do you think the Evils' Remnants are involved with this...?"

"Don't you think it's too convenient to blame them for each and every thing?" replied Anakity.

"But, Aki, I don't think Lefiya's observation is unfounded...Like, this is a huge deal. It's possible that it's part of their strategy..." followed Raul.

Anakity and Raul responded with their respective opinions to the suggestion of the elven girl who'd timidly raised her hand before speaking.

Smack! Tiona pounded her fist on top of her palm to express that she'd come up with a new idea.

"Oh, I get it! That's why the Guild isn't making the information public—because it's all part of the Evils' plan! If they said the Evils were back, people would get scared."

"It's already annoying enough without you opening your trap, ya dumb Amazon," Bete erupted.

"Hey!"

"Use your head. If the Guild knew that, it would be weird that they haven't told us or *Freya Familia*," added Tione.

"If they're dealing with the Evils, it'd be better to work with the strong familias..." explained Aiz.

"Oh..." Tiona froze. "B-but, but even if the Guild hasn't made the connection, it could still be the Evils behind it, like Raul was saying, right?! I mean, it's turned into a big enough deal and all!"

"Now you're just grasping at straws."

"Am not! All righty, my vote goes to Raul and Lefiya's theory!"

""Huh?"" Raul and Lefiya were taken aback when Tiona raised her hand.

"Then I'm with Aki," said Tione.

"Me too," added Bete.

"Erm, I didn't say anything worth noting..."

"What about you, Aiz? Whose side are you on?!"

"Mm...I'm...with Tiona, I guess?"

"All right! That's four to three! What about you guys, Riveria?!"

"Who said you could decide this with a majority vote...?"

Anakity was at a loss for what to do with Tione's and Bete's votes, while Tiona was getting all riled up about Aiz joining her side. Riveria clutched her forehead, as if she had a headache, as they started trying to resolve the discussion by voting.

Gareth offered a shrug, and Loki grinned at Tiona's airheaded-ness, which unarguably brightened the mood.

And inevitably, Finn was thinking, *There's no way this is a trap by the remnants of the Evils,* and discarded that chain of logic, descending into a sea of thought while the others kept yapping on.

And it's not part of the underground forces of the creatures. They're already holed up in Knossos, waiting. When the time comes, they'll unleash the demi-spirit, and that'll be enough to destroy the city. They have no reason to increase tension and vigilance in the city or put themselves in danger now.

Seconds ticked by. He held up his right hand, covering his mouth, while he pensively looked at the ground.

No, this is…a terrible event *that's unrelated to everyone or intended by anyone.*

Finn was looking for a third possibility, far removed from the two choices the group was voting on. In other words, he'd realized that this incident might be the effects of an Irregular.

As Aki said, we'd be selling this incident short if we connected this to what we're chasing, but…at the very least, there's a chance we can catch a glimpse of the enemy's tail.

The first step was to examine the data.

The Guild—or rather, Ouranos and Hermes Familia *are connected…If we go off Loki's investigation, they're keeping some kind of secret. Based on the fact that they've no intention of making it public, this incident isn't part of their calculations…But, given the cover-up, it's safe to say they aren't unrelated, either.*

The mission had changed mid-broadcast not from the brass at the Guild but from Ouranos's divine will. Finn was suspecting the same thing as Loki.

In which case, did that mean that *Ganesha Familia* was also aware of Ouranos's secret?

Finn made a mental note of that possibility.

We can't assume the armed monsters are the same as the violas or the vividly colored monsters, but…we've got a new piece to the puzzle: Ikelos Familia.

This was a valuable clue for solving the case: *Ikelos Familia* was connected to the smuggling of monsters. Given this new information, it was harder to not suspect them.

On top of that, *Hermes Familia* was tracking them with all their resources.

If the armed monsters were originally captured by Ikelos Familia and then escaped...No, that doesn't make sense. It doesn't fit with Bors's reports that the monsters came up from the lower floors. They could have attacked Rivira because that's their instinct as monsters, but...it doesn't fit together nicely.

He kept reviewing and scrutinizing a series of possibilities in his head.

While the others continued making a ruckus, Riveria and Gareth watched Finn as he pondered deep in thought. They'd been around one another long enough to know to wait for him to come up with a solution.

The high elf and dwarf knew that his theory would be the best response.

There's not enough information. My knowledge of the background behind the incident is incomplete. I can't form an educated theory with this, but—

Finn's eyes narrowed.

Would it be too much of a stretch if I say it's an incident at the intersection of Ouranos's secret and Ikelos Familia's *propensity for violence?*

The parties involved would be rattled if they heard his train of thought. His intuition would send shivers up their very spines. If "a certain boy" wrapped up in this incident was there, he would have been wildly sputtering. His heart would be beating out of his chest, without a doubt.

It's all hypothetical. It doesn't matter from what angle I approach this problem. I end up having to make an inferential leap. Is it too early to tie Ikelos Familia *to the center of this?*

Finn examined his own thoughts from an objective perspective and shook his head.

No, I have to assume this is true. Ikelos Familia *is at the center of this. If I don't work under that belief, I can't do anything. This Irregular is outside the expectations of all sides...If we don't intervene before this is resolved, we'll lose our first and only opportunity.*

Strategy valued speed. This time, Finn was going to make use of it.

In this situation, it was more important to move quickly than to worry about risks or mistaken judgments.

More than anything, Finn was sure that the current uproar would tie back to Knossos and allow them to break it open. The ache in his thumb was pointing him in that direction, too.

Our area of operations is limited to aboveground. If we try to force our way into the Dungeon, the Guild will set Freya Familia *against us.*

Other than *Ganesha Familia* on their suppression mission, Babel was off-limits to all familias, making it impossible to enter the Dungeon.

Freya Familia had been brought in to fill the gap in the reserve forces caused by the absence of *Ganesha Familia*, Orario's main security force. The faction of the Goddess of Beauty had been penalized for their destruction of the red-light district, and they were obeying the Guild's instructions for the time being.

Even if Finn tried to mobilize his forces, they could not set foot on the scene of the incident on the eighteenth floor.

"Bete."

Everyone in the parlor froze at the sound of Finn's voice. The ears of the werewolf twitched as Bete looked back at him.

"I heard you fought with a curse user when we were in Knossos… a male human with smoky quartz goggles…Is that correct?"

"…Yeah. He was concealed under one of those Evils robes, but you've got it down. He was using a disgusting, creepy-ass spear," added Bete.

Finn started thinking again.

If I'm right…that would be Hazer, Dix Perdix.

The name of *Ikelos Familia*'s captain.

That confirms Ikelos Familia *has joined forces with the Evils…and*

their headquarters are in Knossos...If they carried monsters through
the labyrinth to smuggle them via the underground route and out of the
city, then...

As everyone focused on Finn, he began to weave a hypothesis connecting all the small pockets of incomplete information. And at the
end of that chain of thought was the epicenter that gave rise to the current incident.

The eighteenth floor...The eighteenth floor, huh?

That was where they had found a connection to Knossos just the
other day.

"...Everyone, get ready to move."

Finn had come to a conclusion.

Everyone stood up at once with bug eyes.

Amid mounting tension, the prum leader spoke.

"We're going to Daedalus Street."

It'd been several hours since *Ganesha Familia* had left Central Park
for their mission.

Loki Familia took up position on Daedalus Street.

They'd moved quickly, quietly, and in secret to not be noticed by
the Guild—more specifically, by Ouranos, who'd handed down the
standby order. They left it to the other familias to control the chaos
on Main Street, meeting up with Alicia, Cruz, and the rest before
deploying their members along the giant labyrinthine district.

"It's Thousand Elf! You were here last time, too, right?! It's a dream
to see *Loki Familia* this often!"

"So cute and pretty...I wish I could be like that..."

"...Will you shake my hand?"

"U-um, you see, we're on patrol at the moment..."

Nominally, their goal was to calm any disturbances among the
residents of Daedalus Street.

With the other familias prioritizing the main streets, the residents
of the slum were grateful for *Loki Familia*'s presence, especially since

they were left to deal with the situation on their own—even if their patrols were only a front for the true objective of the familia. Like the rest of her familia, Lefiya was surrounded by orphans—a human boy with flushed cheeks, an animal-person girl with a yearning gaze, and a half-elf asking for a handshake.

"I feel bad, since it's kinda like we're tricking them."

"S'not like Finn speaking with a forked tongue is a new development."

"Hey! Quit complaining about the captain! And besides, we're not doing anything wrong! If everything goes according to his predictions, we'll have to protect them!"

""Quiet!""

Even though some of them had difficulty simply accepting the gratitude of the slum's inhabitants, the *Loki Familia* patrols made sure to keep an eye out for any strange occurrences along the wide swath of Daedalus Street. As they proceeded along the mazelike black-bricked roads, Tiona punched and Bete kicked Tione for being too loud.

"Is it okay to move out in the open like this, Finn? Guild chaos aside, the guys in Knossos will notice our movements, no doubt."

"Even if we try to conceal ourselves, they would still have the advantage here. As long as we're on Daedalus Street, they'll always catch us. It's better to just show ourselves in plain sight and draw their attention to us."

They were on the roof of a multistory building that looked jumbled and pieced together. The wind carried Finn's and Gareth's voices as they looked over the Labyrinth District.

"Placing a check on the enemy? But won't that lead them to retreat farther into Knossos?" Riveria's jade hair rippled in the breeze as she stood behind the prum.

"At the very least, they'll be on guard, I'm sure. In any event, if they haven't recovered Ishtar's key themselves, our deployment... might be mistaken for preparation for a large-scale attack, tricking them into thinking we've found the key."

Save for a few familia members at the manor with Loki, Finn had deployed a substantial fighting force to Daedalus Street. A large section was placed in the ancient underground passages beneath the Labyrinth District—the location of the hidden passageways to Knossos. Raul and Anakity were commanding those groups.

What would the Evils' Remnants think of *Loki Familia* positioning squads around the confirmed locations of orichalcum doors?

"And if the enemy is wary of us, they *won't be able to spread their forces* to deal with the situation inside Knossos," said Finn.

Gareth and Riveria furrowed their brows in surprise.

"...Is something happening inside Knossos?"

"It's a hypothetical at the moment, but the migration of monsters and the armed ones making their way aboveground haven't moved from the eighteenth floor."

Ganesha Familia had left for the eighteenth floor. That much was known.

If *Ikelos Familia* was trying to patch things up, they wouldn't be able to ignore an entanglement between *Ganesha Familia* and *that thing*. This scuffle causing issues inside Knossos might be nothing more than wishful thinking. But with Finn aboveground and with a situation erupting on the eighteenth floor, the Evils would be caught between a rock and a hard place.

The enemy had lost a skilled commander in Arachnia, Valletta Grede. With pressure, there was a good chance they would make a misstep.

"And also, the fact that we can *see adventurers besides us*, that would lend some credence to the idea that the area around Knossos is in a tizzy."

As Finn glanced down, he noticed a single shadow ducking behind the cover of a building. His blue eyes narrowed.

"Daaaaamn it...Whyyyyy, oh why is Braver here?"

——The shadow was *Hermes Familia*'s Lulune, pressing herself against a wall and letting a small whine seep out.

"Has he found out that Ikelos is hiding here, or...? If it's not that, he has to know something! Otherwise, he wouldn't be setting up his guys!"

Braver is crazy scary, the chienthrope girl thought as her tail bristled and her eyes welled with tears.

"This is bad, Lord Hermes…! If we don't hurry up and get this all sorted, our secret is gonna get out!"

Her intuition was setting off alarm bells as she started to move away.

"…I can't find it," muttered Aiz, talking about the suspicious shadow.

She was alone on a giant tower, observing the surrounding area.

If Finn was correct, the Evils' Remnants or *Ikelos Familia* or *something else* should show up around Daedalus Street. If they could put pressure on whoever appeared, they should be able to get significantly closer to their enemy.

While the members aboveground were frantically searching for clues, Aiz continued moving on her own.

I guess she isn't going to come out?

The creature Levis—the red-haired woman who was obsessed with Aiz.

Aiz had the idea that if she moved around Daedalus Street on her own, Levis might try to make some kind of move. But she hadn't felt anyone's eyes on her so far, let alone Levis's intense pressure. It seemed she didn't have any intention of leaving Knossos.

Aiz inadvertently furrowed her brow when something caught her eye.

"That's…"

She saw the back of something wearing suspiciously tattered clothes scurry into a narrow alley. Aiz kicked off the moment she recognized this figure, slicing through the air like the wind. She touched down on a roof before leaping out again, landing at the entrance of a narrow alley.

The buildings overlapped one another as if this was an optical illusion. The area was dimly lit. A broken lamp made from magic stones was barely clinging to where it was hung on the wall.

Watching out for movement from above, Aiz raced down the narrow path, leaping up the staircase that appeared in front of her in one bound and landing in an elevated area surrounded by blue sky.

There's no one here...?

In a space the size of a garden, Aiz scanned the area from side to side.

"Daedalus Street is restless today."

"!"

Aiz heard the voice of an old woman and spun around to see a goddess making her way down from the path that Aiz had sprinted through.

"Putting me under surveillance. Hounding a goddess. Sheesh, what a troublesome lot you all are."

"...Lady Penia?"

Aiz recognized that long, disheveled white hair. With her tattered clothes, everything about her looked unkempt.

Aiz's eyes widened in surprise upon seeing the goddess Penia—a physical manifestation of destitution. They had met when *Loki Familia* had come to Daedalus Street before they knew about the existence of Knossos.

The Goddess of Poverty.

Or, as Loki put it, poverty on legs.

Aiz wondered if the goddess had access to a hidden passage. After all, Penia had sauntered out of the narrow alley after noticing that Aiz was following her.

The old woman smiled as she approached.

"Searching for something? Or stealing? Takes guts to come here when the whole city is in disarray, wouldn't you say?"

"..."

"Say something! I went out of my way to start the conversation! Sheesh, just standing there with your pretty face like some doll!"

Her lips shifted from the smile of an old, depraved witch to the downturned mouth of a mother-in-law screeching complaints about her daughter-in-law.

It wasn't uncommon for narcissistic deities, but Penia's mood

swings were practically violent. In fact, it was harsh enough that Aiz had a feeling that Penia's outward appearance and intense emotions were more *human* than of those living in the mortal realm.

"...Lady Penia, what were you just...?"

"Answering a question with a question? Deary me. Loki hasn't taught you any manners! If you were in my familia, I'd kick you out in no time at all! Though it's not like aaaaaaanyone wants to follow me!"

"...We're investigating...the current incident...around here. We thought there might be something...we're looking for..."

"I see! I was just taking a stroll myself!"

"..."

I'm not sure how to put it...but she's difficult to deal with.

Aiz was no good with words, but she suspected she simply wasn't compatible with the goddess standing before her to begin with.

Penia loudly sniffed, as she often did. "...Has there been anything strange going on in Daedalus Street recently?"

"Anything strange? Like?"

"Like a suspicious person hanging around..."

"This is a slum. A cesspool in the heart of the city, full of has-been adventurers with violent streaks and fools of—"

"...A monster...or the Evils," Aiz interjected.

Penia cocked an eyebrow, her wrinkles drawing toward it. Aiz didn't want to worry the residents, which was why she hadn't said it plainly before, but with a god, she decided to get to the point.

"Do you know anything?"

Penia had settled into the labyrinthine district centuries ago, and she was the ruler of Daedalus Street.

It was possible that she'd caught on to something.

Aiz looked into her ashen eyes.

"I don't know anything," the goddess quipped.

A familiar smile spread across Penia's face.

A smile that a resident of the mortal realm could not see through.

The smile of a god.

"Hey, Sword Princess…what do you think of Daedalus Street?"

"…?"

Aiz was puzzled by this sudden question and quiet for a moment, thinking as she looked out over the complex labyrinth town unfolding under her.

"…It's a strange place. It's dizzying, dungeon-like…The strangest area in the city…"

"Ohhh? And?"

"And…the poorest area…" Aiz managed to say with some hesitation.

"Well, if you ask me, it's far too rich." Penia sneered.

What? Aiz froze.

"There's no way a slum should be as clean as this one. Sure, it's difficult to get around, the ups and downs of the roads are tiring, and you'll get lost without the ariadne. It has some inconveniences, but those are trivial."

"…"

"There are parentless brats who are completely filthy running around smiling. I've heard that some goddess is supporting them. No clue who…But even in this cesspool, there's love, you know, and cooperation." Penia continued, spitting out her words. "I'd say the same for Orario as a whole, but it's definitely too happy here."

"Happy…?"

"Happy people shine all the brighter. It's like they have no choice but to be so iridescent. That's what it feels like here. It's claustrophobic for someone like me. Makes it hard to call it home."

The people, gods, and, above all, adventurers.

The old goddess concluded that the Labyrinth City had too many people too full of dreams and aspirations.

"It was better before. When monsters were running amok, everyone was unhappy…and they shone even brighter than any do now."

Aiz's heart stirred upon hearing those words. The goddess seemed to genuinely believe that, and her eyes narrowed in reminiscence, but Aiz couldn't accept it for some reason.

"It wasn't like this rotten luster we have now. It was an honorable poverty. Is there anything more glorious than a spirit without any excess flab? The people of the world shone because they were caught up in that harshness. The poverty I rule over was one side of it."

"…!"

"I had a conversation like this with some god before, I think… Who was it?"

Penia ignored Aiz and carried on, her shoulders quivering in delight.

"Yes. It would be good to have more…hardship."

That smile on her face again. That look in her eyes as she revealed a certain truth.

Aiz spat out a response to all of that head-on. "That's not true."

"Hmm?"

"That it was better long ago, when monsters were running wild… There's no way that's true."

Aiz's eyebrows furrowed as she let out a more assertive tone of voice. Penia opened her eyes a bit wider, as if she thought this was a surprising reaction, despite having limited interactions with Aiz.

The existence of monsters is a poison.

Their very existence is evil.

Even in this incident with the humanoid monster hiding out and living somewhere in Orario. It's enough to stir a commotion.

Aiz wasn't speaking about justice, but she was entirely sure that the monsters doing as they pleased was indisputably a disaster. It would be impossible for happiness to come out of it.

Underneath the blue sky, time passed as she locked eyes with the goddess. After a few moments, the old goddess readjusted her smile.

"…Heh-heh. I guess you'd call this the fundamental difference in the point of view between a god and a mortal. But that's interesting in itself, too."

"Ngh…"

"Well, gods are prone to know-it-all sorts of utterances. From your point of view, it might sound wrong or even illogical."

That's fine. It's better that way. Penia looked in adoration at the girl defying her.

There were too many emotions in Aiz's heart, and she leaned in, trying to say something.

"_____—*Ahhhhh?!*"

The repulsive shout of a beast roared out, sounding almost like the shrieks of a girl whose throat had been torn apart.

"?!"

"Oh my…Isn't that a monster? Could that be the thing you're searching for?"

Penia's smile deepened at the sight of Aiz frozen in place. The Sword Princess glanced at the goddess's upturned lips, enduring the irritation welling in her heart, and pivoted away from the smile. She broke into a run before kicking off the banister.

"Live like your life depends on it—no matter what's waiting for you. Because that's something the gods can't copy, the way the inhabitants of the mortal realm ought to be."

Aiz could hear Penia say that from behind her the moment she leaped into the air. Soon, she was descending into the townscape of Daedalus Street, pulled down by gravity.

Below her, she could see fleeing people and a half-human, half-dragon monster rampaging in the city.

Finn was the first one to arrive on the scene.

"‼"

He broke into a sprint before anyone else the moment the scream rang out, and the site of the commotion quickly came into view.

Dust rose into the air from the demolished corner of a building as the residents of the Labyrinth District struggled to flee. An unsightly monster stood beneath the open sky of the surface.

Finn was slightly startled to see some adventurers standing against the monster, but he didn't waste another second before readying the long spear in his right hand, cocking it behind his back like a loaded ballista. As he leaped across the rooftops, he stepped in with all his might and unleashed the golden spear.

A single line flashed.

The spear accelerated with enough speed to not give the monster any time to react—or the adventurers protecting the residents, for that matter—striking its target deeply without the slightest error. It pierced the monster's raised left hand, knocking the beast back.

"A—aaaaaaaaaaaaaaaarghhhhh—?!"

Losing out to the momentum behind the Fortia Spear now buried in its hand, the monster crashed into the building behind it.

There was a roar and the echoing crash of impact, the deserted house collapsing, the dragon's undulating, long body. The spear smashed into the ground along with the monster's left hand, pinning it down like a live specimen.

——Significant damage to the neighborhood but no casualties.

Finn's top priority was to keep the people as far from the monster as possible. He quickly analyzed the situation as he landed atop a wide roof.

Thump! Thump!

With Aiz leading the way, Bete, Tiona, Tione, Riveria, and Gareth all arrived next to him. The tumult quieted as if the moment was frozen in place, creating a blank moment in time. Finn's eyes narrowed as he scrutinized the half-human, half-dragon monster.

"So that's what's been causing all the commotion, I take it?" he murmured.

Loud cheers broke out an instant later.

"——————————Gh!!"

"Hurray! Hurrrrray!"

"Adventurers!"

It was hasty but prompt—it was a flash of glory when they saved the populace consumed by terror at the sudden shattering of their peaceful lives. The residents of the Labyrinth District exploded in cheers at the sight of the city's strongest taking the stage.

It was a preemptive surprise attack—fast enough to not allow the *concealment* of a certain boy. The faces of the adventurers and goddess filled with despair as he rushed into the frame.

"The residents haven't sustained any casualties yet."

"What's this? Somebody got here before us."

"Wait a sec, isn't that…?"

"It's Argonaut!"

"That rabbit bastard again…?"

As *Loki Familia* continued to gather, Gareth, Tiona, and the others noticed the adventurer standing in the street.

Bell Cranell.

And *Hestia Familia* with their patron goddess.

They made it here faster than we did—No, were they on Daedalus Street this whole time? Finn was suspicious of the coincidence but disregarded it in the face of his top priority.

"A vouivre…That matches the reports of a winged monster."

A reasonable analysis suggested that the monster before their eyes was the same as the one involved in the incident five days ago: the humanoid monster that had shaken the city. Its female dragon body and tail were a bit much to call humanoid, but the wings sprouting from its back matched eyewitness reports.

A subspecies? Or maybe a variant?

And what's with this timing?

Finn predicted that was the real trigger of this incident.

"That monster…Do you think it's connected to the thing on the eighteenth floor? It looks like it's got a restraint on it, but is it armed?" wondered Tiona.

"I can't be certain about that…But the Guild must have planned for this possibility when ordering all familias to stand by," suggested Riveria.

"Tsk, a heads-up would've been nice," snapped Bete.

The three stared at the wide street below them.

When Riveria said *the Guild*, she really meant Ouranos. Finn deduced that her statement was probably half-right. This situation was the worst possible outcome for Ouranos's side. That monster was the secret that Orario's creator god wanted to hide—without a doubt.

As Tiona said, there were manacles on its arms, right where chains had been torn off—proof that it'd been captured by humans. Were those captors *Ikelos Familia*?

There are still some unresolved questions, but for now...

As the breeze tousled his golden hair, Finn looked down at *Hestia Familia* standing stock-still in the street and past them at the suffering monster.

"Captain, the monster..." started Tione.

"The stone in its forehead is missing. *Dispose* of it immediately." Finn made a snap decision.

Vouivres were a rare species of monster. They possessed a drop item, the Vouivre's Tear, said to bring wealth and fortune. But when they lost it, vouivres were known to go into a rage and rampage until they got the stone back. Using the latent potential of a dragon, they became a whirlwind of destruction. With the residents of the Labyrinth District around, the only option for dealing with it was elimination.

But a corpse would do. It would be more than enough physical evidence to use against Ouranos. And it would be more important to preserve the lives of the general public. That was Finn's conclusion.

But...why are you there?

A single boy raised a trembling gaze up at Finn.

It was Bell Cranell.

Why are you looking at me like that?

Upon exchanging a glance with those quivering rubellite eyes, Finn noticed something: an unmistakable unease.

Bell...? At the same time, Aiz felt it again as she stared at his pale face.

She felt an odd chasm. It was the same with the rest of *Hestia Familia*, too. While the residents were celebrating *Loki Familia*'s arrival, they were uniformly speechless, in despair.

She couldn't understand why her eyes were fixed on Bell and not the monster that had appeared aboveground.

"If monsters had a reason to live—"

She suddenly recalled their earlier conversation. Aiz didn't understand why, but she couldn't take her eyes off the boy standing at the threshold of an internal discord.

"Aaaarghh...?!" shrieked the monster, letting out ugly lamentations while its blood ran free.

"Ooooooooooooooooooooooooooooooooooooooooooh!"

The people cheered in expectation that the monster would be struck down, erased from the surface of the world.

The second hand on the clock advanced slowly as the Labyrinth District roared.

The deities in the vicinity silently watched the progress from outside the playing field.

The goddess's followers froze in despair, losing the will to fight back.

The strongest adventurers prepared to eliminate the monster.

And that boy standing on the border of it all.

That boy.

That boy.

That boy—

"_____"

Aiz would never forget that scene.

It would never disappear for all eternity, a scar etched into her heart.

Aiz's golden eyes opened wide.

On that day. At that time. In that location.

A single decision took place, a resolution that loved destruction, too irredeemable, too foolish, the gods would say of it later.

On that day, at that time, in that location, it was a turning point that made a historic impact—the unknowable moment in between eras, as the gods would lament.

On this day. At this time. In this location.

A widely respected up-and-coming *hero* would fall—and in his place, a *fool* was born.

*   *   *

"Oooooooooooooo————...?"

The thunderous anticipation of the crowd turned to a stunned murmur and then to silence.

"Huh?" Bete furrowed his brow at the sight.

"Wait...what's...that?"

"A-Argonaut...?"

Tione and Tiona became flustered.

"Are my eyes playing tricks on me?"

"Finn..."

"...What is he thinking?"

Gareth, Riveria, and Finn coolly narrowed their gazes.

"_____"

And Aiz was at a loss for words.

"...Ngh!!"

The boy confronted them, turning his back to the writhing monster and challenging *Loki Familia* attempting to subdue it.

He shielded the monster, as if to protect it—sweating bullets, breath quivering, turning pale.

Brandishing his jet-black knife, he stood before them, blocking their way.

What are you doing...? For the life of her, Aiz couldn't understand what she was seeing.

Somewhere along the way, the boy who'd been so close to her had ended up so far from her. There was nothing she could do. The only thing Aiz knew was that the two of them were perfectly at odds with each other.

Bell Cranell—

As for Finn, his thoughts were kicking into overdrive—despite his composed tone of voice.

A human was protecting a monster.

But that's exactly what was happening in the scene unfolding

before his eyes, in a series of events that shouldn't have been possible. It was the real motive of the boy blocking his way.

Even with his mind clear, he could only process an error. Finn was
faced with an answer that he couldn't have predicted or deduced
and focused on those rubellite eyes.

What if?

Seriously. What if?

If he worked from the hypothesis that Bell Cranell actually
intended to protect it…

He couldn't accept this in the current situation. It would be a
meaningless discussion. But hypothetically, if it was just the two
of them and the monster had any value, some kind of negotiation
might have been possible.

But they'd been seen by a bunch of people. As the hope of the
prums, Braver had no choice left except summary execution. There
was no acceptable reason to let the monster live.

Meaning if Bell Cranell intended to save the vouivre, then his
decision was the correct one—and an irredeemable *folly* leading to
his own destruction.

"——You really are foolish," murmured one of the gods, the faint
whisper fading into the wind.

In front of the civilians, adventurers, a monster, and the gods, a
single boy threw himself into ruin.

"I saw this vouivre first; it's mine…!"

That was the only excuse he could wring out for all those people.

"Hands off…!" Bell threatened *Loki Familia*, taking on the mask
of a simple, greedy adventurer.

As the vouivre pulled the spear out of its hand and fled from its
restraints with a shriek, the white-haired boy pursued it by himself.

"Ummm…Say what?" Tiona cocked her head in confusion as she
watched Bell run away from them.

"It's against the rules for one adventurer to steal a kill from another..."

Aiz was barely able to say that much. It was the only possible explanation excusing his actions, but she said it as though she was trying to convince herself.

"Ah...Well, vouivres are rare, I guess," Tiona empathized.

"Are you kidding me...? That only matters in the Dungeon. You can't bring that weak shit up here!"

Tiona sounded as though she could be convinced that was a reasonable explanation, but Bete closed his eyes and scratched his scalp with his right hand as he made his retort.

His response was the most obvious and natural one. It was absurd to bring up the regular rules of adventurers in this kind of crisis. In the blink of an eye, animosity spread among the members of *Loki Familia* and the residents of the slum.

Aiz couldn't stop it. There was no way it could be stopped. She could not even put the brakes on her own bewilderment.

"Captain..." started Tione.

"We've no responsibility to go along with a child's selfishness. Follow the vouivre."

As Tione looked to their leader with some hesitation for their next instructions, Finn maintained his poise as the commander and immediately responded. The rest of the familia nodded at the decision of their unwavering prum leader and started to chase them down.

"—*Ooooooooooooooooooooooh!*" roared the monster at a volume that assaulted their ears, as if it was trying to discourage their pursuit.

The vouivre and boy disappeared down the wide road as monsters started appearing one after another.

"Armed monsters!"

"It looks as though there was a connection to Rivira's destruction, after all..."

There were more than twenty of them in total. The majority of them had armor without access to weapons: a lizardman with bloodshot eyes and a monstrous appearance, a gargoyle screaming without pause leading a flock of winged monsters, a red-cap goblin wielding an ax that dwarfed its diminutive body, an al-miraj straddling a hellhound. It was a jumble of species.

Tiona and Tione couldn't believe their eyes, which tensed sharply.

Bringing up the rear, a golden-winged siren danced through the air.

"Bows! Loose!"

"Let's go!"

The residents of Daedalus Street began to scream at the sight of the monster swarm.

The leaders of the secondary forces—the Level-4 chienthrope Cruz and human girl Narfi—moved to protect the noncombatants, loosing arrows at the monsters in the sky as the rest of the familia dashed out in the wake of Narfi's charge.

Seeing them respond on their own judgment without hesitation, Riveria turned to Finn for a confirmation that would be unnecessary in an emergency.

"Finn, what shall we do?"

"…If at all possible, capture them alive," Finn said after a moment of contemplation.

"Alive?" Bete parroted.

"Yeah, I'm curious about something."

Just as he was about to dash off himself, Bete whipped around, the wind taken out of his sails. Finn had not once stopped looking ahead and noticed the damage done to the armed monsters. The bulk of them had sustained wounds, as if they had already fought a battle before their arrival.

Finn had hastily and naturally judged that these armed monsters were the same ones that had appeared on the eighteenth floor. And if they'd come from that floor to the surface, that meant they had traversed Knossos.

Had they been unleashed by human hands or had they opened the door themselves in their march to the surface?

Either way, a Daedalus Orb must have been involved. Finn was working under that assumption.

"Tione and the other vanguards, intercept them. Avoid using magic if possible. It'll cause too much damage to the surroundings."

"Understood!"

"Got it!"

"This is a pain in the ass..."

"The rearguard mages, protect the townspeople and help them evacuate. The safety of the civilians is our top priority. Now go!"

"Yes, sir!"

The orders were to obtain the key or information concerning it and protect the citizens. He handed down these instructions in the hopes of accomplishing both at the same time.

Barred from the use of artillery and supporting fire, the mages focused on rushing to the residents while Tione, Tiona, and Bete descended onto the battlefield.

"Arcus! Don't use the main road. That way, the monsters won't notice you. Take a four-man squad and follow the vouivre. Bring Lefiya with you."

"Eh? Uh, yes, sir!" Lefiya was shocked by the follow-up order but obeyed immediately.

They moved toward the rear, entering a hidden back alley once they could no longer be seen by the monsters.

After every other member of her familia had sprung into action, Aiz moved for the first time in a while, shaking her head slightly as if to switch gears.

"Aiz, you stay here."

"...?"

"Riveria, prepare a barrier. I know what I said, but there's no way the townspeople will be able to get away that quickly."

"...Too much renown poses its own problems. I understand. We must be cautious."

"Thanks. Gareth, sorry, but can you set up a perimeter over there?"

"Hmm? Fine by me, but...will they be okay against the armed monsters?"

"Yeah, Bete's group should be enough."

Finn tacked on more instructions to the pile for Riveria and Gareth specifically. Aiz was feeling impatient about being left to her own devices, looking out over the battlefield with him. Honestly, it was difficult for her to stay still.

"...Finn."

"Yeah. Sorry, Aiz, but you stay here just in case," Finn responded when she finally looked at him to complain.

He had on a vague strained smile that didn't betray whether he could understand her feelings. And his face tensed as he quickly looked over the street.

"...Is there...something coming?"

"My thumb is a bit...you know..." His blue eyes narrowed as he licked his thumb.

Moments later, the adventurers clashed with the armed monsters. The battle had begun.

The sound of weapons clanging against one another and the violent screeching of the monsters was deafening. At every turn on the wide street, there were adventurers working together to intercept the monsters with the most potential to inflict damage. The battle progressed as Finn anticipated—with *Loki Familia*'s forces superior from start to finish.

"...This doesn't seem like your regular lizardman," Tione murmured as she distanced herself from the monster that had broken free of its shackles.

The lizardman had taken significant damage from her haphazard attacks, stumbling unstably as it gripped a longsword and scimitar, but she could see that the will to fight was burning strong in its deep-orange eyes.

"*Grooooaaa!*" It roared wildly, obstinately, and attacked with a precise slash.

It possessed unmistakable skill and command of tactics, though its sword techniques evoked the image of a self-taught warrior. As an Amazon, Tione could tell it was a style that had been nurtured through frequent combat. At the same time, she had never run across a monster that possessed learned techniques before. And to take it a step further, such a monster shouldn't even exist.

Tione licked her lips at the thought of fighting this monster. It unleashed various techniques one after another—instead of relying on instinct alone. That said, her beloved's orders needed to be carried out, and she dispassionately battered the enemy in front of her eyes.

"Quite the looker for a monster, aren't you?"

Meanwhile, there was a single siren collapsed at Bete's feet. He'd won in an instant.

A portion of unsightly blood fell away from its face, revealing one beautiful enough to rival an elf.

But Bete mercilessly stomped down on the siren's stomach.

"*...Argh?!*"

"Monsters can go to hell."

His smile stretched and twisted the tattoo on his cheek, which was dyed red with a mix of scorn and rage. Bete couldn't accept monsters walking around aboveground like they owned the place—or flying around in the sky or swimming around lazily in the seas.

It was unforgivable.

He would never say it out loud, and he wouldn't think back on his past, but the cold hard truth was that Bete's family—the people who were most important to him—had almost all been slaughtered by monsters.

Bete stamped his foot down, unleashing the full extent of his wrath on behalf of all the people in the world. Even if it was female, even if its face looked vaguely human, it wouldn't stop him. He had no mercy for any type of monster.

You bastards deserve to be destroyed, he thought as he beat the siren that had dared to come aboveground.

"*OOOoooooooooo!*" A gargoyle swooped in as Bete continued to punt the monster.

"One pain in the ass after another." He met it without any difficulty, easily brushing it aside.

"*GOOAGH?!*"

"You dumbasses are a long way from home."

Bete ripped off the stone claws of the enemy, slamming his metal boots into its body. The expression on the werewolf's face remained contorted.

Bete realized the feeling filling his chest: *This is pissing me off.*

That was because their howls sounded as if they were protecting something. He couldn't shake the feeling that these monsters crying out and thinking of their comrades closely resembled his family on the plains. They were despicable, loathsome, detestable.

"Just stay down already!"

"*Gaagh?!*"

He slammed a brutal kick into the gargoyle to avoid confronting his feelings.

"Come at me!"

"*Grugh?!*"

As Bete vented his frustrations in a violent rampage, Tiona knocked back a goblin. By using hand-to-hand techniques from her studies in Telskyura, she rendered it incapable of fighting back.

"I'm not Bete or anything, but it's hard to hold back using Urga."

She was dragging her feet to her job, working her way around the intense battlefield with the other familia members. She knew there wasn't a weapon more unsuited to the task of capturing monsters alive than Urga. And above all else, she was hesitant to use it on them.

It's kinda…hard to fight these guys. What's with this horde of monsters…?

She neutralized the al-miraj, sending it flying with a flick to the forehead as she frowned slightly. This horde was different from the beasts they usually killed in the Dungeon. She couldn't put it into words, but it felt bad. She was finding it difficult to fight.

If Tione heard her line of thought, Tiona would probably catch a slap to the back of the head. But she couldn't explain it, and it wasn't based on anything, seeing as she was an idiot. Despite being an airhead, Tiona was struggling to resolve it when the ground shook.

"Waaah?! What's that?!"

The stone pavement welled up, and a lump of metal appeared from underground—a kind of metallic monster resembling a giant flame rock. She hadn't seen anything like it before. The others fighting nearby paused to look on in shock.

Tiona quickly realized its body was made of adamantite—just like her Urga. As if to prove her right, it deflected the attacks of Tione and Bete. Its movements were slow and efficient, knocking away the vanguard wall, shields and all.

"—Yeah, yeah, thaaat's what I was looking for!"

Tiona's eyes sparkled as she swung her sword. A sudden rush of enthusiasm bubbled up within her—if for no other reason than the hunk of metal not causing the same lump in her throat as the other monsters.

With this thing, I don't have to think about anything when I'm swinging my sword.

To push past her doubts, Tiona split the golem in a single slash.

Interest, annoyance, and delay.

Each holding their own thoughts, *Loki Familia* proceeded to neutralize the armed monsters.

"…What is this?" Aiz whispered amid the chaos.

Her whisper went unheard as she watched the battle unfold before her eyes. She was standing above it all, overlooking the battlefield. Because of that, it was easy for her to understand—much more clearly and distinctly than Tiona and the others fighting.

The monsters were covering one another. They were *working together* to fight—as if they were adventurers.

What's going on? That's impossible.

There were monsters with enough intelligence that had been known to cooperate with one another for the purposes of attacking mankind—but protecting one another? That was unheard of. To devour people, they didn't care whether others of their species or anything else got killed in the process. That was what a monster was: a beast.

And yet.

Aiz hid her bewilderment and agitation behind her emotionless expression.

Is there anyone else who's noticed it? Tiona? Tione? Bete? Anyone else?

What are you thinking, Finn?

The prum leader beside her was wearing a commander's mask, hiding his feelings.

Her mind was a mess.

Her heart was filled with confusion.

She couldn't get the image of that boy protecting the vouivre out of her head. Aiz realized her palms were sweaty as she looked out over the battlefield.

"OOOOOOOOOOOOOOOOOOOOOoooooooooooooooooooooooooooo oooooo!!"

That's why Aiz was relieved when she heard that overwhelming roar, when she saw that pitch-black body, the very image of fear and menace.

And even though the piercing howl immediately rendered the residents unconscious, even though its arms as thick as logs blew away several of her comrades, even though its brutal Labrys battle-ax was glinting in the sunlight, sowing destruction in its path, in the corner of her heart roiled by shock, Aiz felt reassured.

Because this was the kind of monster she knew.

"Uooooooo!"

It was a pitch-black minotaur.

Tiona, Tione, and Bete barely managed to hold their ground, while the other members were cornered by its restraint and unable to intervene. Just as the Level 6s were about to take control of the battle by leveraging their numbers, the titanic monster unsheathed a second ax from behind its back.

""""?!"""""

The colossal weapon ripped through the ground, kicking up a

storm of electrical discharges and scattering the dried clots of blood on its blade to reveal its golden color. It was a magic blade with the lightning attribute.

Bathed in a net of thunder, the first-tier adventurers couldn't help but freeze for an instant.

The black minotaur swung the ax upward, piercing the heavens as it flipped into position to mercilessly attack them.

"Riveria, the barrier!" Finn shouted, abandoning all pretenses of composure.

"*Via Shilheim!*" rang out a resonant voice, casting the spell to form a magic barrier in the shape of a dome.

It protected the unconscious residents at the same time as the minotaur unleashed its next blast.

"—*OOOOOOOOOOOOOOOOOOOOOOOOOOOOOOOOOOO OOOOOOOO!*"

Lightning flooded the area like a crashing wave.

Bete stuck out his Frosvirt to absorb the impact, but the thunderous explosion of lightning couldn't be contained. Bete, Tiona, and Tione bore the brunt of the attack and were sent flying back as the other members were swallowed up in a whirlpool of light.

The undulating rays of light ripped up the cobblestones, leaving rows of houses obliterated in their wake. Other than Riveria's barrier, nothing escaped destruction.

This was the largest amount of damage that had been dealt since the start of the battle against the monsters. Once the thunderous bombardment passed through, the smoke cleared to reveal a demolished street with the members of *Loki Familia* collapsed on the ground.

Everyone had been wiped out—except for Bete and the two sisters.

"No more trying to catch them alive—"

The black minotaur stood in the center of the street pulverized from that location onward to the western end. Everything had been turned to rubble, save the eastern end of the street where the defeated armed monsters lay in a crumpled heap.

Finn's eyes narrowed at the scene of destruction—and Aiz dashed out, unseen, alone, without saying a word or making a sound.

She moved as though compelled by something, welcoming something, as she kicked the roof and whirled through the sky, landing behind the monster.

"—Do it, Aiz!"

Tap.
The beast's back stiffened at the sound of her boots lightly striking the ground as she drew her trusted sword.
"Understood."
Aiz didn't take notice of the tone of her voice. There was a quality of serenity to it. And her gaze was calm as she stood before the roaring minotaur spinning around to smash its ax down onto her.
"*Tempest,*" she chanted in a sonorous voice, signaling an intent to kill.
"*Airiel.*"
The wind whined.
A tremendous flow of air rushed up, and her sword flashed.
And in the next moment, the monster's right arm flew through the sky.
"_____"

Her comrades, *Hestia Familia*, the armed monsters, and the black minotaur were silent.
The flash of steel stole all their breaths away. A gentle breeze blew by, and the severed arm crashed to the ground.
Even as the screech of the monster reached a fever pitch and its blood spattered onto its surroundings, the wind shielded the girl's body from it all, functioning as her armor. Her heart was calm.
There was no doubt—straightforward to the point that it surprised her.
As her long blond locks rippled in the wind, Aiz held the beauty of a goddess on the battlefield, swinging her sword at the giant monster before her—mercilessly, even cruelly.
"Here I come," she warned.
The dark minotaur sent spittle flying as it furiously started to

counterattack, but Aiz kept her composure, playing a melody by slicing her sword through the wind.

"_____*Argh?!*"

She unleashed seemingly thousands of slashes from all angles. Sheathed in the wind, Desperate cut through the armored enemy's body, sending splashes of blood flying. But her sword didn't stop. Aiz's whole body flitted around, slicing up a storm into the enemy standing before her.

"*UOOOOOOOOOOOOOOOOOOOOOOOOOOOOO!*"

In the blink of an eye, it was covered in blood, but its eyes flared, ready to fight back—as a monster that surpassed human intellect. It pushed forward, abandoning its defenses. With one arm and one foot in its grave, it forced itself to launch a counterattack. Unloading a single strike with enough force to turn everything to dust, it knocked back her stream of slashes. Her field of vision quivering, Aiz was shocked for a moment but regained her fighting spirit—and awe.

Ah.

How strong.

How terrifying.

How dreadful.

Yes, this is—

"Th-that's…"

Her sword growled as she accelerated, and the world around her seemed to freeze in time. As her eyes lost sight of everything but the black monster before her, Aiz was no longer capable of noticing someone murmuring.

As the person witnessed the frozen features of the Sword Princess and the furious slashes filled with black flames, their voice quivered.

"That's…the War Princess."

Someone had called her that long ago: the War Princess, monster slayer in a girl's skin, the one who'd built untold mountains of monster corpses, the reckless fighter who never tired of descending into the depths of the Dungeon over and over.

As her sword danced, she reverted to her appearance as the Doll

Princess, one she'd long ago left behind—all the more beautiful for the perilousness of it. She inspired fear and terror in the monsters and *Loki Familia*.

But Aiz didn't notice that she was unconsciously using the skill she'd forbidden herself from using on others.

"...Aiz."

She didn't process the murmur of a high elf watching as she became possessed by the battle.

Good—

Aiz felt relieved before the pitch-black minotaur, the incarnation of violence.

This is a monster.

This is a beast.

I'm not in the wrong.

The image of the boy protecting the vouivre faded from her mind.

I knew I wasn't wrong.

Monsters must be killed.

As the minotaur joyously roared for more combat, Aiz danced, unleashing a loud hum with the wind.

The young version of Aiz in a corner of her heart was peering at her, lonely, but she pretended not to see her as she tore into the pitch-black minotaur.

INTERLUDE

THE FAIRY'S RAGE

Гэта казка іншага сям і.

Фея была лютасьць

"Lefiya, get a move on!"

"O-okay!"

While *Loki Familia*'s main group was clashing with the black minotaur, Lefiya and the others were headed to the southern end of Daedalus Street. Following Finn's orders, they had formed a four-man cell to hound the fleeing vouivre.

"Little Rookie, you bastard. Showing your true colors!"

"Thinking about making money at a time like this...Can you believe this crap?!"

"..."

The human and elf familia members voiced their irritation as they sprinted. They had endless insults for an adventurer who would invite unnecessary chaos by protecting a monster.

How greedy did an adventurer have to be to aim for a rare monster's high-value drop item at a time like this? That's how Bell Cranell appeared to them. That was the only way they could rationalize his actions.

Their incandescent rage took the form of open disdain. It was an obvious conclusion.

Lefiya alone kept quiet, lips pursed, face unreadable.

What was that human thinking?!

Lefiya wasn't feeling the same anger as the others. She was perplexed.

She didn't want to acknowledge it, but compared to the others, she'd had more interactions with Bell Cranell and, at the very least, understood his nature.

A selfish desire. A vision clouded by riches. Those words could never be used to describe him.

A greedy adventurer? It was so uncharacteristic that instead of bursting with rage, she was more likely to look to the heavens for some explanation. If he was that kind of adventurer, he could have gotten through life a lot easier.

That was why she couldn't figure it out.

Why would he go this far to protect a monster? Even if it resulted in him being reviled as a greedy adventurer?

Lefiya was trying to process a comparable feeling of shock to Aiz and Tiona when she saw him protect the vouivre. Instead of criticizing him, she was unsure how to respond even now.

Why do I have to be worrying myself over you…?!

That was why she was so unhappy with him—acting in a way that would invite misunderstanding.

Or maybe she was actually feeling anger.

"Other adventurers are…!"

The light from the setting sun shone on Lefiya's face as a bunch of adventurers from all different familias started appearing on the scene upon hearing the uproar on Daedalus Street. They'd gathered to get the situation under control: If they were going to take out the monster, they needed to act now. Lefiya and the other members from *Loki Familia* split up and jumped into the forest of interlocking buildings, rushing in the direction from where the cries and dust clouds were originating.

"Eep?! Noooooooooooooooo!"

"Whoa, hey, adventurers?! Over here! Over here!!"

The howls of the monster's advance were without end, and its piercing wails echoed all around. With the others, Lefiya became uneasy as they witnessed weeping prostitutes and their children clambering to escape before them.

Their group accelerated, stepping out onto a straight road.

"There it is!"

They confirmed the sight of the vouivre's titanic body in the distance. And just before it, the back of a white-haired boy as he pursued the monster.

"We're going to circle around! Lefiya, hit it with your magic from here!"

"Yes, sir!"

The other three people in her cell moved ahead as Lefiya raised her staff, Forest Teardrop. She could see that the vouivre had already been injured—the adventurers lying in wait must have hit it with their own attacks. The dragon tail hanging from its lower body had a javelin sticking out of it, and from its slender back sprouted arrows.

The monster unleashed a pained roar as Lefiya prepared to chant when she saw something unbelievable.

"*Firebolt!*"

It was magic.

The boy had cast magic—*at the adventurers.*

"?!"

She couldn't believe her eyes. The electrical fire crackled, blowing away the adventurers trying to intercept the monster.

"Wh—?!"

"*Arrrrrgh?!*"

None of them were able to deal with it—because none of them expected to be attacked by a fellow adventurer, not here, not now. Their weapons were shattered while their bodies suffered burns as they plunged from the collapsing rooftop. Lefiya was at a loss for words at his eccentric behavior—something that far surpassed simple barbarism.

Bell Cranell's magic was a menace.

He didn't have to worry about chanting to unleash the Swift-Strike spell, which had the force of a short-trigger cast to match. But it was a Level 3. After becoming a second-tier adventurer, he had magic on par with a Level-2 mage. Its firepower was not an insignificant thing. It shot off at a speed that hardly anyone could hope to block—the members of *Loki Familia* focused on the monster were no exception. They took a direct hit when they were about to attack the vouivre, and their heads smacked into the wall and the ground upon impact.

"Wh—?"

——*What are your intentions?!*

——*What are you doing?!*

——*If you do that…!*

As her mind fogged over, Lefiya's apprehensions became reality.

"Little Rookie, you piece of shit!"

"Are you out of your damn mind?!"

"You want the rare drop that badly, you greedy rat?!"

"At a time like this?!"

A violent swirl of rage and abuse welled up among the adventurers.

Lefiya's hands started to tremble, feeling as though the abuse and slander hurled at Bell was aimed at her. The residents who had been desperately trying to flee froze in place, dumbfounded, and the children started to bawl at an increased urgency, adding to the chaos of the situation.

But despite all of that, Bell kept firing off magic.

He was pushing everyone away from the vouivre as if to protect it while chasing after the rampaging monster.

"Ngh!" Gripping her staff, Lefiya sprinted with all her might.

Taking the shortest path along the top of the roofs, she finally raced fast enough to line up alongside him.

"Bell Cranell!! What are you doing?!!" she screamed.

"Gh…!"

He glanced over at her once, but that was the limit of his response. His twisted face didn't allow for a dialogue as he sped up, trying to leave her in the dust.

—*Are you ignoring me?!* Lefiya seethed.

"Wait! Answer! My! Question!" she huffed, shouting over the wind whipping against her body.

But the boy refused to meet her eyes. He was focused on the monster making its escape, and he'd discarded everything except for that.

"Why? Why…?!" Lefiya growled.

Why do you look like you're suffering?!

Look at me!

Explain yourself!

If you don't, I won't be able to understand anything!

She screamed in her mind at the boy whose face was clearly conflicted and distressed.

What happened to your usual excuses? Turn red already while you shout You've got it all wrong! *Hurry up and say something! Just like when you make excuses after angering me by getting involved with my beloved Aiz! Do it now, and I'll get a little mad, lecture you, give you a warning, and then forgive you—just like usual!*

Don't make a pitiful face!

That expression doesn't fit you at all!

She couldn't hold together the list of all the things filling her heart. Lefiya certainly didn't want to see him in this sad state. It wasn't disappointment or despair but unpleasant.

As a competitor, as a rival, as an adventurer aiming for the same aspiration, she wanted to ask about his true intentions. At this point, she wasn't even chasing the monster.

She was chasing him.

"*Guaaaagh?!*"

"—?!"

With the screams echoing around her, she had no choice but to give up on questioning him. Adventurers kept collapsing, blood flowing freely from their wounds, and the vouivre continued to rampage. Without the red stone on its forehead, the dragon had become entirely indiscriminate, no more calculating than a storm now.

Her eyes wavered, and Lefiya had to destroy the monster.

"*—Unleashed pillar of light, limbs of the holy tree. You are the master archer!*" She cast concurrently, sprinting at full speed.

Bell's shoulders quivered as he felt the magical energy building, and he looked back at her for the first time. He hesitated to fire off a spell—possibly because she was an acquaintance—then he began screaming as if he were being split in two.

"Please stop!!"

——*Don't be unreasonable!*

If I let it go, more people will get hurt. In the worst case, the ordinary civilians will get tossed around like the adventurers are now. This is long past the point of trivial grievances.

If I fail to stop it, you're the one who's going to face a tragic future!

"*Loose your arrows, fairy archers. Pierce, arrow of accuracy!*" cast Lefiya, thrusting out her staff and firing her spell with a contorted face.

"*Arcs Ray!*"

A single shot of magic homed in on its target. After it was released, the missile would not disappear until it hit home. This was an arrow that would never miss.

The ray of light shone with enough power to lay low a large-scale monster.

Upon seeing that dazzling light, the boy turned around in despair.

"?!"

He leaped *into the path of the magic*, spreading his arms, trying to intercept the ray of light before it hit the vouivre.

Lefiya gazed in wonder as he attempted to physically shield the monster.

"*A-Alio?!*" He immediately chanted a spell to disperse it.

When it was hit by the homing spellkey magic, Arcs Ray scattered just before reaching him.

"Grrrrrrrrrrrm?!"

Even though he wasn't directly hit by it, Bell was blasted away when it exploded directly in front of him. With smoke rising from his armor, the battered boy leaped to his feet and resumed his chase of the vouivre.

Lefiya was left behind, dumbfounded.

"...Why?"

In the middle of the road, the legs of the elf stopped moving.

Why would you go that far?

Why would you go to such lengths to protect a monster?

Why do I feel this way about you when I'm right and you're wrong?

She couldn't wrap her head around it.

"...Wait, Bell Cranell!" she screeched at the back moving away from her position on the street.

But the boy didn't pay her any heed. It was as if he didn't want to waste a second in his pursuit of the vouivre. He persisted in playing the fool.

Lefiya clenched both fists, ignored again and again, her body starting to tremble. Her long ears turned red to their tips, and as if she could bear it no more, she closed her eyes, roaring as loudly as she could.

"Your reason! Your situation!…Explain yourseeeeeeelf!!"

The sun dipped below the city walls. As dusk set in, the screams of the bright-red elf echoed across the evening sky.

THE MELANCHOLY OF A HERO.

THE ANGUISH OF THE SWORD PRINCESS.

Πριγκίπισσα του σπαθιού.
θα αναλωθείς σε πράξεις εκδίκησης.

Χρόνε, σταμάτησε.
γίσαι όμορφη.
το σπαθί,

Σε παρακαλώ.
Χρόνε, σταμάτα.
Μέχρι την ημέρα που θα εμφανιστεί ο ήρωάς σου.

Είσαι όμορφη.

Гэты казка іншага сям'і.

Опо меланхоліі жанчына фехтавання Tsukai адважных

"Lord Ikelos, we don't have time to go back and forth here. Just answer our questions," demanded Finn, face-to-face with the god.

The location was a run-down, deserted house. The red sunset was visible through a hole in the wall, lighting the rubble on the floor. It was evening, immediately after the battle with the armed monsters.

The black minotaur and all the other monsters managed to escape by using clever ploys. *Loki Familia* was dealing with the cleanup—repairing the destroyed street, keeping watch for monsters, assisting and guiding the residents.

The vouivre had been killed at the hands of adventurers. The ashes from its corpse had been found in a secret underground path. A more detailed investigation was ongoing.

While the familia members were carrying out their duties, Finn had Loki with him as he questioned one of the persons of interest connected to the incident.

"You say that, but you guys already know about Knossos, right? That means there's not much for me to talk about." The god chuckled, which echoed through the dilapidated house.

He had navy hair, dark skin, and was wearing mostly black clothes. His face was well proportioned—a clear indicator that he was a god—with an insincere, superficial grin etched onto it. It was the smile of a hedonistic, ephemeral, destructive, stubborn god.

He was Ikelos, the patron god of *Ikelos Familia*, captured in the dragnet that Finn had asked Gareth to set up.

"When the folks from the Guild get here, they'll arrest ya. Once they do, we can't twist your arm anymore, so cough up what we want now."

"Don't glare at me, Loki. And twisting my arm? I'd never have guessed you to act that way."

As Loki glared down at him, Ikelos responded playfully, perched on an uncomfortable-looking piece of rubble. He locked eyes with Finn, who was sitting in an ancient-looking chair in front of him.

"Do you have a key to Knossos?"

"I don't. Come on, I swear. After the thing with Ishtar, the Evils took it when we went outside."

As a key witness to this event, Ikelos would undoubtedly be taken away by the Guild. And he would be dealt with: sent back to the heavens or banished from the city for eternity. Either way, if *Loki Familia* let this opportunity slip by, they would not see him again.

Finn intended to get information out of him before they handed him over to the Guild.

"What's the size of the remnants of the Evils? How many familias are there?"

"No clue. It's just the odds and ends that Thanatos managed to draw to himself. I was just using them to get a place to sleep, so I didn't have much interest in them at all. It was just in passing. But if you're thinkin' about them in terms of familias, then it's really just Thanatos's people."

"'Enyo'...Do you know a god going by that name?"

"Oh, the city destroyer? I don't remember any god going by such a stupid name," Ikelos answered Finn and Loki.

His responses were all along the lines of *I don't know.* He apparently amused himself by watching over his own familia—making them put on interesting performances—and was not at all connected to the plot to destroy Orario. At the very least, Loki could vouch for the fact that he wasn't lying.

"Why'd you join up with the Evils?" Loki spat.

"Just the way the cookie crumbled," he responded with a shameless grin.

Ikelos Familia spearheaded the plans to smuggle through Meren as a way to fund the construction of Knossos. When asked why they were smuggling monsters, his answer was that they sold for a high price to aristocrats with an interest in monsters.

They ended up with information about things they already knew, and they made paltry progress on the parts they didn't know. But—they did learn the origin of that strange man-made labyrinth.

It was a monument to human tenacity, dreamed up by the great craftsman Daedalus and built by his descendants.

Loki visibly grimaced while Finn managed to hold in his astonishment when they heard that Knossos had been built over a span of a thousand years to reach its current scale.

On that fateful day when Knossos first beat them, they realized it was extraordinary the moment they set foot in the area. And it was apparently connected to a deep-rooted delusion far greater than they'd imagined.

"That's how that den of devils originated…Then, where is the notebook that fascinated Daedalus's family and compelled that madness? Is there a blueprint mapping Knossos?"

"Heh-heh…Braver, do you really intend to clear that absurd labyrinth?"

"Just answer Finn's question already, dumbass."

"I don't have it. Really. Dix had it. But if there aren't any traces of his Blessing anymore, he must already be dead."

"…"

"Maybe someone took it. Or maybe it just fell somewhere in Knossos."

Finding a single notebook in the middle of that complicated and mysterious labyrinth…It was a dizzying prospect. A metaphorical needle in a haystack.

"But if it's been burned into the heads of the other descendants of Daedalus, you might find it if you pry open their skulls," Ikelos joked, earning a kick from Loki.

"…Lord Ikelos, final question."

The sun was sinking, and the sound of footsteps was getting louder outside the deserted house. Guessing that people from the Guild had arrived, Finn narrowed his blue eyes as he broached the subject.

"The armed monsters…Just what are they?"

"…Heh-heh-heh-heh-heh. What do you mean by that, Braver? What are you tryin' to ask?"

Ikelos's smile broadened, and he seemed to enjoy himself from the bottom of his heart as he peered into Finn's face.

"Do they have emotions? Do they possess not only cognition but some kind of higher reasoning? Have they formed a community of sorts?" Finn continued probing, approaching the crux of the matter.

They were speculations that an ordinary adventurer—no, that anyone living in this world would laugh off. He was assigning savage monsters traits that should never describe them. But that was exactly what Finn was suggesting in all sincerity and earnestness.

Aiz had sensed that the monsters were cooperating, too. Despite the fact that they were all different species, they were supporting one another in a way comparable to humans, fighting to achieve a goal that went beyond simple slaughter. Specifically, they were fighting in order to buy time for the vouivre to get away.

Finn was the only one who had fought them in the Labyrinth District, observed them in detail, and still attempted to broach this topic.

"Is it possible for people and monsters to come to a mutual understanding?"

The dilapidated building was silent. Loki watched Finn silently. Ikelos smirked, his lips curling into a crescent.

"No clue."

"…"

"When I tried to hold a conversation or wave at the monsters locked up in the cages, they wouldn't respond at all."

He wasn't lying.

Certainly, he wasn't lying, but he wasn't being honest, either.

It was as if he was saying, *Why don't you see for yourself?* His navy eyes narrowed, and he looked back at Finn with a smug grin. Finn's face became expressionless, and he was silent for a moment.

"Is *Hestia Familia*…Is Bell Cranell connected to them?" Finn spilled out unconsciously, asking the question before he realized it.

"Who knows?" Ikelos played dumb, blowing smoke as before. "Maybe he's friends with that vouivre?"

"Isn't that the magic blade you made?"

Tsubaki's mouth curled down in distaste. Her visitor was Riveria, the jade-haired high elf. They were in the workshop in *Hephaistos Familia's* branch store on Northwest Main Street.

Riveria placed a certain item on the workbench between the two of them: a bloodstained battle-ax with gold ornamentation—an ax-style magic blade.

"…Where did you find this?" Tsubaki responded slowly.

"I'm sure you've heard about the incident the other day on Daedalus Street. We recovered it there," Riveria answered smoothly.

She closed an eye, peering with the other at the face of the master smith trying to conceal her agitation.

"I know Gareth has a direct contract with you, and he said it was one of your works without a doubt."

"Hmm, I see…And what of the dwarf?"

"Right now, he's completing a high-priority construction project—in the middle of it and unable to leave. Hence why I came."

One day had passed since the armed monsters had emerged aboveground. The city was on edge, and the residents had been calling for the Guild to hold a question-and-answer session and present a response plan. The monsters had not yet been apprehended, either. The disturbance in Orario was ongoing.

"And this magic blade is one of yours, correct?"

"Yes…It's from my smithy. There's no way I could mistake one of my own creations. Its name is Kaminari-Ikazuchi-Maru. I started by attempting to copy an impertinent magic blade smith to surpass him. For starters, I studied that unintelligible naming sense of his, but good grief, now I just regret—"

"Tsubaki." Riveria softly cut her off, silencing the smith. "This was used by the armed monsters…by a black minotaur. Because of it, several in our familia were more than a little injured."

Her tone of voice was vaguely accusatory.

Or was it just Tsubaki's imagination hearing it that way?

"Can you explain why a monster would be using this?"

"…And you suspect me, Riveria?" Tsubaki asked nervously, rooted in a fear of being suspected of associating with the monsters.

"What is there to suspect you for? I'm merely asking if you have any idea why a monster was holding your magic blade. Nothing more, nothing less." Riveria responded without missing a beat or displaying any trace of emotion.

Her jade eyes watched Tsubaki and certainly didn't seem accusatory. They were only looking to acquire information. But it was clear they wouldn't forgive lies.

With a noble presence, the fastidious high elf pressed the question.

"…Gaaaaaaaaaaaaaah." Tsubaki let out a full-bodied sigh.

"The transaction was supposed to be handled in utmost secrecy, but I guess there's no point in holding back if it's come to this. I've no interest in keeping my silence and being suspected by you all… And the buyer has already passed on."

"…? What do you mean?"

"I sold this magic blade to *Ganesha Familia*…to Hashana Dorlia."

"!"

Riveria could not contain her shock.

"That Hashana? The one killed in Rivira…?"

"That's the guy. At the time, he mentioned getting a quest that required absolute secrecy. He couldn't reveal it to anyone and needed to descend to the lower levels solo."

"And he came by to commission a strong magic blade?"

"That's right. If there was no rearguard, he'd have to cover it himself. And because it required absolute secrecy, I kept my promise not to reveal it to anyone. Until today, at least.

"I was shocked when I heard what happened to Hashana, but…" Tsubaki added with a frown.

"That's all I know. Of course, I've got no guess as to why a monster was using it, either."

There was no lie in what she said. After observing Tsubaki's face, Riveria covered her mouth with one hand as she pondered what she'd heard.

Hashana Dorlia had been sent to recover the crystal orb fetus from the thirtieth floor.

Did the magic blade cross the Dungeon by some means before making its way to the armed monsters...? If Finn's supposition is correct, does that mean the armed monsters have a connection not just to the Guild but to Ganesha Familia, *too?*

Did Hashana know something about those armed monsters? Riveria decided to limit the scope of her musings for the moment.

In any case, her suspicions had more or less been answered.

Given it was a magic blade crafted by one of Orario's master smiths, it wasn't surprising that Bete and the others had been hurt by it.

After careful deliberation, Riveria looked up again at Tsubaki.

"Is there anything else you haven't told me?"

"Hey, quit the cross-examination already! That's everything! I've got nothing to be guilty about!"

Tsubaki placed both hands on her hips, puffing up her chest, emphasizing her voluptuous bosom covered by a bleached white cloth. It was as if she was saying, *Dig all you want; I've got nothing to hide. No matter how much you feel around—or search.* Her unpatched right eye glared sharply.

...I can see she doesn't feel troubled about anything else. After taking in her childish pose, Riveria sighed.

"Very well. I'm sorry for taking up your time. As for this magic blade...should I return it to you?"

"Ah...yes, if it's lost its user, I'll take it."

After handing over the magic blade, Riveria left the room, exiting the shop to report her findings to Finn and the others deployed in the Labyrinth District.

"…Good grief. That was a bit tense."

As she looked out the window at the high elf walking away down Main Street, Tsubaki felt drained.

"It did seem like my goddess knew something about those monsters…Should I ask her about them?"

All things considered, it's good I don't know anything yet, she thought to herself as she massaged her neck. *If I'd known, those green eyes would have seen right through me trying to hide it just now.*

"………"

Lefiya was sullen.

Her mood was so dark that the other familia members nearby averted their eyes, trying not to broach the topic.

"…Lefiya. We're monitoring *Hestia Familia* right now. Keep it together, please."

"I'm properly keeping watch."

"Er…That's not what I meant…Your mood…" trailed off the Level-4 chienthrope Cruz as he tried to work himself up to say something.

Lefiya didn't even glance at him, remaining focused solely on a certain manor.

They were in the sixth district, the southwest quarter of the city, and inside a building constructed in one part of that district, located on a block filled with high-class residences on large lots.

Loki Familia was monitoring *Hestia Familia*'s home, Hearthstone Manor. This was because Finn had concluded that Bell and the others had been involved in the incident where the armed monsters appeared aboveground.

Report any moves that Hestia's followers make, the prum leader had ordered.

The surveillance squad led by Cruz had borrowed an abandoned building diagonally opposite the manor to observe their movements. And Lefiya had personally volunteered to be on that squad.

"Hey, Elfie…What's up with Lefiya? She's been kind of off since that incident, hasn't she?"

"That's what I want to ask, Cruuuuuuz! I'm her roommate, but she won't talk to me at all! Which means I've got no clue what's going on!"

"Just say that to begin with..."

Ignoring their idiotic banter, Lefiya continued to peer out from the slatted window blinds. As she scanned their surroundings, she could see other adventurers hiding around street corners and in other buildings. It wasn't only *Loki Familia* that was watching *Hestia Familia*. They probably suspected Bell Cranell of knowing something, as did Finn. But Lefiya couldn't care one way or the other.

She glared at the manor. It showed no signs of movement—or rather, she glared at the boy she was certain was somewhere inside it.

"Hey, what are you so mad about, Lefiya? Just tell me already!"

"...I'm not particularly angry about anything."

"You are, though! Like, it's so obvious! Look at your face! It's scary!"

Elfie's comments elicited only a surly response from Lefiya, since she hadn't been able to figure it out herself, either.

Why was she irritated? When she thought about it and asked herself...her answer was foolish.

Doesn't that mean I'm...I mean, Loki Familia *are the bad guys?!*

At the present moment, *Loki Familia* had the support of the public for protecting the Labyrinth District, and the populace was speaking ill of Little Rookie for protecting the monster.

Lefiya couldn't resolve the suspicion bothering her.

They needed to prevent the plan that would pulverize the town, to eliminate the armed monsters roaming aboveground—all in service of supporting the Labyrinth City. They were on a mission, a noble cause. Or at the very least, that's what Lefiya thought as an elf. *Loki Familia* was delivering justice.

If we're doing the right thing, why do I have to feel this bad?

Lefiya saw that scene: The boy had thrust himself into danger to protect the vouivre. And for some reason, that action had felt justified when she saw it—as if the scorned act of protecting a monster wasn't *wrong*.

That was how desperate and earnest he appeared in his endeavor.

And because that human won't explain himself, I can't understand why he did any of it!

——In the end, that was the source of her anger.

Lefiya was upset with Bell Cranell for not talking to her, despite obviously having some kind of reason for his actions. At least she was honest about considering his situation from his point of view and counterintuitively begging him—"I can't understand if you don't talk to me"—at the same time.

After considering everything that had transpired, she set aside slower options and decided on the simplest method available to her.

"L-Lefiya?"

"Oy! Where are you going?"

Lefiya left the room without saying a word in response to Elfie or Cruz, walking briskly and hastily out the building before making her way to Hearthstone Manor.

"Wai—!"

She could hear Elfie's voice from the building behind her but chose to ignore it. Using the leaping ability of a Level 3, she cleared the main gate and metal fence, eliciting a groaned "Oyyy?!" from Cruz.

But she paid no heed to that, either.

Beneath the cloudy sky, she cut through the estate with long strides, climbed the steps, and rang the bell at the front door.

Clang, clang! No response. No one came out.

Clang, clang! again. No trace of a response. Ignored.

Lefiya silently and blankly continued ringing the bell progressively louder and louder.

As time passed, the *clang, clang!* had taken on tremendous strength and turned into *CLANG, CLANG!* at which point there was finally a response on the other side. Someone walked up to the door. Lefiya released the calling bell.

With a *click*, the door slowly opened.

"M-may I ask who's here…?" stammered a cute, reserved renart girl peeking out from behind the cracked door.

She was wearing a maid uniform, and her long blond hair resembled Aiz's. Her face wasn't elven but was extremely beautiful nonetheless.

Is this someone working for Hestia Familia*?*

More than anything, she seemed ephemeral. *There's no way you could be violent with such a frail girl, right? Just withdraw and end things peacefully*—that's what the beautiful girl seemed to emanate.

This sort of person makes people want to protect her. Are you trying to damage my conscience?!

Coward! You're unforgiveable, Bell Cranell!

Lefiya screamed at the boy in her heart, entirely misunderstanding the situation.

She managed with great difficulty to respond quietly. "Please bring Bell Cranell. I know he's here."

"Uh, ummm…Master Bell is not in the best condition…If you have some business, I would be glad to assist you…" replied the renart girl, appearing a little scared as she tried to accommodate Lefiya, who had skipped right past greetings and pleasantries and straight to her demand.

Lefiya could sense several people skulking around behind the girl. It appeared they were on guard against the sudden inquisitor, impertinent.

When she looked closer, she noticed there was a strong chain between the door and the wall that locked to prevent Lefiya from entering.

The question of *Could you come back some other time…?* was practically written on the trembling renart girl's face.

Lefiya sighed audibly, recognizing that she wouldn't be welcomed there.

The next instant, she grabbed the slightly ajar door and yanked it open as she stuck her face in.

"BELL CRANELLLLLLLLLLLLLLL! Meet me face-to-face and explain yourself!"

"Hwhat?!"

The elf lost herself in frustration and resorted to more hardball tactics. The piteous renart's face froze in shock. Lefiya had blown past several limits on her self-control and resorted to pure force, causing *Hestia Familia* to panic.

"Lady Haruhime?! Please run away!"

"She just resorted to force. There's no use trying to reason with her! Lilly's instinct was right! This is why you can't trust adventurers!"

"This isn't the time or place for that! Hurry up and close the door! We have to protect Bell!"

When Lefiya scanned around, she saw a panicking girl of Far Eastern descent and heard the voice of a sulking prum and the shouts of a goddess. She was pushed out of the doorway by the Far Eastern girl, and as Lefiya staggered back, the door slammed shut in her face.

Bam! Ca-chink!

"Huh?!"

Just as she noticed the renart girl had withdrawn, the door closed and locked in a second.

"Heeeeeeeeeeey! Bell Cranell, you coward! Come out this instant! Explain yourself!"

"You guys, stop Lefiya!"

"What are you doing, Lefiya?!"

She was banging on the door with both hands with enough force to break it down when the other members of *Loki Familia* surrounded her. Cruz and Elfie snatched Lefiya and shouted wildly as they tried to restrain her while she struggled against them with a strength that seemed out of place for her slender body.

In the end, it took every member of the surveillance squad, but they managed to drag Lefiya away from the door. The other factions watching *Hestia Familia* saw the commotion from start to finish and were left shuddering.

"*Loki Familia* is crazy scary..."

"Thousand Elf's insane..."

After that, Lefiya was removed from the surveillance squad—obviously.

"Heeeeeeeave-ho!"

The sounds of excessive destruction resounded along with a loud voice as a hole in the wall opened up. Stone slabs clattered to the ground, and a lump of adamantite fell to the floor. When they finished carving out a hole large enough for the passage of a single person, Gareth stepped through the opening, followed by Tiona.

"There's no mistaking it...this is Knossos."

"Owwwwie, my hands huuuurt. Digging through an adamantite wall is hard."

Loki Familia had followed the path where the vouivre had emerged aboveground and found a secret passage below Daedalus Street and an orichalcum door leading to Knossos.

At Finn's direction, they'd dug through the adamantite wall and broken into the area in question. It was a brute-force method that they resorted to solely for the purpose of obtaining any clue they could find about the armed monsters. Gareth and Tiona, the two strongest members of the familia, were assigned to the demolition work.

In order to protect against intruders, the walls near the entrance were thicker than the rest of the labyrinth's walls. It took a lot of time and effort, and they had broken countless tools made of Valmars, but they were finally able to break through. Tiona tossed down a pickax that was no longer usable now that the tip was ruined before looking around.

"It's huge...and this ain't the maze we wandered around in. We're in an actual room. And we walked down a tooooon of stairs to get here. Do you think we're in the mid-levels?"

"Hmm, it's very possible. The atmosphere resembles the Great Wall of Sorrows on the seventeenth floor."

A squad led by Raul was waiting just outside the labyrinth on guard for an attack by the enemy. Tiona and Gareth turned back to examine the hole they'd carved out.

Based on what Finn had learned from questioning Ikelos, Knossos was dreamed up by Daedalus, who had been influenced by the original Dungeon. If his creation's design was based on the original's layout, it would explain Gareth's sense of déjà vu.

"Ugh...dead bodies..."

"It looks like they were killed by monsters...No emblems to identify them, but from recent events, I'm guessing it's *Ikelos Familia*?"

© Kiyotaka Haimura

As they slunk cautiously through the stone structure comparable to a large hall, they came across several corpses—more than ten. Ripped to shreds by claws and fangs, all of them died with their eyes wide open. Dried pools of blood were scattered across the stone-paved floor.

Tiona grimaced at the strong stench, but if evil people were going to die, this was the most fitting scene for it.

"Looking back on it, the stairs led straight here, which means this is probably a warehouse for holding the monsters they were smuggling. Or a checkpoint between the Dungeon and the surface. Like maybe a system of multiple routes leading to the surface with this serving as a base of operations..."

As if confirming Gareth's prediction, there were several black cages, big and small, in the dimly lit hall. The majority of them had been broken, and the chains holding them down had been snapped in two.

"...I'm guessing the captured monsters got angry...and rebelled, maybe?"

"..."

"Mm, in other words...we fought the monsters in Daedalus Street that broke out of these cages...and escaped?"

"It's possible. That would be the simplest explanation..."

Tiona leaned over a broken cage, staring intently at it as her empty head struggled to work. Gareth's response was muddled, as if he was considering other possibilities. They split up and started examining the surroundings to see if there was anything more to be found.

Fortunately, they were on guard for an enemy attack that never came. At the same time, there were no living creatures there, save them.

"Gareth, there's a door this way, too. I can't get any farther. If we try, we can break the wall, but..."

"Hold up, lass. It seems they've already given up on this place and abandoned it, but...provoking the enemy will cause problems. Let's ask Finn for directions first."

There were several doors in the hall itself and several narrow paths extending off it, but in order to go farther, they needed a key. Gareth forbade Tiona from going any deeper in her search of the surroundings before ordering Raul standing by outside to send word aboveground. Then he called the others into the hall to carry out the corpses of *Ikelos Familia.*

"Ah, Gareth, sir…instructions from the captain: We should withdraw. It would be bad if violas or other monsters are on the loose. Make sure to block up the hole…"

"…Finn, you arse…making it sound easy."

"What?! After we went to so much effort to break it open! And how are we supposed to plug it up?!"

Finn wanted to avoid any further complications making their way to the surface. Gareth recognized his intentions, but as the one charged with actually making it happen, he couldn't help grumbling at the time and effort it would require.

Tiona moaned, as expected.

"Give it up, Tiona. If it's just this level of dirt- and woodwork, then a dwarf can just suck it up and do it."

"I'm not a dwarf, though! Fiiiiinn, just do it yourself!"

As the Amazon kept complaining, Gareth sighed and quietly started the work of pulling out. He was of the mind that the prum was in a far more troublesome position than mere manual labor.

"Every unit must maintain a strict guard while you gather information. The armed monsters will appear in Daedalus Street for sure. Watch out for hidden passages in particular."

It was the fourth morning after the armed monsters had appeared. Finn had deployed almost the entire familia on Daedalus Street. They were based a short distance away from the center of the Labyrinth District, near the spot they had let the black minotaur escape.

Many of the buildings had been destroyed, burned down, or turned to ruins, and a swarm of Guild workers was working on repairs, mingling with *Loki Familia* members rushing around.

And along the street, there were adventurers from other familias out and about. Everyone was on pins and needles, observing everything and intently gathering information from the residents.

"I guess it's to be expected, since the other adventurers have noticed there's something in Daedalus Street…" Riveria noted as she walked up.

"Or they were instructed by their gods to come," Finn responded without looking at her.

"Is it okay to let them be?"

"Yes. They definitely haven't discovered the existence of Knossos. It's fine to ignore them."

"…And the evacuation of the residents? With all of us gathering here, their tension is mounting."

"If my theory is correct, this area will turn into a battlefield again. Leave the evacuation to the Guild and continue working to de-escalate the situation. It's too inefficient to do otherwise."

"…" Riveria remained silent.

Finn was correct, but his response was rather indifferent. *Loki Familia*'s pretext for deploying in this area was the reconstruction and defense of the Labyrinth District. Their real reason was to steal the Daedalus Orb that was in the possession of the armed monsters.

"After the monsters were seen on the eighteenth floor, they suddenly appeared in Daedalus Street. They crossed through Knossos. It's indisputable. With *Ikelos Familia* defeated, there's no doubt that the monsters are now in possession of their key. We have to get our hands on it."

Without the key, they couldn't take on Knossos. Finn was doing everything in his power to obtain it. A once-in-a-lifetime opportunity had dropped into their laps. And he wasn't so good-natured that he could let it go.

He was mobilizing the familia with the justification that they were working to prevent the destruction of Orario.

"Captain, there have been reports of monsters in the city's sewers to the north and northwest! And that the adventurers who spotted them were all pushed back…What should we do?"

"Those are decoys. It's the opposite end of the city from us in Daedalus Street…They're waiting for us to fall for it and move out. Don't worry about it. Alicia, where are the doors located?"

"Sir! The vouivre emerged from a hidden passage, which is being investigated as we speak! And we just found a third door!"

"Keep it up. The Evils won't blunder and come out of the doors, but in the event that a fight with them breaks out, getting a key is the top priority. Rakuta, I want you to map the hidden passages in the area around the newly discovered door as soon as possible."

"U-understood!"

The familia members appeared before Finn one after another, reporting their finds.

He ordered Narfi, who reported an enemy sighting elsewhere, to ignore it; he acknowledged Alicia's report; and he had Rakuta continue her mapping of the area.

The image of their reliable leader handing out orders without hesitation comforted the familia members. In the midst of all this uncertainty, a normal person would not be able to determine the correct goal and work toward it, but Finn was different. As long as they had Finn as a guide, *Loki Familia* would never lose track of their path.

Everyone trusted Finn, who never changed.

Everyone commended him, "as expected of Braver."

No one noticed his internal conflict.

"…Finn."

If anyone might have been able to, it would only be the high elf standing beside him—or the dwarf who wasn't there at the moment.

"Riveria, what are you doing? We don't have enough manpower. Head to the sewers and take command there for me."

"Finn."

"It's inefficient for the two of us to stick together. I need to get instructions to Gare—"

"*Finn.*"

Riveria's tone hardened as the prum continued to bark orders without looking at her.

She cut him off. *"You're getting too impatient."*

"..." He closed his mouth.

"I realize that we can't let this opportunity pass us by. But why are you rushing? It isn't like you."

"..."

"I can understand maintaining appearances for the familia. But do not put up a front with me."

"..."

"When was the last time you slept? I haven't seen you leave the command center once in the past four days."

"I can just—"

"'Make do with my skills'? Were you really about to give me an excuse?"

"......" Finn was silenced by the tone of her voice and her sharp gaze.

He'd intended to keep up his usual calm appearance, but he couldn't pull the wool over her eyes. She'd been with him too long to fall for that.

Gareth and Loki had noticed it, too.

"Take a break. Raul and the others can hear your gruffness in your orders. It's rippling outward."

If it became an issue involving the morale of the familia, then Finn didn't have any room left to argue as a commander entrusted with its care.

He shut his eyes, breathing in—and then out. Finn turned to Riveria and smiled wryly.

"...I got it, Riveria. Once they carry out the instructions I just gave, I'll take a nap. Is that okay?"

"Yes, that's fine." Riveria nodded magnanimously. "I should warn you, though—I'll be standing watch beside your bed until you go to sleep."

"And sing me a lullaby? I'm honored, but I think Alicia and the other elves might resent me for it."

"No, I won't be the one singing. That'll be Gareth."

"...Kh—ha-ha-ha! That might be a problem. I think his singing would drive me up the wall, and I'd never fall asleep."

For a moment, Finn stared in complete bafflement before responding, as his reflexive sarcastic quip elicited a sudden, unexpected joke. And then he suddenly burst into laughter.

His laughter was rare enough that all familia members working nearby were shocked. Riveria noticed that Finn had finally loosened up a bit. She wasn't one for jokes normally.

Her eyes relaxed as she smiled.

*I've really done it now...I screwed up and made the others worry about me...*Finn derisively laughed at himself.

I'm in a position where I need to make sure everyone else is okay, but I ended up making someone worry about me instead—a failure as a captain.

That's not like me. That's not like me at all.

He'd intended to hide it behind the outward facade of a leader, but someone had managed to peer into his heart.

"Captain."

He pulled himself out of his thoughts when he heard someone calling him.

Anakity was standing in front of him. "A messenger from the Guild has come...It's the head of the Guild himself."

Upon hearing that, Finn turned back to Riveria.

I'll hold off on my orders of sending you to bed. She gave her permission with a nod.

Finn shrugged, leaving various matters that needed to be dealt with to his second-in-command, and stood up.

"Got it. Bring him here."

"—All right, then, I'll accept your conditions. I'll inform Ouranos...But! Don't even think of trying to get the jump on us! If you try anything funny, I'll wash my hands of you in an instant!"

The Guild's head, Royman Mardeel, gave his warning, spittle flying as he breathed heavily through his nose. His rotund belly quivered up and down in sync with his raised voice.

"I promise."

Finn smiled back sweetly, closing the deal in the guise of a conversation. As he watched Royman leave with his aide, Riveria came in to take his place.

"Good grief…That man hasn't changed, I see."

"Ha-ha. I don't trust Royman, but he's predictable. As long as our interests intersect, we can negotiate with him. In that regard, he's easy to understand."

Royman had come to lay down his complaints: to demand that *Loki Familia* withdraw from Daedalus Street, likely in accordance with Ouranos's will.

"Is this okay? Intel on Knossos aside, you even promised to turn over the key."

"We know there are multiple keys after talking with Ikelos. As long as we can keep one for ourselves, it's fine."

As part of the deal with Royman, Finn had promised to hand over the key to coax Royman into convincing the Guild to formally station *Loki Familia* in Daedalus Street. If their presence was officially sanctioned by the Guild, it wouldn't antagonize the residents or any other adventurers.

Finn wanted to avoid any needless disputes, predicting the possibility of fighting an enemy on top of the ongoing hunt for the armed monsters. Giving up one key was a small price to pay.

"Even if it's a calculated move, is it a good thing to collaborate with the Guild?"

"At the very least, I'd say it's fine to work with Royman. But what happened with the announcement of the mission is fishy. There isn't enough evidence for us to trust the Guild as a whole, at least when it comes to this incident."

While Finn and Riveria were discussing the situation, the girl with golden hair and golden eyes made her appearance.

"Ah, thanks for patrolling, Aiz."

"Mm-hmm…"

"Did you notice anything unusual?"

"…That boy, Bell. He came to Daedalus Street."

Finn's blue eyes narrowed. "He's on the move, huh?"

"Finn...Are you suspicious of Bell Cranell?" Riveria asked in Aiz's stead, upon seeing her attitude.

"I'm sure he's a key witness to the incident. The adventurer who squared off against us is not the Bell Cranell I know."

Yes, Finn didn't know the Bell Cranell they'd encountered on that day—the fool who'd planted a seed of disturbance in Finn's mind.

To prevent others from noticing his internal discord, Finn did his best to speak dispassionately.

"If there's more to those armed monsters than first meets the eye...and if Bell Cranell was aware of that when he acted the way he did, that might explain what happened that day—meaning *something* forced him to stand against us."

Finn chose his words carefully so as to not agitate Aiz, who watched him in silence. Noticing that she was quietly focused on him, he flashed a wry smile.

"Aiz, I'm not going to treat Bell Cranell as an enemy without giving him a chance to explain himself. Despite all this, I still believe in him. As an individual and as an adventurer."

"..."

"But for the purposes of handling this incident, it's a different story. Is he our ally? Or is there a chance he might become our enemy? That's what I want to determine."

That was his honest opinion. He managed to skillfully hide the doubt in his heart, even as he spoke the truth. As he looked toward the clusters of tall towers and buildings, he spoke again.

"Riveria, I'm leaving this area to you. I'm going off by myself for a bit."

"What?"

"I don't want to stand out or put him on guard. Aiz, did he come to Daedalus Street by himself?"

"...He was with his goddess."

"Hmm, got it. Tell me where you saw them." Finn announced without hesitation, "I'm off to meet Bell Cranell."

With a smile plastered on his face, Finn looked up at Riveria, who met his eyes. The high elf nodded back after a while.

"…Very well. I'll take charge here for a bit."

Aiz was shocked to see Riveria accept him heading out as Finn said his thanks and left the headquarters.

I made her worry about me again, he murmured to himself as he walked away.

Finn followed Aiz's directions to make contact with Bell Cranell. There was no trace of anyone on the intricate web of roads. Finn was equipped with his spear and armor, and his footsteps echoed against the gray sky covered in clouds.

Along the way, Finn tried to look at himself again from a disinterested observer's point of view. His thoughts had been lacking composure—enough to warrant a talking-to from Riveria.

Why was that?

Was it because he had to do whatever it took to get his hands on the key?

Or because the city was on the brink of destruction?

Or because his comrades in the familia…Because Leene and the others had been killed?

There had to be a bit of that, too.

But the main reason was…

"Bell Cranell…"

That boy.

Finn couldn't get the image from four days ago—Bell turning his back to the vouivre and standing in their way—out of his mind.

That image introduced static into Finn's mind, which should have been more composed than anyone else's, and created a disturbance in his heart.

"Hey, look…"

"Bell Cranell…Did he come back? To hunt monsters?"

"Just like ya'd expect of a top-tier adventurer. He wants that Guild reward money for himself, apparently."

The chattering residents of Daedalus Street cut off his thoughts.

Their gloomy voices led him in a certain direction. Finn eventually found the white-haired boy standing at the focal point of people's glares. He was looking at the ground as he walked, as if desperately trying to flee from the scornful whispers and disdainful gazes of the crowd.

The Little Rookie's reputation had plummeted—for no other reason than Bell Cranell's own actions. In the eyes of the public, he had been utterly idiotic choosing to protect the vouivre and claiming it as his own prey as justification to attack adventurers attempting to take out the monster.

Some called him an adventurer who cared only for his own selfish desires; others said he exposed the city to danger to advance his own standing. Orario was filled with voices criticizing and denouncing him. The fact that the Little Rookie had been the talk of the town before only intensified the disappointment of the city's inhabitants, which verged on hostility and malice.

How pitiful. How foolish.

There was no room for sympathy after he took things that far.

——*It would be so much easier if I could think like that.*

"Bell Cranell," Finn called out, stepping away from the people spewing bitter remarks.

The boy froze in place, his rubellite eyes filled with an intense shock when he turned to see who called him.

"Mr....Finn...?"

Finn gave Bell a once-over, his eyes narrowing.

"Only a knife for self-defense, huh...? That's a light load out in this situation."

"!" Bell clearly winced at Finn's observation.

Every adventurer in the Labyrinth District was fully equipped for self-defense purposes at the very least. Even Finn had weapons and armor to deal with the impending attack of armed monsters.

And amid all that, the young boy before his eyes wasn't in battle clothes, let alone armor. It was as if he was absolutely sure there was no danger in the city—that the armed monsters wouldn't inflict any further harm.

As the boy displayed a level of agitation that Finn found almost humorous, Finn spoke in a voice that bore no hostility.

"Are you by yourself? Perfect. I'd like to have a conversation with just the two of us."

The neighborhood had been on edge from the moment they started talking. Everyone was focused on them: the captain of *Loki Familia*, whose members were putting all their effort into protecting the city, and the captain of *Hestia Familia*, who had insisted on acting selfishly. On one side, an ally of justice; on the other, the villain who single-handedly earned the derision of everyone in the city. There were even some glares condemning Finn for trying to have a chat with him.

I want to have a private conversation where no one can interrupt us, Finn implied as he asked again with a friendly smile.

"What do you say?"

"…Oh, uh, okay," Bell responded stiffly as he nodded awkwardly.

They headed toward a back alley, walking for a while before arriving at a cul-de-sac that seemed like it was being used as storage. Casks and wooden boxes of all shapes were haphazardly placed around the scene. There was no trace of anyone nearby. Perfect for his purposes.

Bell looked as though he had something to say as he trailed behind Finn. To not give Bell enough time to regain his composure, Finn began to talk as he spun around.

"I intend to turn a blind eye to what you did that day. The priority is resolving the current situation. I want to have a productive conversation with you."

Finn was looking up due to their height difference. Bell looked down, shocked by his suggestion.

"A conversation…?"

"Yes. You know *something* we don't about those armed monsters, right? To take it further, I'd venture a guess that you know the whole truth behind the recent incident."

To put it even more precisely, Finn had a decent grasp of the full story, though it was only conjecture. That line was a calculated move to lower Bell Cranell's guard and create an opening in his mental defenses—a tactic to drag more information out of him.

"I consider the events of the other day a small misunderstanding. If we'd been sharing information, things would have gone differently."

If Bell had made that choice, the current situation would have been different. The end results would have changed as well: Finn would have undoubtedly killed the vouivre in front of the boy as he screamed and cried.

After extracting all the useful information out of it, of course. As was fitting for the Braver.

Because Bell had realized that subconsciously, his face became taut as he frantically tried to read into Finn's words. Bell Cranell was a fool, but he wasn't stupid.

"Plus, things are different now."

"…!"

But Bell was still inexperienced.

His heart wavered visibly at Finn's offer. If he was to stand by his goal, he should have ignored Finn when they ran into each other and just walked away.

But the boy's true nature was innately good. He had the virtue of believing in people.

He's the exact opposite of me. Finn mockingly laughed at himself.

"Bell Cranell. If you know something, I want you to tell me."

"I, uh…"

He stepped right up to the boy—to get conclusive proof of his connection to the monsters and hear his true motives.

Bell wavered in indecision but started to open his mouth.

"Hey, Bell! What a coincidence!"

"""!"""

The voice of a cheerful god resounded in the cul-de-sac.

"Lord Hermes…?"

"Yep, yep, it's me, Hermes. What are you doing back here? Are you lost, perhaps? Or maybe young Bell is out gathering information in Daedalus Street, too?"

A dandy god appeared from behind Bell's back, wearing a winged travel hat and acting as if he just so happened to be passing through at that moment.

"Oh-ho, Braver. Were you two in the middle of something?" Hermes smiled and squinted at Finn, whose eyes tensed in response.

——*That's settled.*

Ouranos, Hermes Familia, and Bell Cranell are all connected in their involvement with the armed monsters.

"...No, I'm done here, Hermes."

Finn didn't get any proof per se, but he'd gotten enough to make his decision.

In which case, there was nothing left to do here. Getting greedy would only increase the risk of the smooth talker of a god gleaning some information from him. More than anything, he didn't want a god getting a glimpse into his mind—into his heart.

"Bell Cranell, do you have a key?" Finn lobbed one last question, passing right by the flustered Bell, as he was about to leave the cul-de-sac.

First, suspicion crossed the boy's face, followed immediately by apprehension.

He apparently recognized that the question was referring to the Daedalus Orb. *And judging by his face, he doesn't have it on him now.*

"Never mind. If you don't know what I'm talking about, forget I said anything." With a harmless smile, Finn finally left with that, proceeding down the complicated tangle of streets. Finn didn't immediately return to the operation headquarters, instead picking his path at random, roaming around the Labyrinth District looking for a place to be alone.

On one street, he came across a broken fountain with no water coming out and sat there.

"...Haaaah," he sighed.

His exhalation was full of various emotions that Finn would never reveal in front of other people. Finn had been behaving in a manner befitting a commander ever since the armed monsters appeared, acting to protect Orario as it fell into a state of upheaval. And all the while, he didn't know what to do with himself.

That was why he wanted to take a little time to be alone, even though he felt bad for leaving the familia members to their own devices. Only when he was alone could he step out of his role as captain, and he needed time to reexamine himself.

"...I came with the intention of scoping out Bell Cranell, but I guess I'm not fully composed myself, either, huh?" he murmured.

Finn's heart was wavering.

It wasn't just because of the boy's actions four days ago. And if he'd heard only Ikelos's story, he would still have been fine.

But when he came up with a single hypothesis that tied those two points together, Finn's heart became uncertain.

He had arrived at a dangerous speculation that he'd become convinced was not wrong.

It was the theory that the armed monsters might be intelligent life-forms, like humans.

They had emotions—not just simple cognition but a higher reasoning. They'd formed a community. Finn had a suspicion that they might be intelligent, self-aware organisms capable of reaching a mutual understanding with humanity.

With this hypothesis, all the oddities came together in an instant: the monsters who covered for one another in the battle and Bell Cranell protecting the vouivre in a supremely eccentric display.

It could be explained under the assumption that the monsters had hearts and minds comparable to people.

If my theory is correct…that's an insane Irregular.

He couldn't talk about it with Aiz—not when she was more unstable than he was at the moment.

He couldn't talk about it with the familia members. That would just invite chaos that couldn't be resolved.

Finn had arrived at a grim reality.

I can understand why those on Ouranos's side were trying to keep this hidden. If it came out, the truth would shake the world to its core. Orario would cease to function.

If they found out that monsters and people didn't have to kill each other but could talk things out, the city's residents would either be filled with doubt—or fully embrace their hatred.

The adventurers who were supposed to exterminate monsters would lose their edge.

And there would be those out for revenge that get killed by monsters acting in self-defense. Casualties were inevitable.

This affair was an earthquake that would rock the world.

But I don't give a damn *about that.*

Even if they could learn Koine, or if it truly is possible to reach a mutual understanding.

All of that was trivial to Finn.

Monsters had to be eliminated.

He didn't have the slightest bit of doubt on that one point.

Same as Aiz, Finn would kill monsters without hesitation.

It didn't matter if the monsters were different. He knew their very existence was a poison afflicting the people of the surface.

As Braver, as the object of admiration and envy of an untold number of people, he understood that defeating monsters was the only choice.

"...I don't give a damn about that...Or that's what I thought. So why am I so shaken up?" he whispered.

And in response, a sneer seeped out from the bottom of his heart: *You already know why.*

He closed his mouth.

Finn had already realized and acknowledged that he was a man-made hero.

As an easy example, he had negotiated with his patron goddess to have the title of Braver. It was nothing more than another tool in his quest to achieve fame, which he had sought out. Of course, Finn had conducted himself in a manner deserving of the name, which demonstrated his belief and strength. He had put in the effort and work to become Braver—both in name and substance.

However, it was all a calculated scheme he had come up with, a phantom that Finn had created.

Put simply, Finn was not a true hero. He was a hypocrite.

That's why...

That was why Finn's heart wavered when he saw Bell Cranell's foolish behavior.

When he strung all the information together, he realized the full picture of the various interrelated incidents, and the static flared. There was no choice but for it to run wild.

—Heroes aren't built. They appear because they're desired, right?

A person doesn't just become a hero...Intention and calculation have nothing to do with it. They're born of the people's desire for a hero, right? They're the ones who opened that last door of their own volition, in response to the longing, tears, cries, and voices pleading for help.

They're those who would take the same actions as Bell Cranell.

It wasn't the tears of a person but of a monster that—

"Ngh..." Finn shook his head.

There was no end to that train of thought. It was a dangerous conjecture. But he couldn't stop now.

Is it a feeling of inferiority? Do I feel jealous of Bell Cranell?

That boy had shown Finn youth, or perhaps it was dumb honesty, or ideals, or something along those lines. It was something that Finn had left behind, something he'd lost.

When he'd hardened his resolve to face reality head-on, Finn had weighed many things on the scales and discarded a great number of them.

He'd grown up. He'd gotten to know the world. He'd become famous, come to terms with society, and lost. That's how he felt.

It wasn't as if he'd always been "Finn."

Just like Bell, he'd been a stubborn child once—no, he'd almost certainly been even more immature than Bell was.

With a lust for knowledge, he'd frantically committed himself to changing the very meaning of what it meant to be a prum. Back then, his stage had been the small village where he'd been born, nothing more than a tiny sandbox. But there was no doubt that was when Finn truly struggled against the world.

But now, he'd accepted that world, trying his best to bring about a revolution from within the confines of its rules. He wasn't holding his ideals aloft but fighting while hiding the true scope of his ambition. And it was a fight grounded in callousness.

Finn used the word *ambition*. He would never say *ideals*. Even if he thought it, he would never say it aloud. As a man-made hero, he was fully aware that *ideals* were just a tool used to inspire or encourage others—not something to ever take seriously.

He'd always been and would continue to be correct. His choice wasn't wrong, he was sure of it. But when he'd faced off against the boy protecting the vouivre, he was struck by the suspicion that he was horribly superficial.

A realist would scoff at Bell's folly. That was the appropriate response. He would never have chosen Bell's actions. That was how it should have been—or perhaps it was precisely because he wouldn't have done the same thing that Finn was shaken, and fascinated.

"I see…This feeling is…"

It wasn't jealousy or envy or inferiority. Something dazzling. Finn thought Bell Cranell was noble for doing something he could no longer do.

"…This is a problem."

He would much rather feel shameful, a sense of inferiority. If that was all it was, Finn would have been able to simply accept this feeling for what it was or find a solution or get over it.

"And…a bad influence…"

But the fact that Finn was thinking about him was proof that he couldn't ignore Bell Cranell. While Finn was disappointed and judged the boy for his foolishness, he found Bell blindingly radiant. He couldn't help feeling absolutely ridiculous in comparison.

A smile appeared on his face. It wasn't a sneer.

"F-Finn? Is that really Finn Deimne?!" a young voice called out.

He quickly snapped back to being "Finn," standing up and looking in the direction of the voice, where a fellow prum stood. Even among their small species, he was clearly a child, a good head shorter than Finn and topped with curly brown hair. When Finn smiled and started to respond, the boy beamed, trotting over.

"Braver! Hero of the prums! I-I've always been rooting for you!"

His clothing wasn't clean by any means, and he was an orphan without a doubt. The boy looked up at Finn with eyes filled to the brim with admiration.

"I always wish I can become a prum like you someday! That's why, um…!"

It was what Finn had been wanting, his reason for fighting as Braver, the goal of his efforts to restore his species. This encounter should have been vindication of all that, but he felt empty…maybe because his heart was uncertain.

"I'm honored. Hearing that from a young fellow prum encourages me to continue my adventure. Your words help me fight with the pride of a prum," responded Finn with an exemplary answer.

With a smile lacking even a single hint of gloom, he managed to perfectly pull off the answer he'd recited countless times for his fellow prums. As he shook off the melancholy he'd been feeling, Finn fulfilled his role as Braver, responding to the expectations of the prum.

He was the sort of man who could do that much, as pathetic as that sounded.

"Ah!"

And he was rewarded for it. The boy's cheeks turned red, and he smiled in delight, eyes shining with excitement, celebrating a chance to talk to him.

"I-I'm short and not very strong, and I'm slow, and everyone at the orphanage makes fun of me, but when I hear about your adventures, I feel like I could be brave, too. And when *Loki Familia* returned after getting to the fifty-ninth floor, everyone changed their minds, and they were all saying that prums are amazing! I was so happy! And—!"

"Ossian! What are you doing going off on your own? Hurry up and come back!" another voice called out.

A human, chienthrope, and half-elf—all children wearing ragged clothing—appeared. *They're probably from the same orphanage. Even after considering that he's a prum, they're probably older based on their stature?*

The orphans from various species ran over to the boy called Ossian.

"Lai! Look! It's Finn! The real Braver!"

"Eh? Braver...?"

As Ossian started to introduce Finn, the human boy froze, gazing in wonder. The other two had similar reactions. Lai looked as though he was about to say something, but he pursed his lips and remained silent.

To Finn's eyes, it seemed as if Lai wanted to celebrate meeting a first-tier adventurer, but for some reason, he could not bring himself to be happy.

Ossian tilted his head in utter confusion at his friend's response.

"...Ossian, don't go off by yourself. You know that...there are lots of adventurers around here right now...One of the monsters might show up," Lai cautioned, seeming distressed and grabbing Ossian's arm to drag him away.

The faces of the chienthrope girl and the half-elf clouded over at his warning. Ossian stopped moving. He seemed to hang his head as if brooding but immediately snapped it back up to look at Finn.

"Hey! You're...you're not like—like Bell Cranell, right?"

That question came out of nowhere. Finn's blue eyes were full of shock, an expression he almost never let anyone see.

The young boy spoke as though he was pleading, saying, *I don't want to be betrayed again.* The three other children were dumbfounded, and Lai leaned forward, his face twisting.

"Hey, Ossian!"

"But you all said it! That Bell hurt the other adventurers to get money!"

"—!"

"And that because of Bell, the monsters got away, and now everyone's scared!" the prum child shouted as tears welled in his eyes.

It was as if he blamed Bell Cranell. The human boy didn't respond to his angry glare.

"Bell is just like the other thugs living in Daedalus Street!"

"You take that back!"

"Lai?!"

In a rage, the human boy lurched forward to grab Ossian, and the chienthrope girl shrieked as she tried to stop him with the half-elf's help. The human looked as though he didn't know why he was so angry—or why he seemed like he was about to cry.

It was likely that Bell and those orphans had interacted before. At the very least, they were friendly enough to have built trust between them.

As a result of that boy's stupidity, he's betrayed these children.

How indifferent and cruel—but Finn couldn't bring himself to ridicule him.

"He isn't a self-interested adventurer by any means, if you ask me," Finn softly offered before he realized, taking the hand that Lai was holding aloft.

As the shocked children turned their gazes to him, Finn began to speak.

"I hold him…Bell Cranell in high esteem. I'm one of the people fascinated by his adventure. Even now."

Their eyes widened in surprise at his statement. Finn didn't know why he'd said that. But he felt like it had naturally slipped from his mouth and displayed his true feelings.

"B-but…he let the monsters get away and put everyone in danger!"

"There was probably a reason why he couldn't back down. Even if it was something that should be despised…he made his decision and followed through—for the sake of his beliefs."

Finn explained with a clear voice his perspective on the entire situation as Ossian leaned forward. He couldn't share the truth, but Finn sincerely spoke of what he imagined Bell was feeling.

Ossian and the other children were anxious. In particular, Lai's eyes wavered, and the half-elf looked back at Finn, as though seriously mulling over what Finn was saying.

Why am I trying to cover for Bell Cranell?

In order to manipulate his public image, he could have criticized Bell to his heart's content. And people would have agreed with him.

But Finn could not bring himself to do that in the end—not because he was pretending to be some saint but because he thought it would be pathetic, ugly, the exact opposite of what a hero would say.

"Right and wrong…It's difficult to define those in absolute terms."

That was why he pretended not to know anything about the situation and solemnly spoke of reality in general, knowing that his words could be applied to him just as well as Bell.

The children lowered their hands, unable to think of a way to respond.

"—Laaaaaaai! Where did you guys go?" said a voice, and a figure appeared suddenly as though having been waiting for the right spot to break in.

She was wearing a white dress, and her blue-gray hair was bouncing—a human.

She's…

She was one of the people who worked at The Benevolent Mistress, a tavern that *Loki Familia* used for post-expedition celebrations. Her name was Syr Flover.

She stopped in front of the children and smiled sweetly.

"Miss Maria is getting worried. Why don't we all head back?"

The children nervously raised their heads and quietly nodded, starting to go home.

As they were leaving, Ossian swung around as if yanked by his hair. After glancing back at Finn one more time, he followed Lai and the other two.

The only people left were the girl and Finn.

"…Is it okay not to go? It seemed like you know them."

"Yes, after I thank you, I'll be returning as well." Syr smiled as she spoke.

Her eyes—the same color as her hair—narrowed softly as she looked at Finn.

She was the person who required the most vigilance at that bar, not the owner, Mia. Finn had been warned about her by Loki. While he didn't rise to the level of being on guard, he chose his words carefully so she wouldn't notice his conflicted feelings.

"I don't think I did anything that merits appreciation."

"Lai and the others have been troubled by Mr. Bell, and you spoke to them about it. Thanks to that, I think they won't hate him."

"..."

"Thank you very much," she continued, showing her feelings for Bell.

It was a side of her that he hadn't seen once in all the times he'd been to The Benevolent Mistress. She politely bowed with a different sort of grace from the movements on display at the tavern.

It was hard for Finn to accept her frank thanks, given his own feelings. He ended up glancing away reflexively.

"It's about time for me to take my leave. There are things I have to get done. Pardon me."

"Okay. Keep up the good work, Mr. Hero."

Finn had turned to leave, but his feet stopped in their tracks when he heard her.

He turned around, staring at Syr, who was still smiling.

It wasn't ironic. She meant what she said.

She didn't notice. No, she does *know the relationship between Bell and the others.* Finn realized he'd opened his mouth, looking as if he'd seen something strange.

"I'm fighting against Bell Cranell, you know. Are you still cheering me on?"

"Yes. Because Mr. Bell and you are both—" the silver-haired girl responded as she bore a radiant smile.

"The children's heroes."

The rain fell from the sky in scattered drops before transforming into a drizzle and pelting one girl's long blond hair.

On the roof of a building on Daedalus Street, Aiz was standing, staring out at the dungeon town shrouded in rain without really processing her surroundings.

"Aiiiiizuu," called out the easygoing voice of her patron goddess.

Aiz had already noticed her but didn't turn around, continuing to look down on Daedalus Street.

"Tiona and the others are worried. They thought you might be broodin' over something."

"…I'm sorry," Aiz managed to say, but she still refused to turn around.

Her back conveyed her desire to be left alone. But Loki didn't leave—nor did she do anything else. Loki simply stood right behind her.

Aiz opened her mouth, unable to bear the gaze on her back.

"…What do you want?"

"I came to see how you were doin', Aizuu. Watchin' the sunset all by yourself," Loki responded playfully, glancing over in the direction of the base camp. "Seems like Finn's got some doubts about something, too…but I was more worried about you."

And then she lowered her voice to a soft whisper. "Hey, Aizuu, you ran into Itty-Bitty and the boy earlier, right?"

"Ngh…"

Right before she'd reported to Finn that Bell had appeared in Daedalus Street, Aiz had run into him while he was with his patron goddess, Hestia.

It had been so sudden that she never got the chance to put her thoughts in order or ask the pale-faced boy anything. Immediately after, Loki had suddenly appeared, and Aiz had obediently followed her instructions to head back to Finn.

Aiz suspected that Loki had intentionally separated them. She was worried about Aiz.

"After that, I didn't get to ask the kid anything, but I got an interesting story out of Itty-Bitty…Wanna hear?"

"I don't want to hear it," Aiz responded tersely, appearing scared to hear the truth from Loki's mouth.

It seemed that she was only pretending that she hadn't noticed it herself.

She kept thinking about his expression when he asked her a question. The image of the strange monsters in the Labyrinth District kept running through her head as well. That was the reason Aiz's heart was troubled even after so much time had passed.

The relief she felt when she saw the black minotaur appear was ephemeral, disappearing as soon as she no longer had to wield her sword and fight.

Right now, Aiz was conflicted.

Loki wasn't annoyed or sad in the face of rejection. With a short "okay," she let it go.

"All right, then, how about something else? Let me ask ya about somethin' that happened a little while ago, Aizuu."

But she wouldn't allow Aiz to run from reality, so she switched to a different tack.

"When Itty-Bitty got kidnapped and you were chasing after her, there was an incident in the Beor Mountains where you were helped by, what was it, Edas Village? What do you think of them now?"

Why now of all times? Why bring that up? Why here?

Why are you asking me like this?

Edas Village, a community that worshipped the dragon, established and maintained by the protection of the dragon's scales, a hidden village of those abandoned by the world.

She'd intentionally forgotten about it, desperately tried to put the memory behind her.

She was struggling to hold on to the determination to wield her sword—and faltering. Aiz couldn't answer Loki's question, instead squeezing her hands tightly into fists.

"Aiz...whichever path you choose is fine. That's your right." Loki said those words to Aiz's back as if to test her.

"You'll destroy yourself if you don't make the decision for yourself. Worry to your heart's content.

"If ya listened to us gods now, you'd only be led astray," she added. "Whatever answer you come to...I'll still go buy Jyaga Maru Kun with ya."

Even turning around, Aiz knew Loki was watching her with a faint smile and a kind face.

"Hey, Aiz…that boy's pretty interestin'."

As the ripples spread in Aiz's heart, Loki changed the topic with a cheerful voice. By *the boy*, she meant Bell.

The goddess put her hands behind her head and cackled childishly. "At first, my only impression was that he was cheeky for choosing that shrimp of a goddess, but…he's fascinating. A true fool of a child. I can understand why that pervert got interested in him."

"…?" Aiz finally turned around, her eyes questioning, *When you said* that pervert, *did you mean…?*

Loki smiled back, her vermilion hair soaked by the rain, before finally turning away.

"But…I don't want ya to lose. Not you, Aiz. And not Finn, either." Leaving those words, Loki got down from the rooftop.

Aiz was left behind, alone with the rain.

"…I…"

As she stared out over the cityscape again, Aiz reflected on Loki's comment—rethinking, looking back, questioning herself…But she wasn't able to come to a different answer.

She stuck with her determination, what she had told him before.

That was all there was. That was all there could be.

The young Aiz in the back of her mind didn't say anything, hanging her head, her bangs covering her eyes, standing there like a ghost.

In other words, that was her answer.

"Finn is…unsure, too…?" Aiz considered, thinking back to her conversation with Loki.

Aiz lifted her eyes to the sky.

If Finn started saying the same thing as Bell, asking about right or wrong and killing or sparing monsters, then—

Aiz would surely turn against them, abandoning herself to the black flame inside her heart.

Night had come. The ashen clouds filling the sky prevented the sunset from breaking through and gradually got darker. Finn opened his eyes in silence. He was in an empty room that he'd borrowed to nap. He pulled aside the blanket and posed a question to the two other people in the room with him.

"How long was I asleep?"

"Exactly one hour."

"You'd do well to sleep a bit longer... You've been working nonstop."

The two people in the room responded—Riveria with exasperation and Gareth with a sigh. The pair should have been taking command for him, but they were keeping him company instead. In other words, they were concerned about Finn enough to stay behind. The only saving grace was that they hadn't said anything to the others in the familia and kept it to themselves.

Finn smiled bitterly and sat up.

"They found a door to Knossos in the southeast area of Daedalus Street. It's the fourth one we've managed to run down."

"We searched up and down the hidden passage underground. That might be all of the entrances. Whether the other doors connect to the Dungeon...and whether that underground passage is the only connection...we don't know. As expected, we can't cover everything."

"I see..." Finn listened to their report on the edge of the bed.

After making sure that no one else was around, he started to speak again. "Riveria, Gareth, listen up. If my prediction is right, this should cover everything regarding this incident."

He explained the reality of the armed monsters and Ouranos's and *Hestia Familia*'s connection to them, reviewing his deductions to Riveria and Gareth alone—only to those two, his comrades-in-arms and equals.

"...If your theory is true, Ouranos's goal of trying to hide the self-aware monsters is..."

"Yeah. Given the current situation, he's definitely trying to get the monsters back to the Dungeon."

"Big picture...No. In the end, how does Ouranos want this to turn out?"

"Who knows? Something along the lines of people and monsters living together hand in hand or something like that?"

"...That's absurd."

Finn's eyes were half-serious, half-joking when he fired back with his suggestion, and Gareth's beard twitched as he groaned.

"...Setting aside dreams of reconciliation between people and monsters." Riveria prefaced her thoughts before continuing. "What about a cease-fire in this one instance...? Wouldn't it be possible to negotiate with intelligent monsters?"

Use Ouranos at Guild Headquarters as an intermediary to negotiate safe passage for the monsters in exchange for the key. Riveria was bringing up that option as a potential resolution. If the monsters really didn't have any intention of bringing further harm to the city—which seemed believable, judging from Bell Cranell's words and actions—then wouldn't it be possible to contact them secretly to negotiate?

Finn responded, *"It's impossible."*

He denied the very possibility.

"Colluding with monsters in order to get the key might work. But what happens next?"

"..."

"Won't morale drop in the familia? Will no one be alienated? There are many in the familia who have lost family and loved ones, comrades. Can we really get them to accept the truth?"

"..."

"Will she—will Aiz accept my decision?"

No.

That was exactly why it was impossible.

Riveria and Gareth silently confirmed his assessment. There would undoubtedly be internal conflict in the familia. If it leaked that they had secretly made a deal with the monsters—if they betrayed the others in the familia, Bete would lead the pack rushing to denounce them. The strife between people and monsters ran deep. The word *misfortune* didn't even do it justice. It was a tragedy.

If the situation were different, he might have been able to actually consider the option. But it was hopeless. He couldn't have *Loki Familia* in disarray with the impending destruction of Orario so near.

"And if we go along with Ouranos's divine will even once, he'll hold it over us from then on."

If they rolled the dice on this chance, once they agreed to a negotiation with the monsters, Ouranos and Hermes would have Finn on a leash.

Gods wouldn't abide by something so weak as "trust." They would manipulate the mortals to achieve their goals. If Ouranos knew that Braver, the hero of the masses, made a deal with the monsters, *Loki Familia* would be blackmailed into his camp.

That would be a serious obstacle to Finn and his ambition—a road to ruin, with only his self-destruction waiting at the end. As soon as it came out that he'd dealt with monsters, it would be the end of Braver.

The populace's hostility toward Bell Cranell was a perfect example of what was potentially awaiting him.

…*Don't lie, Deimne.* He was disgusted with himself.

These were his true feelings but also an excuse for others. The greatest wishes rooted in the deepest crevices of his tiny body were tied to his success as Braver and his ingrained hatred.

Both of Finn's—no, *his* parents had been killed by monsters, murdered before his eyes by monsters' claws and fangs as they'd scrambled to protect their child.

On the same day the monsters had taken his parents, he swore to rebuild the prum race.

If monsters had never existed, *Finn* would never have been born.

If monsters had never existed, he would've lived his life as a cocky child in his small hometown.

Cooperating with monsters would mean turning his back on that day, the beginning of everything.

It would be a denial of *Finn's* entire existence.

As for me…As Deimne, that's the one thing I cannot do.

That was absolute. He couldn't do something that would negate the hero—Finn.

" "
…

" "
…

He recognized that Riveria and Gareth were looking at him, worried.

But it wasn't with sympathy or pity by any means. Like their patron goddess, the two of them had stood by his side as he fought and devoted himself to his ambition. What they felt was resignation and respect.

When it came to his ambitions, he would never seek assistance, unlike when it came to advancing the interests of their familia. He would never hesitate to say that it was his own goal or try to share that heavy burden with anyone else.

Riveria and Gareth would occasionally admonish him, occasionally advise him, and always watch over him—but that was all they could do.

"I understand…I'll abide by your judgment."

Riveria was the one who broke the silence.

Beside her, Gareth closed his eyes and nodded.

"…Sorry."

"Fool." Gareth snorted. "What are you apologizing for? Your answer was perfectly reasonable. No one said you were mistaken about anything."

Finn's response was more realistic than negotiating with the monsters, let alone an absurd proposal like coexistence. Gareth said as much when he tried to apologize.

Looking up, Finn smiled wryly as if to thank his two friends.

"But a secret deal is a nice train of thought. Pretend to negotiate to draw out the monsters and wrangle the key from them by force. That would make things easier. Gah-ha-ha!"

"Gareth…I completely misjudged you. Even if they're monsters, there's no way I could approve something so cowardly."

"It's a joke, a joke! Sheesh, this is why inflexible elves are just... Even if we were willing to open negotiations, we'd have no choice but to go through Ouranos. And if you've any qualms, the eyes of a god will see through it immediately. Even if we wanted, we'd have no way of pulling off a surprise attack."

Gareth and Riveria started bickering as if a switch had been flipped, intentionally criticizing each other in a joking tone to lighten Finn's mood. Finn was grateful for their concern, descending into thought to determine their next moves.

"At this rate, there's no avoiding a clash. Daedalus Street will be the battlefield. In order to get the key, we'll have to contend with..."

"*Hermes Familia*...and *Hestia Familia*? In addition to the monsters."

The static hit again. The image of Bell Cranell's face flashed through the back of his mind, which could be due to the fact that he'd just reaffirmed he couldn't discard his persona as Braver.

...But that boy didn't hesitate at all, did he?

That boy didn't worry about losing everything he'd built up, as Finn fretted.

The people had faith in him; the adventurers had placed their trust in him; he had his social status and honor. He hadn't considered this in the balance against that monster's life, had he? Had he committed that folly thoughtlessly and without regret?

Finn couldn't say for sure, other than one thing: Bell had done it.

He hadn't cast it aside but protected it—that monster.

If it were Finn, he would have abandoned it.

For the sake of his ambition, Finn would have made the sacrifice, but Bell had thrown away his position as a hero and chosen the path of the fool.

Finn couldn't do that, as he fought for possibly the most meaningless thing in the world—fame.

That was why Bell Cranell's behavior was noble.

That was why he was dazzling—to the extent that Finn wished he could be like that, too.

"...I'm surprised. To think I harbored such a destructive desire."

"Finn?" Riveria turned to him when that slipped from his mouth.

He just smiled, replying, "Nothing," and looked down at the palm of his hand, laughing at himself.

His right thumb ached like never before.

It was as if it were pleading with him. That train of thought was dangerous. It would be the death of "Finn."

——*I know.*

He never had the option of taking the wrong path from the start.

Ever since he decided he would become the light of his race, he knew he had to swallow everything for that.

He was aiming to be a man-made hero, a hypocritical hero, a hero of the masses.

Maybe Finn was being narrow-minded.

He would use everything and discard whatever he had to. If that starstruck young prum could see this side of Finn, he would be crushed by disillusionment. That much was certain.

But—

"—I'll get past this."

That was Finn's path, the one he'd chosen long ago when he was a young man like Bell Cranell, the prum adventurer.

There was no more doubt in his eyes. The throbbing in his thumb and the image in his mind disappeared.

As he stood up and raised his head, Finn announced, "Call a strategy meeting. Gather everyone for me."

"*Loki Familia* is focused on Bell Cranell—I bet that's what our opponent is thinking."

The sky had gotten dark, and the curtain of night was drawing closed over the city. The meeting had started in *Loki Familia*'s encampment in a corner of the Labyrinth District. All the leaders and almost all the lower-tier members of the familia were in attendance.

"The armed monsters will use Bell Cranell as a diversion to sneak into Knossos. We'll pretend that we've fallen for their trick and lay a trap in a different location. But the most important thing is to pay attention to what's happening in the opposite direction of Bell Cranell."

The magic-stone lanterns lighting the camp illuminated their faces. A restless buzz filled the air as Finn announced how things would unfold.

"Hey, Finn, is that mangy rabbit boy working with the monsters?"

"You're certainly in a bad mood, Bete."

"Piss off!" Bete snapped back at Riveria.

Finn chose his words carefully, since the werewolf didn't seem aware of the fact that he was focusing on the boy.

"At the very least, Bell Cranell is in a position where they're making use of him—whether of his own volition or because he's being deceived."

Bell Cranell was at the crux of the situation, a fact that evoked a range of reactions from the members of the familia. There were those who were grimacing sourly and others who looked unsure how to feel, including Tiona.

"........."

"D-did something happen to Lefiya? She's making a really scary face..."

"No clue."

And in an entirely different direction, there was an elf practically overflowing with rage. Raul was frightened, and Anakity could only hunch over in response to his question. Lefiya had been this way since she'd been removed from the *Hestia Familia* surveillance squad. The others were keeping their distance, leaving a big berth between them and her.

"At any rate, Bell Cranell will not be our ally in this situation... Keep that in mind," Finn warned—aimed particularly at Aiz, who was still brooding.

"Mm, I don't really get it, but I'm guessing that you're trying to say not to get distracted by Argonaut?"

"Yes. We can't simply let him do as he pleases. Right now, Cruz and a couple of the others are watching him."

"Better yet, Captain, why don't we capture him before he has a chance to do anything? You know, use a bit of force."

"Even with everyone treating Bell Cranell as a villain, there's no definite proof against him. If we resorted to preemptive force, I think we'd end up becoming notorious ourselves. The Guild already has its eye on us. And Hephaistos is friendly with *Hestia Familia*. Getting her worked up is a scary proposition."

After Finn responded to the Amazonian sisters' questions, Tione came back with another.

"And one other thing. I know the armed monsters are highly intelligent, but it's nothing more than that, right? Can they really pull off this strategy...?"

"They've got a leader of some sort. Right, Gareth?"

"Aye. When we were fighting before, I got a good look at the situation from atop the building. It was wearing a black robe, and I can't say whether it was a person or a monster, but...it's fair to think of it as a tamer."

Finn was hiding the fact that the armed monsters were intelligent creatures, concerned about chaos spreading among the familia if word got out. But he still wanted them to be wary of high-level tactics the enemy might use, which was why the pair had arranged this story beforehand. They exchanged glances as Tione and the rest of the members accepted their explanation.

"And on top of it all, we need to be wary of that black minotaur... Even if it's wounded, we can't underestimate its ability to break through our formations."

The atmosphere shifted when Finn mentioned that monster. Bete and Tione raised their eyebrows, and even Aiz's face tensed up.

"If Tione hadn't snapped, we would have beaten it easily."

"Say what?!"

"Its techniques weren't anything to write home about. If we can just get into close range, it won't be too hard to fight. But...it was stronger than every other monster we've pulverized."

"And its resilience was abnormal. It didn't matter how much Tione and the others hit it; it didn't show any sign of holding back—not until Aiz's wind landed a solid hit."

"Its skin was tougher than an enhanced black rhino's hide. If it got any stronger, it would pose a big problem for us. It's better to think of it as a floor boss than a regular monster. But as long as we don't mess up while dealing with it, we can beat it, exactly like Tiona said."

After Tiona, Tione, Bete, Riveria, and Gareth all spoke, Aiz finally chimed in.

"But…that monster…is going to get even stronger."

No one in the upper echelon of *Loki Familia* denied her comment. All the first-tier adventurers were thinking the same thing. The pitch-black monster was still developing, as unbelievable as that might have sounded.

Raul, Lefiya, Narfi, and the other candidates for the upper echelon gulped, along with everyone else who'd been trampled by the monster.

"If nothing else, we have to make sure to kill that black minotaur. The fact that it's still developing is dangerous. Sooner or later, it'll become a menace."

Now that Finn had a full grasp of the incident, he judged that the minotaur's unique condition alone was Irregular. Unlike the other armed monsters, it didn't seem to have any higher reasoning. It seemed to be only a creature starved for combat, a symbol of destruction steamrolling everything in its path. If the monsters were rational, Finn could predict their movements, but that black minotaur alone was unreadable.

It was annihilation incarnate. Finn made clear that enormous Irregular was to be erased.

"If we consider the route taken by the enemy from the eighteenth floor to the surface, there's no question they have a key. We need to defend all the entrances to Knossos we've discovered."

The prum leader raised his head as he gave his order. "Familia members will be stationed throughout Daedalus Street. That's how we'll lay our trap."

Everyone nodded vigorously at the plan.

Finn paused for a moment before his tone of voice changed dramatically.

"Everything up until now will be part of our ostensible plan."

Without waiting for a response, he continued.

"The real plan is to use the armed monsters as a decoy to draw out the Evils' Remnants from Knossos."

"‼"

Aiz and the main forces were shocked—let alone the lower-tier members.

"The armed monsters have a key…The Evils in Knossos can't ignore that. If we defeat the monsters, they'll be forced to watch the key fall into our hands. There's no way any of them will be content to watch from the sidelines."

Lefiya and Raul were taken aback by his explanation.

Finn had predicted that Daedalus Street would become a battlefield. It would draw in not only the monsters but their supporters in *Hestia Familia* and even the remnants of the Evils.

It wouldn't be a three-way battle but a four-sided one.

No, depending on the situation, it might even turn into a five- or six-sided conflict.

The possibility made their throats tremble. The only ones unmoved were Riveria and Gareth, who'd been told beforehand, along with Alicia and Anakity, who were wiser than Aiz and the other main group members.

The latter pair actually broke out into a cold sweat, because despite anticipating that the Evils might make a move, they hadn't expected Finn to plan on it happening.

Their apprehension was due to the difficulty of the proposed plan.

"A plan on *two fronts*…"

"To suppress the monsters and lure out the Evils while controlling every little thing…"

"Uhhhhh?! Wait, what do you mean?!"

"We can't beat the monsters too quickly, and we can't let them get away. We have to keep them busy without killing them until we've reeled in our true target."

"Didn't this just get waaay harder all of a sudden?!"

As Anakity and Alicia groaned, Tiona clutched her head so tightly that it was about to burst. Tione explained it in a way that even an idiot could understand, shattering Tiona's mind.

"Waiting for the monsters to invade Knossos...The enemy won't rely on such a foolishly optimistic strategy. They believe *Loki Familia* will try to capture the monsters outside the labyrinth...They won't be able to think otherwise."

"C-Captain...that means we can't let the monsters get away while guarding the entrances to Knossos...and we have to take care of any Evils coming out of Knossos as well...?"

"Yes. We'll be caught between a rock and a hard place." Raul's face twitched as Finn casually nodded.

They would have to keep track of the monsters making a break for Knossos while maintaining a firm grasp on the movements of the Evils' Remnants at the same time. In particular, the movements on the Knossos side would be troublesome. The enemy would obviously be protecting the inside of their fortress, but they would definitely be mounting attacks outside of it, too. *Loki Familia* would be stuck between the hammer and the anvil.

It would be a complicated affair to maintain communication lines while the plan unfolded across Daedalus Street, which covered a massive area in the city. On top of that, there would be several other groups of adventurers tossed in the mix.

Every member of the familia understood that achieving their goal would be extraordinarily difficult.

That said, Finn was still ordering them to carry it out.

"We can't let this chance pass us by. The armed monsters will be our bait to lure them out of their fortress...This is our first and last chance."

Finn intended to use everything at his disposal.

He discarded the possibility of negotiating with the intelligent monsters, because they could use them as effective bait. The armed monsters tromping around with a key would be a serious source of concern for the Evils.

By discarding all elements of uncertainty, Finn confronted the reality before him and chose to use the situation in a way that had the most potential.

"We'll place sufficient forces at the four doors in the hidden passageway. Riveria and Gareth will take command there. The enemy has been passive up until now, but they will start harassing us. Stay alert."

"Right."

"Aye."

Starting with Riveria and Gareth, Finn began giving each member their orders.

No one cut in. They all abided by the battle plans he laid out.

"Our number one priority is to obtain a key. The destruction of the monsters and the Evils is secondary—if worse comes to worst. Make sure you don't forget the shape of this key."

Finn pulled out a replica of the Daedalus Orb.

It was a copy created from his memory, based on the one he'd seen and the testimony of the former *Ishtar Familia* member Lena. It was just a lump of gold. Everyone stared intently at it on the palm of Finn's hand.

"Finn…What if the black minotaur appears?" Aiz asked.

"I'll leave it to the people on the ground to decide what's best if it happens, but…under no circumstances should anyone try to face it alone. Wait for support to come and stall for time. Got it, Aiz?"

"…Yes."

Finn gave a forceful explanation to make sure she didn't mistake her priorities. Her golden eyes held the prum's blue ones in their gaze before she nodded slightly.

"…I know you're all concerned. This time, our plan carries significant risk and difficulty."

After announcing all the orders, Finn looked around at everyone, speaking slowly. "And what of it?" he asked with a sharp gaze and a strong will.

"Do you remember the faces of our friends who fell in Knossos? If you remember them, we will perform the impossible and give the odds a good thrashing. Aren't I right?"

""*Yes!*"" shouted everyone in the room.

The heat rose under their feverish response. There was no more fear or anxiety in their eyes as they responded to their leader's question with a roaring will to fight.

Braver was alive and well, using even the memory of their lost comrades to bring out the familia's anger and stiffen their resolve.

With a nod to confirm that morale was high, Finn added one last point of warning.

"If anything is going to provoke Irregulars, it would be him. Do not let your guard down and do not overlook him. That adventurer will blow past our expectations as he's done in the past."

It was almost as if he was acknowledging that boy, as if saying that folly was the one source of uncertainty.

Finn's eyes narrowed.

"Finn...'Him'?"

"Yes—" he started, nodding at Aiz as he said the name of a single adventurer, which crashed into her chest, ringing endlessly.

"Bell Cranell."

INTERLUDE

A
PRIVATE
CONVERSATION

BETWEEN
GODS

Гэта казка іншага сям°і.

Хаддл багоў

"Intelligent monsters, huh…?"

"That's right. They're the root of our current problem and what Ouranos has been hiding."

In the highest location of the city, a secret discussion was taking place where no one could overhear them.

On Babel's highest floor, a certain god was visiting the castle where Freya held court.

Hermes stood there, his hat removed and his orange hair swaying.

"And what of it? What's your goal in sharing that information with me?"

It was nighttime.

Hermes had recounted to Freya the full story of the incident that dragged the city into chaos—as well as the true nature of the armed monsters. Plus, Ouranos's will. And the existence of Knossos and the evil hidden away in it and, on top of all that, its relation to *Loki Familia*.

Everything.

In response, Freya mustered a "humph." There were some surprises, but she already knew much of what he had shared. And none of it particularly interested her.

The Goddess of Beauty was fixated on a single boy.

To the point that the fate of the armed monsters and Ouranos's intentions were trivial compared to him.

"Lady Freya, I'm anxious for Bell."

Bell Cranell was falling into ruin. His accomplishments were undoubtedly crumbling, tumbling down the staircase he'd managed to climb. He was on the verge of losing everything after betraying the hearts of the people, just as a certain hero elsewhere feared would happen to him.

That wasn't the end the god had wanted.

"I have a few plans myself, of course, but I'd like to ask for your assistance."

"…"

"You don't want that white light to collapse over something as meaningless as disappointment, right?"

It wasn't a development she'd desired, either.

Upon emphasizing their shared goals, the dandy god made his courteous request.

Freya's response: "Have you forgotten what you did to me during the dispute with Ishtar?"

She wore a smile that could charm the hearts of a thousand men. But the divine intention hidden behind it was entwined with wrath.

In destroying *Ishtar Familia*, which had been connected to the Evils' Remnants, the Goddess of Beauty had been forced to dance to Hermes's tune, and she still hadn't forgiven him for that incident.

Freya was the type to smile modestly, and Hermes's face twitched visibly when he saw her grinning from ear to ear. He quickly raised his hands, indicating his surrender and recoiling.

He didn't apologize, or explain himself, or acknowledge his sin. But he did make a simple request.

"Then, I hope you will find a way to watch over us."

Look after the fate of that boy. And witness what I've prepared to flip everything on its head. Hermes left it implied, unspoken.

"Which means you'd like me to do nothing."

"Yes."

He returned her gaze, and the silver eyes of the goddess bored into his orange ones.

Hermes deliberately bowed deeply.

"If you believe me and if you're willing to entrust it to me…I'd like you to give me the key."

For the first time in their conversation, Freya flinched. She raised a single eyebrow.

"With the key to Knossos…I'll take care of the intelligent monsters. And bring that boy back once more to the role of a hero."

"What do you intend to do?"

"I'll set a stage, one where the hero can return."

Freya contemplated this as Hermes continued to remain bent over before her.

When Ishtar was sent back, Freya had protected one of the exiled goddess's followers, Tammuz. He'd held the key to Knossos, which was now under Freya's control.

To hand it over to Hermes when I didn't give it to Loki...If I'm being honest, I don't trust him...But if that child can overcome it, then this side might be...

A stage for the return of a hero.

A dramatic play prepared by a god—or a farce.

With a firm grip on Hermes's divine will, Freya decided it had the potential to be a sufficient trial.

And setting aside the wishes of the god before her, this would satisfy her own desire: It might be possible for her to witness the great scene. It wasn't her divine will but the boy's fervent wish to overcome.

*In that case, I...*Freya realized that her instincts had been correct when she had refused to yield to Loki and kept the key to herself.

"Ottar. The key."

"My lady," echoed a curt response from a dark corner of the room.

After the briefest of pauses, the boaz attendant approached Freya, respectfully holding out a magic item with the symbol *D* engraved into it.

"Very well. I shall give it to you."

That was the goddess's decision—or whim. Its effects would greatly surpass her intentions, eventually going on to sharpen everyone's branching paths.

"Thank you, Lady Freya."

Hermes smiled as Freya handed him the Daedalus Orb and then hurried toward the door to the goddess's room, as if not wanting to waste any more time.

"Pardon me," he said as he left the room.

"...Hermes? You believe you know everything, but you should be careful. Don't get tripped up, all right?"

The door closed behind him. The god disappeared, and Freya grinned upon giving him a warning that didn't reach his ears.

Standing by her side, Ottar offered a response instead.

"By you, my lady?"

"Not by me...By that child," she responded as she approached the window.

Outside the gigantic, seamless window was a gray and black sky filled with thick clouds.

She stared out at it.

"I have no need for a god-made hero. I'm tired of them."

Ironically, it had the same ring to it as the "man-made hero" a certain Braver had spoken about before.

"I want to see...No, the world itself desires a hero who's never been seen before."

The goddess smiled sweetly, and her eyes narrowed, as if looking at something elsewhere in the distance, as she hooked her hair behind her ear.

"To break the stagnation of the mortal realm, we need...a *heretical hero* who betrays the gods."

Her murmur was swallowed up by the darkness.

THE SKIRMISH ON DAEDALUS STREET: BEHIND THE SCENES

Гэта казка іншага сям’і.

Дэдал перастрэлка і назад

Loki Familia moved their camp to the central area of Daedalus Street.

This area of the Labyrinth District was a jungle of towers and tall buildings. The stairs and narrow paths were jumbled together in such a chaotic mess that someone observing the city from up above wouldn't be able to see the ground. Finn set up his headquarters on the roof of a large building that resembled an old fortress. Its roof was wide, and it was possible to look out over all of Daedalus Street from it.

Directly beneath them, just on the other side of the ground, lay Knossos. The familia members were in position to defend access to Daedalus's legacy.

"Captain, *Hestia Familia* is on the move."

"I see...Notify everyone. It won't take long for things to start happening. Have the squads deploy according to the plan."

"Yes, sir!" replied Anakity, serving as Finn's aide for the operation, after she brought him the report.

When he gave her his orders, the catgirl dashed off, straining her voice as she conveyed them to the members deployed nearby.

According to Cruz's surveillance report, Bell Cranell and his familia went outside to buy equipment and items...He didn't have direct contact with anyone, but he's gotta be moving in accordance with orders from the monster side.

The armed monsters had a commander. From Gareth's report, Finn suspected that this person wasn't a tamer but a mage. And the hunk of metal—the golem—that Tiona had destroyed wasn't a monster but a magic item, as unbelievable as that might sound.

Finn had never heard of an automaton capable of engaging in combat by itself. An incredibly advanced mage had to be supporting the monsters. It must be one of Ouranos's secret pawns—someone selected from his personal forces, presumably.

A magic item would work or even a written note, if he considered going back to the basics an option. Finn guessed that the armed monsters in the city's sewers and *Hestia Familia* were communicating and coordinating somehow. Also, the monsters had probably already concealed themselves in Daedalus Street.

"Finn." Aiz alone came to him, while the members of the familia started to head out en masse after taking a break.

"If he comes to Daedalus Street...I'll watch him."

Finn froze in place and looked back at her. Aiz was asking for the role of monitoring Bell Cranell.

Was it an obsession? Or lingering feelings of attachment?

"Really?...Can you do it? Aiz, you've supported Bell Cranell in too many situations. If I'm being honest, I'm afraid you'd purposely lose sight of him," Finn frankly informed Aiz.

In her heart, Aiz felt turbulent, though she didn't let it peek out of her usual expression.

"I'll be frank with you, Aiz. Objectively speaking, Bell Cranell is a destabilizing force in Orario right now. He's a risk. Given that, we need to do two things. First, be hypervigilant. Second, stop him from acting if need be."

"..."

"Can you really do that?"

Aiz looked down before meeting Finn's eyes again and nodding.

"If he tries anything...I'll stop him. If someone has to stop him, I want it to be me."

"..."

"And if a monster shows up...I will take it down."

In her declaration, Finn could hear both an obligation to her duty and her personal desire. He could guess from her resolute expression that something had happened between her and Bell.

In his eyes, she appeared to display a clear sense of responsibility.

"Got it. I'll leave Bell Cranell to you."

"Thank you...Finn."

Finn had approved Aiz's request upon evaluating her.

As Aiz turned and left, Finn watched her get farther and farther from him before lifting up his head.

"...The rain's stopped."

It'd started yesterday and finally gone away. The outline of the clouds in the sky was visible as the moonlight dimly seeped through.

Night had arrived.

Its dark-blue shroud settled over Orario.

The clouds parted after covering the sky for a long time, unveiling a sea of stars.

The sky peered over the giant Labyrinth District. Somewhere in the fray, a single shadow scaled a building in secret. Belying its large body, it leaped lithely onto a roof.

As if steeling itself, it paused for a second before looking up at the moon like an animal.

"OOOOOOOOOOOoooooooooooo——......"

The howl of a monster reverberated through the dark night.

Its long and rumbling roar resounded all through Daedalus Street, making it out to the edges of the city.

In unison, all the adventurers looked up. The residents became scared. Everyone within earshot froze, knowing the time had come.

"AAAaaaaaaa——..."

Next, a high-pitched voice resembling a girl's cry pierced through the sky.

The monsters exchanged cries that echoed across the sky, yowling something incomprehensible to the humans and the gods.

"What's that?!"

"The damn monsters have come!"

Many of the adventurers in the Labyrinth District began to yell.

"It's starting."

A goddess with vermilion hair stopped and scanned the area from high ground.

"Filvis, follow *Loki Familia*'s movements."

"Yes, Dionysus."

The god with blond locks instructed his elf attendant as he watched over the battle—their opportunity for the taking.

"Captain!"

"..."

And ignoring the sudden movements of his fellow familia members, the prum hero glared at the darkness below as it roamed the ground as it pleased.

The monsters' shouts were a declaration.

The curtain opened quietly. The battle had begun.

The fight with the enemy started in the southern sector.

"I—I think they're coming out?!"

"A monster! In the alley!"

A single al-miraj had appeared, wearing a blue battle jacket too large for its body and a broken pocket watch hanging around its neck. It matched the armed monster *Loki Familia* had fought before. It started running around the backstreets in the southern area of the Labyrinth District.

The adventurers roared, rushing to the identified prey.

"An al-miraj!"

"Over there! Follow it!"

Ignoring the intense clamor reaching her ears, Aiz stuck to her original task.

There's no need to falter. I'm watching him.

On the roof of a building, Aiz was keeping an eye on Bell Cranell in the streets below her. From the moment he'd arrived on Daedalus

Street, Aiz had been marking him. She'd been maintaining a distance that would allow her to subdue him at a moment's notice if he made any suspicious moves or contacted any monsters.

Bell glanced with distress up at Aiz, letting go of the hand of the half-elf Guild member at his side and sprinting.

The game of tag began.

"Go! Don't lose sight of him!"

The more perceptive adventurers hadn't fallen for the distraction—the appearance of an al-miraj—and had chosen to follow Bell Cranell. As she dashed along the rooftops, Aiz could see upper-class adventurers who seemed powerful.

Bell ran to the district's southeast area without slowing down. With Aiz's eyes glued to his back, he raced through the streets before suddenly flipping directions. When he ran into a curve in the road, out of sight for a split second, the boy disappeared without a trace.

"?!"

"Where'd Little Rookie go?!"

The adventurers' confused shouts came at the same time as Aiz's surprise.

Bell had literally disappeared, leaving the others dumbfounded and locked in place. Even Aiz paused for a second.

The opening chords of chaos rang out in the next moment.

"He's here! Little Rookie's here! He went in that house!"

"You're wrong—he's here! He went up the street!"

"What?!"

"I-it's a monster! A monster came out!"

Confusion reigned over the conflicting shouts coming from adventurers searching for their target—not just reports of monsters but also reports of Bell Cranell in entirely different locations. Of course, all of them were false. Everyone was losing track of the monsters and the boy.

In the blink of an eye, their surroundings had become anarchy.

"Did he disappear?" Aiz calmly scanned the area, ignoring the bewildered cries of others.

——*No, he's here.* And she quickly found his presence.

It didn't matter if he tried to erase his scent and disappear; his faint footsteps and other traces would never escape the perceptive powers of a first-tier adventurer.

He's gone invisible! Is this chaos part of his plan, too?

With her wealth of experience, the Sword Princess knew how to follow the boy's tracks, leaving the other adventurers behind.

Was the turbulent situation created by a spell or a magic item? Either way, they would outwit her if she let her guard down. Aiz discarded her haughty belief that Bell Cranell and *Hestia Familia* were a lower tier than she was.

As a lone hunter, she continued to track down the boy.

"Sword Princess."

"!"

Someone was blocking her path.

Someone in tall boots and a long cape with a hood. An adventurer hiding their face behind a mask. The person before Aiz drew a wooden sword worn at their waist.

"I challenge you to a game."

Aiz gazed in wonder. *"Now?...Here?"*

"I'm a creature of the shadows. I can cross blades with you in these types of situations."

There were more than a few people who'd pursued the path of the sword and challenged the renowned Sword Princess to a match. But the commanding voice of the challenger didn't seem to be hiding a lie.

But could this timing truly be a coincidence?

Is this one of Bell's...comrades?

In other words, an impediment.

As she reached her hand to her sword belt, Aiz glanced in the direction of the boy's presence as it continued to move away from her.

"I'm afraid I can't accept no for an answer." The masked adventurer charged, swinging their sword.

——*This person's fast!*

Their wooden sword matched the speed of a first-tier adventurer's, forcing Aiz to draw her sword. A sharp sound rang out as their weapons clashed. The anonymous adventurer put significant force into it, sending them both tumbling from the roof to the alley below.

Aiz gave up on Bell and confronted the masked adventurer.

"Word is that an al-miraj showed up to the south! And there have been multiple monster sightings in the southeast, too!"

"False information is getting mixed in...The area is becoming chaotic!"

The progression of the battle was reported in detail at *Loki Familia's* encampment. They were relying mostly on magic-stone semaphores to communicate. Members standing by on the roofs of buildings flashed their lamps, sending messages to the main base in the center of Daedalus Street.

"Don't break formation! Make sure everyone maintains their positions!"

Anakity strained her voice, responding to the familia members receiving the signals.

She tried her best to not disturb the prum leader as he imagined a board and pieces moving around it in different combinations, deftly handing out orders as his second-in-command.

It's not just Bell Cranell but all of Hestia Familia *who have gotten away from their watchers. Even their goddess. Did they use a magic item or just their knowledge of Daedalus Street? Either way, the enemy is moving freely right now.*

Finn had lost the initiative.

From the start, his two-front plan meant that *Loki Familia* had no breathing room, forcing them into a position where they needed to analyze the enemy's movements and respond almost immediately.

The monsters are using Bell Cranell as a lure, as I expected...but we've brought in Aiz. How will they respond?

Aiz's request had been a stroke of luck. He could neutralize the enemy's tricks with a single stroke using the strongest piece on his side. The enemy would be forced to make a move. But first, he would find out exactly how good they were.

"Bell Cranell was in the southeast! And, ummm, Aiz has lost track of him…"

"As I said before, Bell Cranell is a diversion. Leave him to Aiz and forget about it. We don't need to do anything in the south or the southeast yet."

The report that he'd slipped past Aiz shocked the familia members at the base camp, including Anakity. Finn was surprised but suppressed his emotions and fired off more instructions.

"I think something suspicious is brewing in the west. Elfie, tell Tione and the others in the northwest to move to the ninety-eighth block and take up positions there."

When they saw their captain was unperturbed, the others were able to keep their composure and replied, ""Yes, sir!""

Loki Familia wasn't shaken by the enemy's diversion. They continued to maintain their impenetrable defensive stance around Knossos's entrances.

Something must have forced Aiz to stop. An ambush? The enemy's forces are greater than I expected, but…it'll be fine. Aiz will break out soon.

Placing the shaft of his long spear against his shoulder, Finn meditated.

It bothers me more that our scouts and lookouts haven't been able to pick up on any of them. Did they see through our plan?…No, it feels more cunning than that.

The enemy was surpassing his expectations. Could they be using a magic item?

As he thought about the presence of something he hadn't predicted, he asked a question to a nearby familia member.

"Any reports on the black minotaur?"

"Nothing yet."

"I see…Maintain the formation. Let's watch how it unfolds." Finn stayed in the same stance as he continued watching over the battlefield.

And at the same time, he devoted another part of his mind to a different plan. His thoughts never stopped.

We're still fine. *Everything is still within expected bounds. The problem is—*

——over there. Finn grimaced.

"Violas are coming!" A shout echoed in a hidden passage beneath Daedalus Street.

The adventurers took their positions, faces tense as tall yellow-green figures approached.

"*OOOOOOOOOOOOOOOOOOOOOOOOOOOOO!*"

The monsters howled as *Loki Familia*'s members prepared to fight. They were large-scale monsters, even though they were constrained by the width of the underground passage. There were three—four of them. And more kept coming.

The adventurers were outnumbered against the mass of flailing tentacles and disgusting jaws.

"Which door is open?!" Gareth boomed.

"Southwest! A swarm of monsters is flowing out of Knossos! They just keep coming!" a familia member yelled back in response.

They'd been hit in the length of a single moment. The adventurers had been waiting on standby in the underground passage, redirecting their focus to the report of an al-miraj for a second—when the door to Knossos had swung open without any warning, unleashing a revolting stream of violas.

Unable to hold their ground against the surprise attack, the members had been forced to pull back temporarily.

"The flow of monsters isn't stopping, which means the door is still open! We can force our way in...!"

"Stop! It's a trap! After we enter the Dungeon, we'll be trapped right where they want us and slowly ground down! That's what they're hoping for, since the monsters are all that's come out. There hasn't been a single one of the remnants!" Gareth rejected the familia member's impatient plea.

If a single tamer or creature controlling the monsters had emerged aboveground, there would be a target to capture. But all that came out was monsters. They couldn't noticeably deplete the enemy's fighting forces, let alone get their hands on a key.

Considering the tide of monsters, the goal of the enemy was clearly harassment—a war of attrition.

"Between a rock and a hard place, huh?! Finn, you mule's arse! Choose easier plans next time!" Gareth cursed, grinning odiously as he swung his ax.

"Lady Riveria, monster reinforcements are coming!"

Meanwhile, Riveria's elf squad was exposed to attack, protecting the southeastern side. Her second-in-command, Alicia, manipulated her short bow and magic as impatience started to show through in her graceful features.

"This isn't the time to fall for the enemy's machinations. At this rate, even if we lure out the Evils, we can't do anything here…!"

"Endure it. Don't become agitated, Alicia. It will spread to the other elves. Maintain the spirit of the great tree as you fight!"

Riveria was standing on the front lines, Concurrent Casting and acting as a lure for the monsters while the elves bathed the whole passage in a volley of magic. But it wasn't long before more monsters appeared. Unlike the skirmish aboveground, the tunnel had already transformed into a fierce battle scene.

Closing an eye, Riveria finished chanting and unleashed an ice cannon.

"*Loki Familia*…fools."

A purple robe swayed on the other side of the orichalcum door.

A masked person commanding a swarm of violas and vargs scoffed at *Loki Familia* with an ominous voice. It sounded as though several different voices were overlapping. Holding out their hands encased in metal gloves, they sent another swarm of monsters toward the adventurers.

"Excellent work." Thanatos smiled deep inside Knossos.

They were in a large hall inside the labyrinth, the base of the Evils. There was a pedestal holding a large crimson orb in the center of the room. Using that, it was possible to freely manipulate the doors in Knossos. With that special trait, it was called "the room of the labyrinth master" by the members of the remnants.

As he listened to the reports regarding *Loki Familia* brought in by his followers, a thin smile spread across the face of the god who ruled over death.

"Ikelos's screwup was certainly outside my calculations, but…I see what you're planning. You intend to use the key of the talking monsters as bait to lure us out, right?"

The long, deep purple locks of the god swayed, giving off a degenerate atmosphere as he crossed his legs atop the pedestal.

"We're just going to keep spitting out monsters. You can self-destruct as you please. An easy job. Even someone with no knowledge of battle can do this."

Thanatos had seen through Finn's plan. And in doing so, he'd recognized that it put a large burden on *Loki Familia*. As he said, Thanatos only needed to unleash a stream of monsters to harass them. With that alone, the members of *Loki Familia* in the underground passage would incur losses. Meanwhile, on the side of the Evils, they wouldn't suffer any lasting damage, no matter how many of the dispatched monsters were defeated.

Thanks to the help of the creatures, there were countless vividly colored monsters in Knossos.

"Keep the monsters flowing!"

"Ha-ha!" Thanatos's lazy voice broke into a resounding laugh, as if he might break out into song at any moment.

The followers of the God of Death dashed off in response.

"Barca, I'm counting on you, too."

"…This is a waste of time. But it's also an effort that cannot be spared."

At Thanatos's side stood Barca, a descendant of Daedalus, manipulating the crimson orb in front of him on the pedestal.

His left eye was hidden by his white bangs and had long forgotten the light of day, but it shone with the light of D, opening the labyrinth's inner walls, unlocking doors to release the violas inside. Opening and closing doors in succession, Barca led the monsters out of the labyrinth.

"*Loki Familia* won't be able to handle it in this situation...And while they're reeling from their losses, our forces can retrieve the key."

Thanatos had already readied his countermeasures for dealing with the armed monsters. He looked up at the ceiling enclosed with stone, grinning in the direction of the enemy base aboveground.

"Being caught between a rock and a hard place is rough, isn't it, Braver?"

For *Loki Familia*, the difficult situation persisted.

For *Thanatos Familia*, the comedy continued.

Thanatos laughed like a child.

While the intense battle was unfolding in the underground passage, the uproar on the surface was just starting to pick up speed.

"Wow...the captain is incredible. The battle has begun, just as he predicted," murmured Raul, who was charged with one part of the formation.

Raul Nord was a second-tier adventurer.

His status as a Level 4 was proof enough that he was strong, but there was an impression among the others that his personality was lacking. From Finn on down, Raul was plainly daunted by the first-tier adventurers who were among the best in the city. He was the spitting image of a normal person who lacked self-confidence. Unlike most adventurers who often got carried away with themselves, he had unusually low self-esteem, which was why he was seen as an ordinary person.

Which meant there were times when enemies facing off against *Loki Familia* saw him as a weak link.

"—Raul!"

"Um, uh…Captain?!" Raul responded in a wild voice, swinging around.

Finn was running toward him, even though he should have been at the central base. Raul was leading the squad to the Labyrinth District's west, which was part of the defensive line connecting to the central area. He was confused why Finn would come all the way out to their position.

"Wh-why are you here?! Who's giving orders…?"

"The main monster force has arrived in the southeast! And the black minotaur! Meet Aiz there and crush them! Tell your unit—we're changing formation! I'll join you there!"

"Y-yes, sir?!" Raul instinctively snapped to attention at his commanding tone and the words *black minotaur*. He didn't doubt the prum in the slightest.

"Also, Raul, do you remember our positions in Knossos?"

"Uh, the one underground? I remember, but—"

"Tell me what they are. Something has been bothering me."

Raul was totally confused as he responded, "Uh, Gareth and his group should be guarding the four doors—northwest, northeast, southwest, and southeast…"

"I see…Well then, I'll head out first. Gather everyone in this area and come to the southeast."

"Y-yes, sir!"

Raul started moving without hesitation upon receiving orders from the great captain himself. He informed everyone to change formation, accepting Finn's intention to prioritize subduing the black minotaur.

Huh? But what happened to Captain's spear…?

Raul didn't notice.

He couldn't realize that as he turned and ran off, Finn's lips curled into a cold smile.

"—Raul?" Finn noticed the change in formation immediately.

The western squad was moving south.

The flickering phosphorescence of the semaphore seemed almost agitated by the unexpected movement.

"Th-the western troops are shifting southward! Raul said they're going to encircle the pack of monsters there!"

"We haven't gotten any reports of that! The captain hasn't given any orders, either. What are you doing moving on your own?!"

"B-but, uh...Raul said the captain came directly to him and gave him the order..."

"*What?!*" Anakity responded in a fluster when she received the report from the messenger, looking back and forth between Finn and the cityscape below her.

The main camp filled with a sudden unease, but Finn alone had a sense of déjà vu.

That's it...This is like the War Game between Hestia Familia *and* Apollo Familia.

He was thinking about the war two months ago between factions that made the name Little Rookie resound throughout the city. In that fight, a single prum betrayed *Apollo Familia* and brought victory to *Hestia Familia.*

If that wasn't an actual betrayal but a disguise...No, a transformation—

"So that's what happened..."

"Captain?"

Disregarding Anakity looking at him in curiosity, a single prum came to Finn's mind.

It's her, isn't it?

The truth was that there was a fellow prum who had caught Finn's eye ever since Bell had impressed him during the minotaur incident. It was the girl who'd sought out help for the boy's sake even at the risk of her own life, a girl whose bravery Finn had acknowledged.

Finn guessed it was the work of the girl who had the keenest mind in all of *Hestia Familia.* With the use of a magic item or spell, she'd beaten both Raul and Finn. It was a failure on Finn's part for being on guard only against Bell Cranell.

"Draw the squad back. Fill the hole from the north with Narfi's… No, that won't work. Too slow."

Finn was about to tell another squad to fill the hole, but he shook his head before he could finish the order.

Immediately after—*clang, clang, clang!*

As if affirming his resignation, the warning bells of monster sightings in the west started ringing.

"C-Captain! A large group of monsters suddenly appeared from the west. They've breached the gap where Raul's troops were earlier and are heading for the central area!"

"I know. Calm down. I'm guessing Tione's unit noticed what's happening, but I want you to call them back. We'll pincer the enemy using the remaining garrison forces."

Agitation raced through the base, but the sight of Finn's resolute leadership kept his allies from panicking. As they regained their composure, they started carrying out the things they needed to do.

"What route is the enemy taking? What part of Knossos are they headed for?"

"Uh…straight ahead! They're moving straight east from their point in the west!"

"—*Straight ahead?* Meaning toward the west of Knossos?"

For the first time, Finn's face clouded over at that report, looking at the confused messenger as she nodded. He glanced back out across the Labyrinth District.

If they appeared in the west, I would have expected them to angle northwest or southwest…There isn't a door to Knossos in the west. Or at least not one we could find in four days of searching…Is it possible they know a route that we didn't uncover?

Finn's thoughts raced, recalling a certain conversation as he considered the worst possible case.

Ikelos touched on the existence of Daedalus's notebook, which had a blueprint for Knossos…Do they have that?

During the interrogation, Ikelos had definitely said, *I don't have it…Maybe it just fell somewhere in Knossos.*

Loki was on hand, so Finn had believed him.

But if he'd managed to pull the wool over their eyes…or if the notebook had changed hands in a place where Ikelos couldn't see it…

"This is bad," Finn whispered as he looked down at his right hand.

His thumb that foretold his apprehensions hadn't begun to ache yet.

——*I relied too much on instinct without realizing it.*

Finn was ashamed of himself, but he quickly switched gears. His original plan had envisioned them luring the armed monsters into the underground path, but he started adapting as the situation changed. He discarded the possibility of using them as bait to lure out the Evils, prioritizing capturing them aboveground. They couldn't afford to let them advance into the central part of the district now that they knew there was another possible route that had slipped past their investigation.

His thoughts accelerated at a dizzying rate.

"Heeeey, Finn!" The goddess's drawl rang out.

"Where've you been, Loki?"

"Here and there." Loki made her appearance in the hectic main camp, approaching Finn from behind.

He didn't bother to glance back.

"Mm, thinking about something, Finn?"

"Yeah, I guess I was a little conceited. I'd appreciate it if you left me alone for a bit."

Loki looked intently from the side as he continued to weave his thoughts.

And then the corners of her mouth twitched up—ever so slightly.

Loki placed her hands on Finn's shoulders and whispered.

"Finn—get to the bottom of this."

"—" Finn's thoughts ground to a halt.

Did she mean Bell?

Or was she talking about the monsters?

Finn couldn't understand her divine will. She was intentionally making Finn think about it.

She watched from his periphery as just his eyes moved, and the goddess smiled faintly.

"With your own two eyes. Don't rely on anyone else."

"..."

"I'll leave the final decision to you. I won't say anything else."

As she released his shoulders, Loki smiled thoughtlessly as always, swinging her arms playfully and walking past Finn.

"..."

A small pause.

As the uproarious bustle of the main camp continued, Finn drew in a long breath.

As he stored the goddess's words in a corner of his mind, he prioritized dealing with the current situation. Donning the mask of the leader again, Finn looked out over Daedalus Street.

"Call Raul here. At once."

"Y-yes, sir!" responded the messenger Elfie before running off.

Finn started to issue orders without hesitation.

"We're shifting the formation. Reposition Gareth's forces from the southwest back aboveground with the monster-assault squad."

"Is that okay, Captain? If we don't have them underground, it will be harder to check the Evils' movements..."

"If the monsters know another route connecting to Knossos, it'll be a bad plan to leave them belowground. Our goal is the key. What's the point of trying to use them as a lure when we're letting what we're actually looking for slip away? The Evils' attacks are getting more intense, which is why we're moving Gareth to shake them up."

"U-understood!"

Anakity realized that Finn was shifting the priority to the armed monsters, which had originally been intended as bait. While he was explaining it to her, he was working on another plan, too.

I knew we'd be relegated to taking a defensive position, but I might have given them too much of an advantage. To come at me without any hesitation...First, there's Bell Cranell, and then, the rest of you. You're really out to get on my nerves.

As he continued to whine internally, Finn smiled at the situation, as if his heart was rejoicing at the unseen opponent on the other side of the board moving their pieces shrewdly.

She'd deny it, but our lines of thought really are similar. In which case, her next move would be...

Finn looked up when he finished his thought.

"Aki! I'm giving you a squad, so head out."

The base stirred as Finn hammered out a new set of deployments.

"I don't mind, but...what should we do about your logistical support?"

"I'll have Raul take over for you. You're the only one who can do what this plan needs," Finn said with his full confidence in her.

Anakity responded with a nod, and her expression remained unchanged.

He explained the mission details to her as fast as he could, and she crammed them word for word into her head.

As he looked out over the Labyrinth District while the semaphore's light flickered intensely, Finn gave her an order.

"I'm about to tell you where you need to spread a net."

"Loki, where did you go?"

After leaving Finn, Loki went to the location where Dionysus was observing the battle—a spire near *Loki Familia*'s main base, looking out a window inside it.

"I went by the Guild for a bit."

"What? Did you go to Ouranos?"

"Who knows." Loki giggled as Dionysus looked at her reproachfully.

Loki glanced around once she was satisfied by the discontent of the god who was cunning under normal circumstances. The narrow light of a lamp made of magic stones was barely visible, sending an unending stream of signals going back and forth. Was that bonfire in the northwest actually a watch fire in the plaza where the evacuees were gathering?

Filvis wasn't with Dionysus. Loki had two members of her familia as bodyguards, but they were keeping their distance.

"...How does the situation look to you?"

"No clue. Without clairvoyance or the divine mirror, there's no way to know what's goin' on out there."

"That's true."

Loki stuck out her tongue at Dionysus peering into the darkness. But she sniffed as if she could sense the minute changes through the air of the Labyrinth District.

"But they're done with feelin' one another out."

The warning bell in the west was still ringing.

Its chime seemed to confirm Loki's comment, declaring the end of the opening skirmish and announcing the beginning of the real battle.

Loki opened her crimson eyes just the tiniest bit.

"The real fight starts now."

She was a young animal person, one of the many shameless adventurers aiming to make a killing from the rewards the Guild had put out on the armed monsters.

As she pretended to play that part, she scampered around among the other violent people, gathering information and occasionally shouting, "Outta my way!"

"Th-this's awful…"

"Shit, how many people is that?!"

There was a sea of blood—adventurers collapsed at every turn on winding roads, bodies piled up as far as the eye could see. It looked as if they'd been crushed, broken, their blood splattered from an excessive amount of brute force. Among the fallen were some bearing the jester's emblem.

Gasping at the awful scene, she left the place without being noticed by the other adventurers, from 277th Street to the sign for the back alley of 278th.

As she slunk around the eastern side of the Labyrinth District, she made extra effort to ensure that no one was nearby before she crouched and stealthily held her hand to her mouth.

"This is bad. The *Xenos* aren't here. They were probably noticed by some adventurers at the meet-up point…Yes. Yes…Yes, give up on meeting with them and start another diversion—" she softly whispered into the crystal in her small hand, even though she was alone.

She stopped murmuring, stood up, and scanned the area, about to run off again.

"Just as Captain predicted—"

Huh? She was stopped by a shadow floating above the ground.

"—you were passing from the south to the east."

The shadow leaped down on the girl's head, silently and in a feline fashion. Without allowing her a chance to get a good look, the shadow woman held a blade to her slender neck.

"——Gh?!"

Her left hand was twisted behind her back. She could feel the cold blade against her skin. She was rendered helpless in an instant.

The animal person's eyes widened in shock, unable to process what had happened.

"*Supporter? What's wrong? Did something happen?*" called out the crystal in her right hand, giving off a dim glow.

It was painfully quiet in the middle of the alley. A single crimson drop seeped from her neck under the pressure of the blade.

The cold steel commanded that she lie. The girl breathed in and responded with a quivering voice.

"There are…adventurers here…I'll be caught…Please cut transmission for the time being…"

"*Okay, got it,*" replied the goddess on the other end, withdrawing without noticing anything and mistaking her hushed voice for nervousness about being near other adventurers.

The light dimmed, and the crystal went silent. At the same time, a sudden cold sweat drenched her entire body.

The distasteful insignia on the hilt of the shortsword was that of a certain familia: the emblem of a jester, its lips strung up into a crescent smile.

Thump. Thump. Thump. Her heart was beating wildly in her chest. *Wh-why…?*

Why did I get caught?

Did they see through my disguise?

No way! Why? How?

This isn't my real body—

As if to answer the questions running through the girl's head, the woman standing behind her, Anakity, whispered in her ear.

"You, and only you, *don't smell like anything.*"

The girl's body temperature instantly dropped.

"A scent-erasing item, right? I noticed it when I was investigating with Bete…Were you the one who hid the monster in the west?"

"…?!"

"When you're alone, it's one thing…But when you're in a group, it *stands out.*"

Is that it?

Is that all?

Did she find me hidden among all the adventurers from that alone?

As the emotions swirled on her face at a blinding pace, her small body started to quiver.

"And…you're the same height as the fake Captain who fooled Raul."

Anakity Autumn.

A Level 4, just like her uninteresting colleague Raul Nord.

But despite being a second-tier adventurer, she was a little *too skilled.*

With Finn's prediction about the girl's transformation, she managed to narrow down her target and find her among all the adventurers running around.

Several members of *Loki Familia* appeared around them.

This time, all the blood drained from the girl's face.

"I'll have you come with us."

—Bell.

As if sensing her end, she whispered his name.

THEIR RESPECTIVE BATTLES

The sound of a blade parrying a wooden sword, an intense clash, rang out as Aiz landed in the alley.

"Guh!"

As she fell on the ground from the roof, Aiz faced off against her attacker, the masked adventurer.

The stranger's long, hooded cape fluttered, and they wore boots that extended halfway up their thighs. The svelte adventurer held a wooden sword as their lower body shifted into a battle stance.

The location was a backstreet in the southeast of the Labyrinth District.

The street was unexpectedly wide at seven meders with wooden boxes and casks and mounds of scrap wood haphazardly scattered around. The skirmish between the boy and the adventurers chasing the monsters was in the distance. That one corner of the Labyrinth District became a battlefield all their own, as if the rest of the world had been closed off.

"Who are—?!"

"Unfortunately, I cannot identify myself. Please forgive what practically amounts to a surprise attack," the anonymous adventurer interjected sincerely as Aiz started to question their identity.

It was a resolute, honorable response, and the face behind the mask could be that of an elf. Their polite tone had an apologetic tinge to it, but it also revealed their readiness for battle, a declaration that combat couldn't be avoided.

"Against an opponent like you, I can't take a wait-and-see approach—I'll be going all out from the start."

The next instant, the masked adventurer disappeared.

"!!"

In one high-speed action, they retreated out of Aiz's field of vision. Her golden eyes were a split second behind, tracking them moving diagonally to the right, and the anonymous adventurer leaned down enough to scrape along the ground before unleashing a strike with the wooden sword from a low angle.

Aiz responded precisely to the attack closing in from her periphery, deflecting it with Desperate.

""—Gh!""

The wooden sword and rapier cut through the air, their impact sending a stinging jolt through both their arms.

The moment they traded blows, Aiz's golden eyes met sky-blue ones.

As if recognizing from the start that the attack would be blocked, the anonymous adventurer darted away, brushing past Aiz, *accelerating further.*

"?!"

As a gale, the challenger blew past Aiz and circled around her, using the wide alley to its fullest to boost their speed. The sound of feet pounding the stone pavement over and over echoed through the street as the occasional cobblestone shattered and kicked up into the air. The attacker didn't stay still for a split second, moving in all directions.

"—Ha!"

"！"

They unleashed an attack in the blink of an eye. A flash of steel managed to block the wooden sword slashing up behind her.

Aiz furrowed her brow at the force transferred through her sword.

The masked adventurer didn't allow her any time to think, taking their distance and attacking from a high speed.

Another attack. Followed by another.

Aiz blocked them as they came from all directions. Her eyes widened as the magnitude of the strikes incessantly resounding through her became clear.

Is the force...increasing?!

There was no mistaking it.

The second attack was stronger than the first. And the third with more impact than the second. The ambush had grown intense, and the impact started to shake Aiz's body through her defenses.

Desperate was quivering from the blows, a testament to their increasing power.

——*Is it a kind of sprinting skill like Bete's?*

Solmani was the name of the werewolf's skill, powerful and rare, that increased strength and agility as it accelerated. Aiz guessed it was extremely likely that her opponent had a skill of some kind that interacted with the action of sprinting.

In a fight between two adventurers, techniques and tactics were obviously fundamental, but sussing out magic and skills was equally important. Failing to see through the enemy's abilities or trump cards could be the difference between victory and a complete reversal at the last possible moment.

Those trump cards would often be the line between victory and defeat, especially in a fight between two people with real skill.

"Haaaaaaaaaaaaaaaa—!" A loud scream accompanied another attack.

Her opponent's body gave off golden particles of light.

Aiz had seen that effect before.

Is it the same as Androctonus, the Man Slayer?!

That was the first-tier adventurer Phryne Jamil, who'd attacked her when they had fought *Ishtar Familia* in Meren.

Phryne should have been a Level-5 opponent, crossing swords evenly with Aiz at Level 6. At the time, she'd been giving off a large number of light particles. The scene before Aiz's eyes stirred memories from a month ago.

Had her opponent been given a boost equivalent to a level-up?

Was this masked adventurer a former member of *Ishtar Familia*?

——*No, that's not it. This isn't one of Ishtar's followers.*

Aiz discarded the speculation in her mind, because there was a memory that came back, far beyond a month ago.

I know. I know this person.

I—We've fought before!

If I remember correctly, they hid their identity that time, too.

A mask. A wooden sword. A cape. That sharp follow-through. The strong gaze in those blue-green eyes.

Past Aiz had been desperate to become strong and could remember only vague symbols.

Why had they been fighting? Why had they had such a serious fight?

Just who had won that fight—?

"—Hyah!"

"Gh!"

As she remained half-immersed in her past recollections, Aiz engaged in a fierce dance, darting with her sword. As the masked adventurer unleashed attack after attack, she accepted the challenge head-on.

The battle bloomed with intensity. The swift movements of her assailant knew no limits as they conducted a sonata with the sound of their mighty sprint, accelerating fast enough to break the stone pavement. Just when they were about to clash, the masked adventurer would drop their speed for a split second before accelerating to slice at Aiz. By manipulating their speed, the assailant added in tens, hundreds of feints—tactics interwoven into the high-speed battle. They were the smallest of movements, but their precision was unlike anything she'd seen before. The force of those tactics was enough to make the Sword Princess slow to judge for a second, to overcome the level handicap between them. It inspired awe.

Aiz lost the initiative and tried to use her own speed to chase the masked adventurer.

"Ngh...?!"

The enemy's wooden sword smashed the wooden crates and barrels nearby, sending fragments of wood flying.

A blast of projectiles blocked her vision. Aiz was forced to intercept them. The rain of shattered wood didn't allow her any opening for pursuit. The masked adventurer used the terrain to its utmost potential and kept the Sword Princess from closing in.

The hotly contested battlefield had been a storage area for scrap wood. The stacked wooden crates and rows of casks transformed into obstructions blocking Aiz's line of sight.

The anonymous adventurer would escape to the left. But the moment they entered a blind spot, they would come from the right to take Aiz by surprise. From Aiz's perspective, the movements were otherworldly, totally betraying her expectations.

Barrels burst, crates danced, and just when she thought countless splinters would be coming from the front, a blow from the wooden sword came in directly from the side.

"Khhh?!"

Aiz just managed to guard against it, but the masked adventurer had already retreated out of her range.

They weren't greedy in their assault, cutting in with an attack in passing and then leaving Aiz's field of view as they endured Aiz's counterattacks with a range of techniques and a tireless sprint.

A super-precise, super-high-speed battle. A transcendental hit-and-run.

The masked adventurer's tremendous speed and orbit increased as they passed through their surroundings, breaking casks and crates as if a gale. A hail of fragments assaulted Aiz from all directions, accompanied by a series of tremendous booms, to the point that she could imagine herself being trapped inside a windstorm.

They're really going all out...using every last thing to face me.

Their skills, the boost from that light, the terrain. Aiz could feel the conviction in her opponent's stance as they used every last card at their disposal: It was a desire to pin her down in this location.

As she deflected the enemy's attacks, Aiz thought.

They can't maintain this kind of attack for long. If I wait for their stamina to run down, I can break through, and given time, my eyes will adjust to their speed, and I can deal with it.

But that's a bad plan.

If the masked adventurer was connected to Bell, their goal was to buy time. Since Aiz had lost sight of him, more time here was a loss for her.

"..." Aiz was troubled.

If the situation were different, she would have enjoyed continuing the swordplay. If neither of them had their own obligations, they could have clashed head-on to their hearts' content.

If they'd been the same level as Aiz—they could have had more close-range combat.

Aiz drew Desperate's sheath from the sword belt.

"‼"

Sword in her right hand, sheath in her left. As the masked adventurer continued to move at high speed, they gazed in wonder at the Sword Princess's form.

Sword and sheath in both hands...Can the Sword Princess dual wield? Impossible. I've never heard of her doing that before.

The challenger was perplexed and suspicious but never stopped their feet. The masked adventurer continued their sprint to take full advantage of their skill while observing the movements of the girl with golden hair and golden eyes.

In the center of the alley, enclosed in a gale prison, Aiz closed her eyes.

She lowered both arms, holding them loosely by her side, as if to say, *Strike however you like.* It was formless.

Is this a waiting stance...?

Aiming for a counter. A passive tactic.

Did she give up on following my movements? Is she intending to bet it all on a single attack?

For the masked adventurer, it was exactly the sort of development they should have wanted to buy time. If the assailant kept running and continuing to divert without attacking, they could maintain the stalemate.

But the Sword Princess should realize that I'm aiming to buy time... Is she trying to lower my guard? Is it a trap?

The storied warrior behind the mask tried to read into the intentions of the swordswoman. The assailant had been attacking nonstop. And in that smallest of gaps, they adopted a defensive mind-set.

That slight gap in the force of their gale could hardly be called a defensive posture—but it was enough for the girl.

The next instant, Aiz dashed.

"Urg?!"

Discarding the camouflage of a counter, she came in with an instantaneous approach. The masked adventurer was visibly shocked as the golden-eyed swordswoman appeared before their eyes, charging into their projected path.

It had all been a feint—a strategy that Aiz devised to create a single instant of doubt in the masked adventurer. The anonymous challenger realized that the time needed to think had in itself been the trap, and they gathered all the strength in their body to intercept the oncoming blow.

"Hy—?!"

Even as the assailant had been caught off guard, they still maintained the sprint, unleashing a sweeping horizontal slash with the wooden sword.

It carried the force of their skill and the boost brought about by the light particles.

It was a single attack with all their might, combining every blessing they'd been granted.

Crack.

"_____"

The Sword Princess readily repelled the attack with her sword without difficulty and with the precision of threading a needle.

Not enough strength.

Not enough speed.

Not a high enough level.

Even with the masked adventurer's ability and strength, it was meaningless before Aiz, even as a Level 6.

There was an insurmountable difference in combat experience.

The masked adventurer was strong without a doubt. Their movements were more refined than the ones of the person in Aiz's memories.

But Aiz had grown far more than they had.

She'd gone into the Dungeon again and again without rest. She'd continued defeating monsters without end.

She'd gotten mixed up in the incident with the vividly colored monsters, the demi-spirit, and the mortal combat with the creature. She'd accumulated all that experience.

On one side was a person of true strength who'd retired from the front lines; on the other was the Sword Princess, who was fighting out at the very forefront even now.

The number of difficulties they'd overcome on their path to this rematch was the clear deciding factor between them.

They had been equal only in the realm of techniques. Aiz reluctantly lowered her eyebrows, slashing with her remaining weapon.

"Fortunately, it was the sheath side—"

"It was a good thing you attacked from the right," Aiz whispered as she parried the wooden sword, the masked adventurer swinging their sword diagonally down with all their might using a single hand.

"If I used the sword, I couldn't have held back."

Aiz was relieved that it ended *without her cutting her opponent in half,* dispassionately unleashing an attack with the sheath in her hand.

"—Gggggh?!"

A single flash smashed into her opponent's side at extreme speed—a scathing and decisive blow. When the air was forced out of their lungs, they spat up blood as they were blasted away with the force of a river bursting through a dam.

Fragments of wood flew into the sky as they were thrown back into the boxes and barrels behind them.

That slender body smashed into a wall.

The masked adventurer left cracks in the brick wall, exchanging a final glance with Aiz right before losing consciousness.

Their searching sky-colored eyes filled with regret as they slumped over.

The sonata of the gale died down. And in its place, long golden locks fluttered in the alley.

"...I'm sorry."

Three minutes.

That was the amount of time spent to reach a conclusion to this battle that no one would know of.

The slight time that the anonymous adventurer had managed to buy.

Aiz didn't look back at the unconscious woman as she left that place.

"What was that wind just now?!" Tione was in a fit of rage.

She'd been ordered by Finn to scout and raid, following his instructions when the armed monsters appeared in the Labyrinth District's southwest area. She approached the throng of monsters from behind as they marched directly east toward *Loki Familia*'s main base in the central part of Daedalus Street. In hot pursuit, she saw the parade of monsters and commenced attacking them from behind with throwing knives and other projectiles.

The large group of monsters lost its edge—there was no escaping from a first-tier adventurer. They were just about to be captured.

At least if it hadn't been for that divine wind.

"I thought they were hiding and shooting off ice when all of a sudden that weird-ass wind started blowing! Don't screw with me!"

"Amazing! We flew through the sky, Tione! That must be what birds feel like!"

"Shut the hell up!" Tione snapped at her sister's easygoing observation and subconsciously smashed a wall with her fist.

There was an invisible defense around the armed monsters. Two of them. They were invisible with one ability or another, hitting the Amazons with their ice and obstructing their movements. The sisters quickly saw through the invisible enemies and the ice attack without too much difficulty, but they'd been removed from the battlefield by the enemies' hidden trick.

An unbelievable typhoon.

It was unlike anything they'd experienced before, a wind cannon that Aiz's Airiel couldn't even have matched. They'd literally been blown away by it. While they were high up, soaring through the starry night sky, they witnessed the monsters moving farther away, just as the two sisters had managed to catch up with them.

The first-tier adventurers' hot pursuit was reversed at the last minute.

Outmaneuvered, Tione roared in a furious voice that shook the sky, frightening the people in the city, who could have taken it to be a monster.

"Looking down on us...!"

After they were grandly blown away, they finally landed near the outer edge of the western part of the Labyrinth District. In her rage, Tione had taken the tone of a villain as she punched the wall one more time.

The trick up the enemy's sleeve, her quick temper that caught her off guard, and, more than anything, her inability to fulfill her beloved Finn's order caused her anger to well up. She devoted her remaining patience to thinking about the enemy.

Was this invisibility a skill of the tamer who Finn had mentioned?

If the invisible things were part of *Hestia Familia*, would that mean it was the effect of a magic blade? The scenes of the siege in the War Game with *Apollo Familia* were burned into her mind.

Was it the work of the legendary Crozzo's Magic Swords—of Welf Crozzo?

Shithead. Tione burned with rage. *If my guess is right, I'm gonna beat his ass when I catch him or give him a good knee to the stomach, at the very least,* she decided with bloodshot eyes.

At about the same time, a certain young man with red hair felt a tremendous chill.

"We're gonna catch right back up! Tiona!"

"Okay!"

As she continued to be consumed by fury, Tione ran for the central part of the district, where the enemies were heading. As she rushed off driven by anger, she smashed the black-bricked buildings and pavement wherever her feet landed.

She was inhuman in her pursuit to the extent that the monsters seemed pitiful. The pair would be able to catch up to the enemy's back lines within three minutes.

If they could pull that off and catch the monsters in a pincer with the defensive squad, the monsters would be out of luck.

But it wasn't to be.

"!"

"Tiona?!"

The other half of her party suddenly turned down a different route. Tione almost telepathically guessed what her stupid sister was thinking, though she was shocked.

A pitch-black fog was released from near the central area where the defensive squad and the monsters were clashing.

That suspicious fog permeated the surroundings, stretching to the northwest.

It would have been fine if it was the southern side of the district, since there were only adventurers searching for monsters there. But Tione had heard there were still residents evacuating in the north.

If the monsters moving around in that fog headed for the northwestern end of the district, it would be bad. That was what Tiona had to be thinking.

"That idiot! Is she trying to disobey the captain?! Hey! Wait for me!"

Because the two of them had been told to move together, Tione chased after her little sister, heading northwest.

"A smoke screen!"

Gareth was fighting in the middle of the area of the black mist that Tione and Tiona had seen.

Near the central area of Daedalus Street, Gareth had moved from his station underground up to the surface to assault the armed monsters who'd escaped the sisters. As he used his Level-6 strength to corner the monsters, the pitch-black mist spread around in futile resistance.

At the hands of the mage leading the monsters, the battlefield descended into a chaotic mess of human and monster screams intermingling.

"Get them—!"

"*Guuuuuuuuuuuuuuuu!*"

More and more of the reinforcements for *Loki Familia* piled into the part of the Labyrinth District that'd become the main battle-field. The sounds of weapons and claws clashing wildly rang out.

Amid that, Gareth dashed unhesitatingly in a straight line. His target was the person who'd released the dark mist, the black-robed mage.

"Grr!"

"Guh?!"

The mage was toppled by the force of the ax swing. Gareth paid no heed to the other monsters, focusing only on their leader.

If I can just take out this mage—!

The monsters would no longer be able to use any further schemes and *Loki Familia* would have a significant advantage. Gareth had seen through the level of detestable danger the mage posed, lock-ing onto its presence in the awful visual conditions and preparing to smash his war ax into its black robes.

"Hmm?!"

An ice blast interrupted him.

Gareth hadn't heard a chant. It had been an ice-type magic blade, without a doubt.

Frozen in an unnatural position, he managed to break the ice and swing down his blade, but the mage used the split-second pause to escape.

As he saw that black robe disappear into the mist, Gareth made to follow it, annoyed, when a second blast of similar force came at him.

"This magic blade...Is this one of Tsubaki's?!"

Its output couldn't be matched by an average smith. It brought to mind the master smith with whom he had a direct contract. Plus, he thought he heard the words *test fire* from the fog.

I don't know what you're thinking, you asshole. Gareth's lips twisted.

I'm gonna get her good once this is over...That said, Tsubaki's a fool's fool, but she knows the time and place for her tomfoolery. She wouldn't come attackin' just to test the strength of a magic blade. In which case—

Was her patron goddess, Hephaistos, on the side of the armed monsters?

Or could she be motivated by her friendship with Hestia? Or because she'd judged that the heretical beasts shouldn't be killed?

Gareth was trying to think it over for a second, but the rain of ice didn't end. Without giving him any time to think, it was precisely targeting him and him alone.

"Mr. Gareth!"

Noticing that Gareth was being hammered with attack after attack, the other familia members dashed over to him, but that just made things worse.

"_____"

Of all times, an ice blast incomparable to the previous ones came flying toward them. A stream of blue ice shot through the black mist. The blizzard blew past, leaving Gareth no way to evade its effects as it froze over the pavement in an instant.

As he tried to cover the members of the familia, he took out the shield beneath his mantle on his back to absorb the full brunt of the blow.

"Grrrrrrrrrrrrrrrrrrrrrrrrr?!"

The crackling chill sound was so loud that everyone on the battle-field stopped moving.

"M-Mr. Gareth?!"

"…I'm guessing it's on the same level as Riveria's magic, huh? That's got a wee bite to it."

The shield, and the hand holding it, and all of Gareth's lower body were frozen over. He was frozen up to his beard, and his face looked frostbitten, as if he'd been outdoors in a blizzard in an icy country.

If she put everything into it, Riveria's Wynn Fimbulvetr was stronger. But that didn't make this assault any less scary. After all, this one had been unleashed by a magic blade that could cast spells quickly.

"All of you, fall back!"

Gareth couldn't help but grin, despite the fact that he was in a position where he needed to chase after the monsters, and his blood boiled as he took a second cannon blast.

"*Shiiiiiii!*"

"Wh—...Vividly colored monsters?!" The astonished cry of a familia member rang out.

Gareth had seen it as he was blocking the ice blast: the outline of a water spider emerging from the shimmering black mist.

What at first seemed to be one turned into many, indiscriminately attacking both *Loki Familia* and the armed monsters.

"Tch, those bastards...Tryin' to take advantage of the chaos, huh?!"

Upon realizing that Gareth's squad had withdrawn from the underground in the southwest, the Evils had sent them up. Shrouded in dense fog, it was a perfect battlefield for them. They'd come to take advantage of the chaos and steal the armed monsters' key.

The plan had originally been to use them as bait to lure out the Evils, but the current situation was not good at all.

"Narfi, hold back the Evils! Don't let them engage the monsters!" boomed Gareth.

The familia members responded valiantly to his command. It'd turned into a three-sided fight with no way of telling apart friend from foe. *Loki Familia* was chasing after the monsters while facing off against the Evils' forces to secure the key before them.

The main battlefield had gone past the point of disorder, transitioning into full-blown chaos.

"The key! Steal the key! Find the monsters and—"

"Shut up!"

"—Geh?!"

During a moment of relative peace, Gareth sent the offensive forces of the cloaked Evils flying as they wildly swung their swords. These deployed soldiers were sacrificial pawns, no doubt, and wouldn't have a key to get back into Knossos.

Gareth wanted to chase after the armed monsters already, but his situation wouldn't allow it.

"It's Elgarm! Crush him!"

"Hiyo!"

"If we just beat this dwaaaaaaaarf!"

"Hiyo!"

"H-he's a monster! Surround hiiiiiiiim!"

"Hiyo!"

"I-I'm sorry for the sneak attack!"

"Hiyo!"

"Shaaaaaaaaaaaaaaaaaaaaa!"

"Hiyo!"

"This friggin' dwarf won't die! All of you! Get him!"

""""Uoooooooooooooooooooooh!""""

Between ice volleys, the Evils' Remnants swarmed in. He shouted a name that resembled one of a magic blade. The Far Eastern girl launched the surprise attack. The vividly colored monsters charged. A rotten master smith's cackling laughter at the chaos echoed.

Everything centered around Gareth. They were desperately trying to hold him down.

They all viewed Elgarm as a threat and swarmed him.

Bathed in ice, Gareth kept wreaking havoc, his roar ringing in the wind.

"Each! And every! One a ya! Go easy on an old man!"

""""As if!"""" Shooting ice blasts wildly, the smiths and even the Evils' subordinates all shouted back in unison.

If they let the dwarf go, he would wipe out his target, the monsters. And the rest of them.

They were absolutely convinced this was the case, which was precisely why the minor-league players on the side of the Evils fought back as their sweat and tears blended together and the smiths struggled desperately to hold him back.

The two-front plan left Gareth between a rock and a hard place. He was undoubtedly bearing the brunt of the three-sided fight, howling as the veins on his forehead rippled.

"Yer! In! My! *Waaaaaaaaaaaaaaaaaaaaaay!*"

"GYAAAAAAAAAAAAAAAAAH?!"

In the end, *Loki Familia* was forced to let the armed monsters escape while Gareth was pinned down on the main battlefield.

"Yeah, not sure why I came here, but…I can't help it if I found something."

With her bare brown feet stepping firmly on the building's roof, Tiona looked down at something.

As she'd checked out the black fog, she'd gotten separated from Tione. She'd made it all the way to the northwest part of the district, and in her sight was a single vouivre that'd slipped out of the mist roaming around.

It was a humanoid monster wearing a robe, its red stone shining from inside its deep hood.

"Guess I'll kill it," Tiona commented, wielding Urga one-handed as she jumped from the roof.

When the Amazon's shadow danced through the air, the vouivre dashed in the opposite direction, as if spooked.

"Miss Tiona!"

"Arcus! And everyone else! Are you following that vouivre?"

"We are! One managed to get away from Mr. Gareth's squad…"

"Then let's go after it together!"

"Okay!"

Joining up with the others chasing the vouivre, she dashed through the street, steadily accelerating and closing the gap.

Tiona uncharacteristically had something on her mind.

The humanoid monster is a vouivre…but it's different from the others…This is definitely the one that showed up in the city the first time…Yeah. She pondered as she chased after the vouivre that resembled a lamia—a half snake, half human—desperately fleeing.

When she looked at its back, she couldn't help but think it looked like a scared young girl.

But it was the humanoid monster that appeared in the city a week ago, the winged monster that attacked a child.

It'd been the first impetus for the commotion in the city, the starting point of this whole problem.

Anyway, that's what kicked this whole thing off, right? That was about as much as Tiona understood, defining the beast before her eyes with a simple judgment.

That means—if I somehow understand it, everything'll make sense!
Tiona was a raging idiot.

In fact, she was so stupid that Bete, her mortal rival who did nothing but hurl abuse at her, would look at her pitifully if he heard her internal thought.

She was seriously thinking she could get to the bottom of the complex incident, the one troubling Finn and the others, just by probing a single monster.

She believed that the uncertain feeling in her heart ever since their first encounter with the armed monsters would clear up.

To repeat: Tiona was a real idiot.

"Miss Tiona?!"

"Oh snap?!"

But that was why she was able to see that scene without hatred or loathing or any preconceptions toward monsters.

As they approached an intersection, a half-elf child appeared. The child froze as the vouivre pushed toward them. At the same time, a decrepit building started to tremble violently above the child's head, unable to withstand the impact of the nearby battles. It started to crumble.

Just as Tiona got ready to swing Urga to try to save the child—the vouivre sprinted *to the rescue.*

"___"

The monster turned into a silvery-blue arrow, darting forward to push the child down as its wings burst out of its robe and spread to cover both of them from the rain of rubble.

"Ruu!" screamed the other orphans who chased after the half-elf.

The members of *Loki Familia* gasped.

As the avalanche of rubble fell, Tiona murmured, "—Protected."

But it was drowned out by the noise of the building falling.

How did the orphans view this sequence of events? What did it look like to Arcus and the others?

It must have looked like a monster spreading its fiendish wings and attempting to assault a child when a pile of rubble fell on its head by chance.

But it was different for Tiona, whose dynamic vision was far superior.

Only she was able to correctly piece together the movements that transpired in that split second. She knew the vouivre noticed the falling building and pushed the child down to protect them.

And because she was a stupid girl, the plain truth of the situation was etched into her eyes.

"—Loose!"

As the dust cleared, the familia members saw the monster in the middle of the rubble, looking furious as they shot their arrows. The monster's scales deflected the arrowheads as it withdrew from atop the child before dashing away.

"I'm going by myself! You guys protect those kids!"

"Got it!"

With Urga in her hand, Tiona ordered the others to stay behind and chased the vouivre herself, staring intently at the monster's back. She had arrived at an answer.

Finn...Tione...Sorry...

She thought back to the stories from a week before about the monster attacking a child. *But wasn't it just protecting someone like it did now?*

When Argonaut tried to protect it, wasn't it the same sort of thing?

Tiona could feel her questions start to dispel, sense the uncertainty in her heart melting away.

As she apologized to the leader of the faction and her sister, the stupidly instinctual girl squinted.

"I...don't want to fight these monsters, I think."

In the end, just as Tiona cornered the *girl* in an alleyway, she lost track of her movements.

"!!"

When he heard that noise, Bete kicked the ground.

"Wai—Mr. Bete?!!!"

He leaped off the building, leaving the others who'd been ordered to stand by to deal with the black minotaur. His wolf ears pricked up, perceiving the source of the noise and sprinting after it. It was cutting vertically from the southwest of Daedalus Street north. Bete wasn't nice enough to overlook these obvious movements. If it was supposed to be a trap, he'd just crush it.

It would normally be a breach of command, but Bete's anger was pent-up from being ordered to wait even though the western side had become the main battlefield, and his howl rippled through the night sky.

"?!"

"What was that?!"

There were the sounds of a furious acceleration, a tremendous noise of something cutting through the air, and violent footsteps kicking off walls and roofs. The adventurers on the ground turned to the sky one after the other, noticing a presence moving above their heads at high speed. Through all of that, Bete tracked the source of the noise as he kicked the buildings and shot through the sky.

I can't see anything! Are they invisible?

His sharp amber eyes narrowed, locking onto a momentary tremor in the atmosphere before him.

It could be that someone was harboring enough wind pressure to cause the air to quiver. Or someone was wearing a cloth over their body to become invisible.

A magic item. It didn't take long for Bete to realize who it was.

"That rabbit boy, huh?!"

Bete accelerated as he brought up images of this enemy in his mind's eye.

He was irritated. When he'd heard that *Hestia Familia*—that Bell Cranell was supporting the monsters, he'd gotten angry for some reason. He didn't understand why he was so irritated. But this person Bete had recognized for his power had done something incomprehensible to him. It felt like a foreign substance was lodged in the back of his throat. To borrow Tiona's words, he felt iffy.

*Talking the big talk. What the hell are you doing, rabbit boy?!
…Well, either way, s'got nothin' to do with me!*

As the cloaked figure hopped through the buildings of differing heights, he almost looked like a rabbit, occasionally leaping over tall spires, but Bete never let this invisible existence escape his range of perception. The invisible person was busy pouring their all into sprinting and didn't notice this high-speed pursuit.

Bete leaped and sprinted like a wolf chasing down its prey.

There he is!

And in the Labyrinth District's northwest area, he landed in a back alley with a huge impact.

"…"

His ashen hair fluttered from the landing as he looked around the area that had fallen silent once again.

It was a place where several lanes intersected. The road was shrouded in darkness without a magic-stone lamp or the moonlight. Stillness filled the surroundings.

He couldn't pick up a single sound. It was as if the darkness was trying to deny anyone being there.

There wasn't a figure in sight.

"—Get your ass out here." Bete could sense the presence in one of the lanes, staring into the empty darkness.

Even if the figure had become invisible, they couldn't fool the senses of an animal person. He was about to move toward the enemy who wasn't responding.

"What the—?"

"…"

The person who walked out of the darkness was a single renart girl.

She had gorgeous long blond locks, no less beautiful than Aiz's hair. She had an air of graceful beauty and wore a Far Eastern crimson kimono.

Bete remembered the girl who resolutely met his eyes.

Their encounter had been two months prior on the day he'd attacked Meren to help Tiona and Tione. There had been a renart mixed in with Lena and Phryne and the other members of *Ishtar Familia.*

Did she convert to Hestia Familia after Ishtar Familia was destroyed?

Bete furrowed his brow, entirely disinterested.

"I know you're not alone. The rest of you, get out here already."

"I am alone."

As he shot a glance down the alley she was blocking, Bete spat, rejecting her claim.

"Quit screwing with m—"

"—I am alone!!" She shouted this time.

Bete was getting visibly vexed as his gaze started to look more and more threatening. But the renart girl wouldn't back down.

As she held both her quivering hands to her chest, she spoke again. "Please move out of the way!"

"..."

"And fast!!" she shrieked.

But she wasn't directing this at Bete, even as she faced him. Behind her, in the darkness, a second presence moved farther away.

A rear guard.

The girl standing before him was setting herself as a decoy to let her treasure escape.

"...People who can't fight shouldn't be tryin' to act brave."

Bete saw no vestiges of the girl he'd seen in Meren.

She'd been a dollish wisp of a girl who'd only been protected by the Amazons. But now, she could snap her jaw at someone.

Bete was growing increasingly more irritated.

——*I hate weak broads more than anything else.*

He was talking about women who played tragic heroines, despite having no strength to stand up against anything; girls with no real understanding of the gravity of their words, who armed themselves with nothing more than a feeble wish with no resolve; wretched women who started begging for their lives as soon as they were unmasked.

Bete spit out internally, lightly kicking the stone pavement as if to stroke it, and his metal boots, Frosvirt, shot stone fragments into the air, turning it into buckshot.

"Uuuh...?!"

These fragments struck the shocked renart, scratching her cheek and ripping the fabric of her kimono. She staggered but managed to remain standing.

Bete hadn't intended to hit her, wanted to scare her a bit to resolve the situation, but she went beyond his expectations.

"Tch. Beat it."

"I will not."

"I'll pulverize you."

"I won't move!"

And she didn't, even under his sharp glare. The fox rebelled against the wolf.

He easily could've leaped over her head and chased after the fleeing person. But for some reason, Bete couldn't ignore the girl blocking his way. That was why he moved to pummel her, to use his power to punt her aside.

He closed in on the girl with arms outspread in an instant.

As he felt a strange sense of déjà vu, he raised his hand, annoyed at the pointlessness of it, about to swing it down.

"——Gh!"

That's when he saw the unwavering green eyes peeking out from behind her golden bangs. Bete's hand froze in midair.

"..."

And his eyes widened.

He silently looked into Haruhime's eyes, which hadn't turned away even as she was about to be smashed.

It was a strong gaze, a resolute expression that erased all the remnants of the girl he'd seen in Meren.

Despite being scared, despite her fear, she had no intention of backing down.

There was no mask to be peeled off. The fox bared her fangs with all her might.

It was a pathetic figure of a girl.

It was a bluff of a small fry, a rejection of that categorization.

As the two of them froze, staring at each other, it was silent.

The distant sounds of battle reached the ears of the animal people.

The first one to break their silence was Bete.

"—You little shit!" The edges of his lips violently curled up. "Can't even do anything—are you really ready for this?"

"Gwa?!"

Bete was going off on a murderous tirade, causing the renart to begin convulsing in fear. But she wouldn't step down, glaring back at him with heightened emotion. Bete was almost impressed but chose to hurl his abuse at her.

"You're getting ahead of yourself!!"

In place of his lowered fist, he stomped the left heel of his Frosvirt into the ground, unleashing a torrent of explosive noises and shock waves that sent the girl flying. Her back banged against the wall near the entrance of the back alley, where she slumped over and let out a groan in pain.

Bete couldn't hide his smile at the sight of her. It wasn't from his enjoyment of bullying her or a sadistic satisfaction to see her in pain but a chuckle to welcome her to "this side."

"Stop acting like a proud hussy! You only have your power going for you!!"

"Rg!!" The head of the anguished renart snapped up in response to his contempt.

She mustered all her spirit as she glared back at Bete. She stuck her quivering hands in front of her chest as if presenting an offering, and she began to chant.

"—Grow."

Bete grinned menacingly, squinting.

You're gonna do that much to protect some monsters?

Then, show me your resolve!

Hit me with your determination to resist the strong!

Any thoughts of the key and the remnants of the Evils disappeared from Bete's mind at that moment.

The violent werewolf faced the renart as an enemy, as if acknowledging the determination of a simple weakling.

There was nothing to speak of the battle that followed.

The violent, starving wolf mercilessly beat down all who would bare their fangs at him, until there was no skin left unbruised. When the weeping renart tried to howl at him again, he harshly beat his contempt and her powerlessness into her.

As he cackled over the echoing cries of a new weakling, Bete followed the presence who had fled the scene.

BRAVE SOUL!

Гэта казка іншага свету.

Смяльчак!

Daedalus Street came alive.

The hidden armed monsters raised a war cry and began their charge. *Loki Familia* intercepted them. An unprecedented clash began, centered around the Labyrinth District's western side.

The other adventurers kept out of the loop couldn't grasp the situation, left behind by the flow of events and contributing to spreading confusion and uproar among the people.

"Has Lefiya disappeared...?" Filvis was moving alone through the district.

As the sounds of combat boomed out from the west, a number of residents stood still as others ran around in circles like insects entranced by a light. Filvis alone kept her cool and took in her surroundings. Instead of heading for the western battlefront, she observed the *Loki Familia* formation closely.

Their factions had formed an alliance, and she had some knowledge of the events transpiring on Daedalus Street. From that, she knew that observing *Loki Familia*'s camp was a more effective method of determining the sequence of events. As the situation changed from moment to moment, their movements gave the best indication of how to track the armed monsters.

On top of that, Filvis was prioritizing the safety of her kind, foolhardy fellow elf.

If she couldn't make sure that Lefiya hadn't rushed into danger, she wouldn't feel comfortable enough to carry out her original task. She leaped up to a rooftop without a sound.

...? Loki Familia *is...*

Looking down from above, Filvis noticed that amid all the bustle from the crowd of adventurers, *Loki Familia*'s followers were standing frozen in place. They were leaning together, saying something to one another, and then their expressions changed when they left the location.

As she watched silently, Filvis kicked off the edge of the roof.

"Hey, what happened?"

"Wah?! Oh, Maenad, it's you…"

The guy from *Loki Familia* was shocked to see her but lowered his guard when he realized she was part of the alliance between familias.

"The armed monsters were confirmed in the east. The uproar in the west is a decoy."

"!"

"Apparently, the group protecting things over there was wiped out…along with some other adventurers. That black minotaur is connected to it! If they get underground at this rate, things are gonna be bad!"

It was the work of the stray armed monster. That seemed to be the best guess. And at the same time, the perimeter in the east had been stretched thin.

He explained the situation as they made their way. Filvis was astonished and held her tongue. If they didn't hurry, the monsters would slip out of their grasp while still in possession of the key.

"Please help us out!"

"…Got it." Filvis nodded in response to the stressed adventurer, setting aside her concerns about Lefiya for the moment.

"…"

Other people overheard their conversation.

They'd been observing the movements of *Loki Familia*, just like Filvis, focusing their efforts on eavesdropping. They hadn't been noticed, and *Loki Familia* wasn't on guard against them as they stood in the shadows nearby.

They silently departed, slipping down into the alleys.

Directly after that, monsters appeared before Filvis and the *Loki Familia* members as they began to sprint.

"Wh—?!"

"Are they…the six-legged monsters from Knossos?!"

They were a small breed with a red crystal instead of a magic stone, some of the countless vargs unleashed in Knossos. The adventurers who'd set foot in the man-made labyrinth recalled that nightmare. Filvis's crimson eyes widened.

"*Shiiiiiii!*"

From the alley's manhole, from the gaps in the walls, from the underground stairs, the insectile vargs swarmed them, as if they'd been planted beforehand. The group was forced to fight the monsters welling up from the crevices.

A comparable scene unfolded in several other places around the center of the Labyrinth District.

"C-Captain?! There've been several water spider sightings!"

"An enemy trap."

In *Loki Familia*'s main base, Raul cried out as he gathered the reports from the semaphores. He had been summoned by Finn, whose eyes narrowed.

The reports of monster appearances were mostly around the edges of their formation. Most of the other adventurers focused on the main battlefront in the west, which was why they didn't notice the localized movements.

It was clearly an attack aimed specifically at *Loki Familia*.

"The enemy is moving! We have to get control of the east, the location of the monster sightings. Don't let them get away from us!" Finn shouted in a strained voice that echoed through the air.

A shadow proceeded through the underground passage.

There was a small body with slender limbs, wearing a prum-size version of adventurers' battle clothes.

And unlike a normal goblin, it was lean, an enhanced species.

This was the red-cap that had fought Tiona four days prior.

As the bright-red cap bounced on its head, it quickly and carefully moved through the stone passage, watching its surroundings.

It was holding a lump of silver in its hands.

"—Found you."

"*!!*"

When it turned a corner, it realized several figures were standing before it: a group of five humans and animal people.

They were not *Loki Familia*.

They were the followers of Thanatos.

They'd been ordered to find the Irregulars, the armed monsters, before *Loki Familia* did to dispose of them and obtain the key.

They weren't wearing Evils' robes. Instead, they were equipped with swords and armor and *dressed like adventurers*.

"Kaaaaaaa!"

"*Guh?!*"

The crazed fanatics weren't scared of dying as they charged against the red-cap as a unified front. The monster couldn't fight back, getting pummeled through its defense and dropping the key from its hand. The silver orb fell to the floor, and the leader of the group snatched it from the ground.

"We did it, Lord Thanatos! I, Acoz, have retrieved the key!" shouted the human man, crying the name of his patron god with blazing eyes.

It would be fair to say that they'd made sure their hunt went off without a hitch. They'd blended in with the other adventurers, waiting patiently for the opportune moment to strike. They hadn't left Knossos in the past couple of days while *Loki Familia* had kept the exits under surveillance.

They had left *four days prior*.

It was the same day the armed monsters had made their appearance, when they'd taken a route out of Knossos through the Dungeon to get aboveground, disguised as simple, random adventurers.

And they'd been waiting in Daedalus Street all along for the monsters to appear.

As they blended in to the surroundings as adventurers, they were able to carefully observe all of *Loki Familia*'s movements without arousing any suspicion, gathering information about the flow of the battle.

They were the detached force that Thanatos had mentioned.

"Now Knossos will be totally safe!" The man trembled in excitement, sneering at the wounded monster.

"We should erase all evidence of this," he said, starting to point his weapon at the red-cap along with his subordinates.

"Get them!"

"?!"

A sudden order rang out. His squad was slow to respond.

Adventurers leaped out from the web of interlocking passageways, the intersection where they'd caught the goblin.

The Evils' Remnants were taken by surprise, unable to resist and incapacitated in an instant.

"Wh—...*Loki Familia*?!"

"Just as Captain thought. They really were mixed in with the other adventurers."

The human leader was aghast upon seeing the jester emblem engraved on their armor. Anakity had taken out three of the five enemies in the blink of an eye. Her one-handed sword whistled through the air.

It would be fair to say they had made sure that their hunt went off without a hitch—except for one fatal flaw. *They had been led on by Braver the whole time.*

"The report of monsters appearing in the east was...a trap. To lure you out."

Finn had guessed the existence of a detached force, since the Evils had been so passive. He presumed there were several squads pretending to be adventurers and secretly searching for the monsters' whereabouts.

Of course, it was difficult to find the assassins among the thousands of adventurers in Daedalus Street.

That was why Finn spread some bait.

"A-a trap?!"

"Yes. As you heard, we tricked our allies and all."

Anakity's group had focused on spreading the misinformation, even to their own allies.

From the point when the real armed monsters broke through the west, the members of *Loki Familia* had been forced into making flustered responses. And that would look like a perfect opportunity to the Evils watching *Loki Familia*. Anakity had captured them from a handful of adventurers who had moved out.

"Then...then this key is...?!"

"It's just a replica. Didn't you know?"

Anakity disinterestedly pointed out the silver orb in the leader's hands. It was the replica Finn had shown everyone in the meeting. The man's eyes bulged past their limits.

If this was what Thanatos was calling a detachment, Anakity's unit was one, too.

Finn had set out to drag his prey to shore—hook, line, and sinker.

"No way...nowaynowaynoway! Was the monster a lure, too?! Has *Loki Familia* been working with the monsters?!"

As two people pushed the leader against the ground, his widened eyes quivered, staring at the monster, which had been acting scared the whole time.

The monster spoke. *"S-stroke of midnight's bell."*

In the next instant, the goblin's body was covered in a film of gray light, and when the light dispersed, a prum girl was left sitting in its place.

"Wh—?!"

"To tell you the truth, we intended to catch the actual monsters and uncover you with that, but...we cut that for time."

They'd used transformation magic.

The man opened and closed his mouth in total silence as he realized that she'd just been an empty reflection of a monster.

As Anakity continued disinterestedly, she turned her eyes from him to her.

"Thanks for your help. That magic is so convenient."

"Y-y—...you..."

When Anakity turned around, the prum girl—*Hestia Familia*'s Lilliluka Erde—was at the peak of her confusion. She'd been discovered and captured a little while ago. Lilliluka had assumed she'd be killed, but Anakity had a demand of her: "Help us." She'd been brought to this underground path without consent, forced to transform into an armed monster, and run around in circles holding the replica key.

After seeing through her disguise, Anakity, or rather Finn, had changed plans. They had used her power instead of the monsters to draw out the Evils' detached forces.

"What are you doing?! Aren't you trying to wipe out all the monsters aboveground…?!"

"Ah, it's fine. Don't worry—this is an entirely different thing from your little incident."

Though she was unable to collect her thoughts, Lilliluka Erde was able to subconsciously guess what was going on from Anakity's answer.

Maybe. Probably. Surely. Undoubtedly. *Loki Familia* had—No, Finn Deimne had put the familia at the center of two different conflicts, handling it perfectly fine despite the extreme chaos of the battle in the Labyrinth District.

——*Huh? That makes no sense.*

But even then, it was another story to process it completely.

To think there were several different forces facing off against one another in a huge incident embroiling the city.

She couldn't keep herself from asking what the hell was going on.

"I think it's a bit mean to pull in someone unrelated…but," Anakity started.

Lilly was taken aback. Anakity walked up to her, looking straight down at the prum.

"You see, I'm pretty angry," Anakity admitted, raising her perfectly shaped eyebrows and bending at the waist so their faces were almost touching.

"You tricked Raul with the worst possible method, of all ways."

"Huh?!"

"To Raul, Finn Deimne is a symbol, someone who would never betray him. Even if it was a fake Finn, that fool would never fail to obey him…And you pretended to be that Captain and deceived Raul. So yeah, I'm really angry."

Because Anakity and Finn had been together with him since they entered the familia, she knew him best, and her fury was more serious than anyone else's.

The thin cat tail that extended from her small backside swayed slowly.

As if boring into Lilliluka, she pressed her pointer finger into the chest of the pale prum locked in place.

"So—this just makes us even."

And then she smiled sweetly.

Lilly was filled with an unimaginable terror as the black catgirl adventurer put on a broad smile.

"Sorry for using you. You can go now. Even if you're our enemy for the moment, we didn't want to get you wrapped up in our problems."

Anakity Autumn. Her second name was Alsha. A second-tier adventurer.

She was without doubt one of the best among all the Level 4s in the city.

There was a cold fire inside her beautiful figure that first caught Loki's eye. She was a catgirl gifted with beauty and intelligence, a noble feline recognized by the gods.

"E-eep?!" Lilliluka yelped when Anakity spoke with that smile.

This isn't funny. I could do without getting involved with her, she thought, rising to her feet and about to scurry away.

"Ah…that's right. This is from the captain." Anakity passed along a message to Lilliluka just as she was leaving.

"'I'm letting you go once out of respect for your bravery. But there won't be a second time.' That's all."

The prum girl froze in place. This time, she was aghast.

She thought she'd outwitted *Loki Familia*, outwitted Finn Deimne.

But she was wrong.

She'd been dancing to Braver's beat.

"Bye now. I won't let you go next time, either."

"Uuuuuuuugh?!"

Lilliluka Erde dashed away as fast as she could, not even bothering to soothe her wounded pride.

It might have been demonstrating a loser's natural disposition, but she wanted to get away from "those crazy people." She whizzed past, escaping without looking back.

*   *   *

"Is it okay not to find out what all she knows, Miss Aki?"

"We know better than anyone how dangerous a prum's determination can be. Interrogation or torture would just be a waste of time. This is fine."

Plus, one of the reasons why Finn had said to let her go was because they were hurting for time. And more than anything, Anakity didn't have the leeway to be bothering with the prum girl.

"All right, then…We've kept you waiting." Her voice was cold as she looked down at the man pressed against the floor.

"You have a key, right? If you guys didn't have a means of getting back into Knossos, then you're not much use moving on your own."

"Gh?!"

"Trying to steal the key off the monsters was leaving too much to chance. Did you hide it before coming here? Then, I'll just have to force it out of you."

The blade of the sword glistened.

The leader twitched, the corners of his eyes flaring as he tried to break free from the people holding him down with all his might.

"My life belongs to Thanatos—!" He managed to get one hand free and reached toward his chest.

"I'm not going to let you blow yourself up."

Anakity's hand flashed, her sword piercing through his hand and pinning it to the ground.

"Guuu—Gyaaaaaaaaaaaaaaa?!"

He had an Inferno Stone hidden beneath his equipment. She'd stopped him from igniting the self-destructive device.

With his hand pinned down like an insect specimen, he was overcome by intense pain, trying desperately to remove the bloody sword staking him to the ground, but he couldn't remove it one inch.

The silver blade remained lodged deep in the ground, refusing to loosen its grip, no matter how many times he tried to yank his hand free. It was as if the sword itself contained her fury.

"Please don't waste my time. I'm not used to this sort of thing," she warned with cruel eyes, smiling, but a silent, blazing anger smoldered in her eyes as she remembered Leene and the other comrades who'd been ripped away from her.

"But please don't take that the wrong way. Cats can be...cruel, or so I've heard."

After that, everything was a blur to the man. He thought he was enduring it, motivated by his sense of purpose, but once the real torture started, the screams came pouring out.

After screaming for a while, he gave them everything they wanted before being unceremoniously knocked out.

"Violas are coming!"

"Loose your arrows! Alicia's group, begin chanting!"

The elves' song resounded in the underground passage, the southeast of Daedalus Street.

Monsters were streaming out of Knossos with increased fervor, and there were no signs of the flow slowing down.

The elves fought primarily with magic as beads of sweat trickled down their faces. There were untold magic potion test tubes lying broken on the ground at their feet. Farther ahead, there were dunes of ash dotted with vibrantly colored magic stones.

Riveria's instructions were allowing them to maintain the battle lines several hours after the battle had begun.

Fatigue was visible on the faces of the elves as they fought in a circular formation.

Despite the war of attrition that Thanatos had laughingly foisted on them, the elves hadn't chosen to withdraw. It was almost as if they were waiting for something.

"Lady Riveria!"

"!"

Alicia's jubilant shout reached Riveria's long, slender ears.

When she turned back, Riveria saw Anakity emerge from the depths of the passage, along with some other members of the familia.

As she let the elves under her command deal with the monsters, Riveria rushed over.

"Is it finished?"

"Yes, we got it."

It was a short exchange. But that was more than enough.

Anakity took out a magic item in the shape of an orb. The letter *D* was engraved in it. It was unmistakably a Daedalus Orb—the key that *Loki Familia* had been chasing ever since their flight out of Knossos, the key to recovering from their hopeless situation, the key to Knossos that Anakity had acquired after interrogating the leader of Thanatos's detached force.

It was only one key. But it was a concrete reward.

Behind Anakity, the faces of the other familia members were flushed. They couldn't contain their excitement.

"Well done. Leave the rest to us."

"Okay. I believe in you."

Riveria's lips curled up as she felt the heft of the Daedalus Orb in her hand. Anakity smiled back one more time.

Riveria's face quickly tensed again, and she enthusiastically turned back to the elves.

"—Let's go. We're done defending against the monsters!"

""Yes, ma'am!""

The elves responded in perfect unison to Riveria's call. With her eyebrow raised, the high elf spoke with a voice steeped in all her pent-up frustration and anger. As the passage filled with a swirl of battle lust that contradicted her image as a fairy, Riveria singled out one elf hidden away in the middle of the squad.

"Lefiya, are you ready?"

"Yes!…Ready!"

In the midst of the furious battle, there was a single mage *who'd been held in reserve*, not casting a single spell. She'd been kneeling, holding on to her staff, meditating to increase her magical limit and honing it. As she stood, she opened her eyes.

"Unleashed pillar of light, limbs of the holy tree. You are the master archer!"

Her bright-yellow hair whirled up as she created a magic circle of the same color. Her magic power rose in an instant. This girl with her insurmountable magic power was the elves' special lance, a battering ram to blow away impregnable defenses.

"Loose your arrows, fairy archers. Pierce, arrow of accuracy!"

The high elf pointed her staff forward as the other elves crouched.

Lefiya glared at the horde of approaching monsters as she spun her chant.

"Arcs Ray!"

The giant ray of light filled the entire corridor, annihilating all the monsters.

And Riveria quietly, sharply thrust her long staff forward.

When the raging roar of the ray quieted, when it had cleared away all the things blocking the path before them, the elves—no, all of *Loki Familia*—raised the signal to begin the counterattack.

"Charge!!"

The squad composed of eleven elves charged toward Knossos—straight forward in a single line, like a ballista bolt pulled back to its limit being released. The orichalcum door, which had been closed to stop the emission of monsters, opened with the key in Riveria's right hand.

"Huh?"

Thunk! The door flung open with a crash.

The Evils stationed on the other side cried out in confusion. While the enemy was standing dazed before her, Riveria leaped out to the lead and swung her staff resolutely.

"Gyaaaaaaaaaaaaaaaaaaaaaaaaaaaaaaaaaaaaaaaaaaaaaaaaaaaaa?!"

The enemy forces were blasted away like leaves from a tree.

The elves didn't look back as they crossed into the dimly lit labyrinth, advancing without pause.

"E-e-enemy attack!!!" The Evils' Remnants panicked, sounding their alarm bells.

Arrows flew, swords slashed, magic was unleashed. The fairies ferociously kicked aside all who stood in their way—people and monsters alike. Pushing onward, they changed formation. Riveria now stood at the center of the squad.

She let out a savage order unbefitting a high elf.

"Devour them all!"

"Huh?"

Thanatos was dumbfounded.

"I said it's an enemy attack!! The members of *Loki Familia* that have been holding in the passage just charged in!"

Time stopped when he heard the report from his follower who'd rushed into the hall. Snapping back around, he looked at the pedestal in the center of the room, at the watery film displaying images from all around the labyrinth.

Riveria's elves had entered through the southeast door, advancing into the labyrinth at tremendous speed, destroying the remnants of the Evils and monsters in their path.

"…Gh!!"

Barca had been using the giant crimson orb to operate the doors, and he opened his eyes wide in surprise. Even when he lowered a door to block the elves' path, Riveria's key unlocked it immediately, and when he unleashed the monsters from their vaults, the violas and vargs were frozen solid and reduced to ashes.

The fairies were an unstoppable force. Nothing could slow them down.

"They attacked? They attack—? *They attacked?*" Thanatos felt sick from the shock upon seeing it with his own eyes.

"You're kidding, right? Why? Isn't that impossible?"

No one could have predicted that *Loki Familia* would attack from a position caught between conflicting forces. At the very least, Thanatos the god hadn't been able to.

They stole a key. It was unfortunate. The worst possible result, actually. But it was fine up to there. He could understand that much.

But instead of holding on to that precious key and taking it back or even using it as a lure or a trap, they were using it to attack.

How did they catch us off guard? It was our arrogant assumption that they wouldn't attack, even in the worst case. It's our carelessness for looking down on Loki Familia—

——Finn Deimne was someone who could win against all-knowing gods.

It was his experience from leading so many armies. Knowledge and experience were very different things. Thanatos in particular had been a workaholic in heaven, spending all his time purifying souls. He had no knowledge of the subtleties of the battlefield. None but the most battle-hardened warriors who'd crossed countless battlefields could sense the way the wind was going to blow on a battlefield. It would have been impossible for Thanatos to figure out Finn's seemingly reckless plan.

"D-does he see any chance of winning? Anything other than a gamble?"

Not just a reckless, suicidal charge but a planned surprise attack?

Was there some calculation where he could take on the vast labyrinth and get a valuable result from it?

Deplete our forces, map Knossos, obtain another key, or discover the location of a demi-spirit who's hidden away in the labyrinth— Thanatos was still confused as he systematically went through all the possible strategic conditions for victory against the enemy.

He was being led around by an unknown wonder. His doubts kept piling up.

If Finn's old enemy Valletta Grede had been alive, she would have said a few things.

"Dumbass! There's no way Finn would ever just defend!"

"That rotten hero—he'll keep attacking all the way to the depths of hell itself!"

The next moment, Thanatos's eyes opened as wide as they could go.

"—Are you kidding me, Braverrrrrrrrrrrrr?!"

It sounded like a shriek or an acclamation. As he sweated with a smile on his face, Thanatos turned to his panicking followers.

"Call Levis for me! This is really bad!" he boomed in half fear and half delight.

Thanatos smiled, displaying his propensity to cave to the unknown, to the undiscovered.

And then he let out a shout.

"We're going to be swallowed whole!"

"Reporting! Lady Riveria has commenced the raid on Knossos!" shouted the elf, dashing into the room out of breath.

Upon hearing the announcement, Raul and all the other members of the familia froze before unleashing a booming roar.

""""OOOOOOOOOOOOOOOOOOOOOOOOOOOO!"""""

Fists were clenched, and the mood of the *Loki Familia* base was electric.

The wild cry from the center of Daedalus Street was loud enough to make the other adventurers searching for the armed monsters jump out of their skin.

As they were consumed by unprecedented excitement, the prum leader quietly murmured to himself:

"Good."

He uttered a single word. But it contained a flood of emotions.

It was the first time since this battle had started that Finn had the feeling of "bring it on."

They'd latched onto the throat of their enemy, shooting out a silver bullet against the monsters hidden away in that hellhole—in place of a greeting. They'd announced the time to counterattack as the fairies wedged themselves into the battle.

Finn raised his voice at this critical moment. "We're redeploying the defensive squad. Have Gareth turn his team around! Cease pursuit of the armed monsters and secure the door that Riveria opened in the southeast. Defend it to the last! Upon finishing our preparations, we'll launch a follow-up attack!"

The success of Finn's strategy led to a huge increase in morale. Everyone shouted as they received his orders, reaching a fever pitch.

"Astounding…They got us good."

——In a spire overlooking the main base where Finn and the others were gathered, Dionysus was almost moaning as he spoke.

"Finn never had the slightest intention of staying on the defensive," Loki responded next to him as she looked down over the excited camp.

"The enemy will be restless when they obtain the key. If they figure out we've got one, it'll be too late. We gotta crush them before they get any chance to prepare."

They'd turned tail and run from Knossos once before, when the Evils had been able to finish their preparations and invited *Loki Familia* inside.

They'd defeated Finn and the others with their perfectly laid plans.

But this time was different. They hadn't made any preparations at all. They hadn't imagined they could be attacked, which meant they hadn't made any arrangements to engage the enemy.

And even if they had, they wouldn't have any time to mobilize.

It was a textbook example of a surprise attack.

"With their defenses all leaky and ramshackle, we can swallow them whole and bring back some information. This's our first and last chance."

The jester goddess smirked audaciously. And then it slipped into a soft smile.

"Finn, ya seemed to be wrapped up in doubt, which is uncharacteristic of you, but…" Loki trailed off, watching over the prum as he continued to call out orders.

"Yer a pretty monstrous hero yerself."

Loki smiled. She'd known it all along.

"…How rowdy," a woman murmured.

With voluptuous breasts, a beautiful body, and crimson hair reminiscent of blood, it was a monster in the form of a person—Levis.

With her enhanced hearing, the creature could hear the boisterous chaos in a distant part of the labyrinth. As she hunkered down on the floor with one knee raised, she frowned in annoyance.

"—You shut up, too. Aria can wait. First, we blow away the city and make a big hole…Yeah, I'll show you the sky on the surface—filthier than the time before. Tch," she scoffed, holding her head with one hand.

From the outside, it seemed she was talking to herself, but upon listening in, it'd become clear that she'd formed an understanding with *something*.

"*It won't be much longer…*Just a little more. Wait down there patiently," whispered the woman, voice echoing throughout the long hallway inside Knossos.

Before her, a giant pillar of green meat was forming against the tall wall of the labyrinth. Near the top, a silhouette resembling the upper body of a person was squirming, casting a long shadow against the walls and floor.

"L-Lady Levis!" cried one of the main members of the Evils as they rushed through the entrance of the hall.

Levis swung around, bothered by the intrusion, and the man continued to speak as he knelt down.

"*Loki Familia* has invaded Knossos! They have a key, and they're wreaking havoc! At this rate, th-they might reach one of the s-spirit rooms around the labyrinth!"

The man was careful to not lay eyes on the repulsive green pillar, averting his gaze to the stone-paved floor. Beads of sweat kept hitting the ground as his voice trembled.

The pillar writhed ominously, making a ghastly noise as tentacles extended out, surrounding the man, as if observing him.

"Please. P-please help us…!"

"Useless fools…" Levis slowly stood up as her green eyes narrowed.

And as if in sync with her movement, the tentacles began to coil around the man's body.

"Let it go. It's not a magic stone. It'll just make you sick." Levis spoke indifferently as the man disappeared above her head, pulled up by the tentacles.

As if to respond, the pillar released the sound of crushing meat, and a rain of blood splattered against her cheek.

"Sheesh…Incompetent, each and every one of them…" she muttered, wiping her cheek with a rough swipe of her arm and drawing the pitch-black cursed sword sticking out of the ground.

Levis left the hall as the sound of chewing echoed behind her, looking bored out of her mind.

The footsteps of the elves rang out loudly as they rushed down the stairs in the complicated, mysterious, labyrinthine insides of Knossos. *Loki Familia*'s squad of elves didn't allow the Evils in their way to stop them as they delved farther into the depths of the labyrinth.

"Three enemies ahead!!"

"A group of monsters, two o'clock!"

"Break through! Attack!"

As the elven girls searched for enemies, Riveria gave commands from the center of the formation.

Troops of the Evils sporadically emerged, eager to stop them, but they all fell victim to the magic of the elves. As rays of light burst forth from their wands, they blew away the enemies.

They hadn't slowed down once from the moment they entered Knossos, not stopping their movements and continually opening new paths in every direction.

Riveria's mission was to disrupt the enemy in Knossos—one way or another.

If they could manage to turn the main base of the Evils' Remnants into a storm of chaos, the Evils wouldn't be able to intervene in the battle aboveground. At the very least, Riveria's team needed to pin down the enemy in the man-made dungeon until they could suppress the armed monsters.

And their primary goal was to gather information about Knossos: steal a second key or determine the location of the demi-spirit and deal a destructive blow to the enemy's infrastructure.

It wasn't necessary to completely wipe out the enemy to achieve victory. They needed to blaze through as much of the interior of Knossos as possible, laying the foundation in preparation for the full assault to come in later days.

"Advance! Advance!"

With that in mind, they needed to run and couldn't afford to stop.

As they charged into Knossos as a single squad, they were comparable to a lone ant wandering around a giant anthill. If they were cornered, they'd be crushed in no time at all, considering their power imbalances.

To survive and bring the plan to fruition, they had to avoid capture. It was crucial that they spread as much chaos as possible, as this would prevent the enemy from taking the initiative and relegating them to the defensive. An invasion by a single squad was always one misstep away from catastrophe—or as Thanatos put it, suicidal.

As they cut deep into enemy territory, Riveria's judgment was the key to success for the unsupported troops carrying out their surprise attack alone.

"I sense something on the left! Change course to the right!"

"Yes!"

"Alicia, recover Sonia and the others!"

"Understood!"

When Riveria sensed a trap lying in wait, Alicia and the rest of the team followed her lead without hesitation. They could sense the shock of the enemy forces who'd been lying in wait down the left passage as the troops distanced themselves from it. At the same time, Riveria didn't neglect to delegate recovering her team with items as she deftly handled an unending series of decisions.

© Kiyotaka Haimura

In this regard, she resembled Finn.

She was influenced by all the times she'd stood with Gareth watching over the gallant figure of the prum.

And above all, as a high elf, Riveria wielded extraordinary charisma among elves. Even in the heart of the enemy's base, the fighting spirit of the elves didn't drop—but increased.

"Materialize, mighty barrier of forest's light, and lend us your protection—my name is Alf!"

Riveria made her magic stand by, maintaining the magic circle that expanded to a radius of five meders. As she chanted, the elves gathered perfectly inside it in formation as they ran forward.

A jade-colored glow illuminated their faces from below their feet— the light of the fairies' blessing. The elves' chests trembled, as if they were all overcome with emotion, as if they had received royal protection.

"Everyone, stop! Lefiya!"

"—Pierce, arrow of accuracy!"

They dashed out into a wide passage and were greeted by a wall of monsters.

In response to the swarm of violas and vargs filling the hall, Lefiya quickly stepped in front of the squad, gathering the attention of all the monsters—and then she fired.

"Arcs Ray!"

"————————————————*Aaaaagh?!*"

A stupidly powerful cannon erased the swarm of monsters.

"Lefiya, don't stop casting! Prepare the next volley!"

"Yes!"

They immediately began to move again as the particles from the magic cannon spun together with a Concurrent Cast. A giant ray of light filled the width of the passage and washed over the horde of monsters trying to push through with numbers, turning them all to ash. This was the sixth iteration of the same scene.

With that tremendous output, the bombardment of fire unleashed by Lefiya was equivalent to a lance.

It was like a battering ram that blew away all the enemies that gathered, standing across the hardened door.

Draw the attention of the many monsters hidden away in Knossos and then annihilate them with one blast. That was why Lefiya had been held in reserve, why she'd been tempering and refining her magic through meditation.

Riveria was busy commanding the squad, which meant they couldn't rely on her firepower all the time.

To trample Knossos to the ground, Lefiya's lance was essential.

"Freeze, chains of winter!"

"March, inferno boots—"

"As contracted, I command you!"

As Lefiya was dealing with the enemies in the larger passage, the other elves including Alicia were taking out the monsters emerging from the side routes with their own magic.

In Riveria's squad of female elves, every single member was a mage or magic swordswoman who'd mastered Concurrent Casting and trained in high-speed combat with the ability to freely use shortened-cast magic.

Magic rained down on them one after the other, analogous to a fortress shooting off a legion of fairy arrows.

"Enemy squad, from the front!"

"A group of mages…and magic blades!"

The icing on the cake was their defensive wall, which trivialized the counterattacks of enemies lying in wait.

"Via Shilheim!" activated Riveria from its state in standby, halting the concentrated volley from the enemy.

"What?!"

"Our attack…?! Aaaaaaaaaaaargh?!"

The remnants of the Evils shuddered at the jade dome enshrouding the group, but that was short-lived. The elves cut them down with swords in passing, a fairy platoon with eleven members in all.

Even in *Loki Familia*, they were a cut above, as the party was entirely composed of elves who were Level 3 or higher. They didn't stop producing their magic circles.

A main cannon, barrage, and defense. This group went well beyond the stage of mobile artillery.

They were a fortress.

"It's been a while since we've formed a Fairy Force!"

"I'm fine with supporting from the back lines and all, but wow. Rampaging under Lady Riveria's command is truly an honor!"

"Hey! *Rampage?* We're doing nothing of the sort!" Alicia warned the younger elves making a fuss in their exaltation.

Under normal circumstances, it was rare for Riveria to take an active role leading a raid.

As the woman heralded as the city's strongest mage, she would maximize her potential in the back lines: an overwhelming firepower to exterminate enemies without exception, a defensive method to protect allies from attacks, and a healing support that could maintain an entire battle line. She'd filled her role as a pillar supporting large groups. It was like giving a tiger wings to team her up with Gareth's dwarves who bore the full brunt of the front lines.

But once she separated from the main group, running around as a detached force, she changed dramatically, becoming a projectile weapon, turning into a wedge formation of fairies that Finn could drive in at just the right time.

"Don't prattle on! Attack!"

""Yes, ma'am!""

They launched themselves into combat—a high-speed melee with Concurrent Casting.

Magic was versatile if one mastered its speed and adapted to most situations. The elves running amok in the Dungeon wielded an unimaginable firepower—a flower on the battlefield, as though a cavalry squad.

The situation was different from the usual Dungeon, requiring a long-range hit-and-run, foiling the Evils' soldiers as they attempted their suicide bombing.

As the elves kept moving and unleashing their magic, no one was able to pursue them.

"Lefiya, don't fall behind."

"Y-yes…!"

It was Lefiya's first time joining her fellow elves on the squad, and she was out of breath as she continued to cast magic concurrently. With her improving enough to join them, the fairy squad had acquired a main cannon, completing the mobile fortress.

They had all the pieces necessary for a surprise assault on Knossos.

"Front and rear doors have been closed!"

"I'm opening the front! Time your magic to fight against it!"

The doors had been the largest bottleneck, rendered meaningless by the key in Riveria's hand. The orichalcum barriers yielded readily, opening from their firmly locked positions, exposing the flustered enemies to a hail of shots.

It was the rampage of all rampages, the fruits of Anakity's labor. The proud fairies fought to regain their honor and subdue the fury of their murdered comrades.

"Lady Riveria, a second key!"

"Well done!"

Alicia hadn't missed one person wildly trying to escape among the enemy forces firing back. She'd stopped him in his tracks with a freezing spell and knocked him out, stealing away his hidden key, their second one. After Riveria's praise, the elves continued to shout.

Their advance couldn't be stopped.

"...?"

Riveria alone noticed the slight shift as the squad built up increasingly more momentum.

The enemy's attacks had stopped, grinding to a halt, when their desperate attempts to prevent their advance had assaulted them before.

"...Lefiya. Change your cast."

"Wha...? Ah, yes!"

It'd been nothing more than a reprieve for a short moment, but it was enough for Riveria to recognize it as the harbinger of something abnormal.

She gave a new order. And upon seeing the high elf's tense face, Lefiya and the other exuberant elves became anxious as well.

Riveria was wise.

She knew not to let her guard down in the man-made labyrinth—not in the hellhole that had brought Braver to a point of no recovery.

Her vigilance paid off. *It* came out—with a *bang*!

The door boomed as it opened wide, as crimson hair the color of blood fluttered.

"—! I-is the creature here?!"

One of the elves searching for enemies sounded the alarm.

All present swung around, and the figure of the strongest monster in a human form reflected in their eyes.

"After the elves, it's the prum, huh?"

Levis, the creature, approached, more menacing than the orichalcum door.

Behind her were vividly colored monsters, a multitude of fodder soldiers.

A genuine monster was closing in, one that had beaten both Finn and Aiz.

"—Hn…!" Riveria squinted as the red-haired woman charged with the sinister cursed sword in her hand.

"Ummm…is this okay, Captain…?"

Aboveground, the wind was blowing in the home base of *Loki Familia*, which resembled an old castle.

Beside Finn, Raul had timidly opened his mouth, asking the captain who was still looking out over the Labyrinth District.

"Is what okay?"

"Is it really all right to have Miss Riveria and the others break into Knossos…? The demi-spirit is one thing, but that creature there…"

Raul was having difficulty stringing together words, but he felt an apprehension that he couldn't brush aside. Before Raul's eyes, Levis had brought Finn down in a single blow when they'd entered Knossos last time. It was a nightmare.

It had been a shock to see the greatest hero and his idol being mercilessly overrun. It had left a big impact on him when Finn lost.

Even Aiz couldn't stop it by herself. It was an overwhelming mass of unreasonableness.

"…"

Finn fell silent for a moment as Raul remained apprehensive about the creature with red hair.

"Open up!!" commanded Riveria.

All the elves obeyed, discharging a fusillade of magic.

Rays of light—crimson, azure, gold—rushed at Levis.

"Violas."

"OOOOOOOooooOOOOOO!"

The creature gave a terse command to the monsters, disinterestedly holding out her left hand.

They advanced in front of her, becoming a wall of flesh to block the magic, a tremendous number of vibrantly colored monsters. They wouldn't falter from a broadside of that level.

Levis sprinted out, making an opening in the shield of monsters.

"…?"

She had an uncomfortable feeling.

"That's it."

"Huh?"

"Now that we have a key in our possession, that one creature is the only cause of concern in Knossos," said Finn with an unwavering expression, focusing straight ahead.

He turned to face Raul, who was visibly surprised, and continued without any hesitation in his voice.

"Raul, I wanted to be called Braver so much that I negotiated with Loki for it."

"…?"

"In order to be a light, to exemplify bravery for my race…I was prepared long ago."

There wasn't a logical flow to his statement, leaving Raul flustered. But as Finn continued, Raul finally understood what he was trying to convey.

"If I was to freeze up because of one person, because of a single threat—I wouldn't be standing here."

Raul shivered, getting goose bumps—at Finn's quiet face, at his cold eyes, at the magnificence of his resolve.

Yes, Finn had called himself the name "Braver."

He was a hero who'd put up a front, a man-made hero calculated from the very start.

Finn had borne the weight of that second name from the very beginning. He had always carried that pressure, enough to crush a normal person, on his small back with his immeasurable determination to turn a lie into reality.

What was brave about fearing a single creature?

How could he call himself a hero?

He would never have taken the name Braver if he cowered before them.

"Besides, Raul, you're not taking Riveria seriously enough."

He'd put trust in his friend, layered and heavy.

"If it's Riveria—she can drive back *something of that level.*"

What—?

Levis's discomfort grew at the constant hail of shots that the elves unleashed to keep her from approaching.

Their effect was a little—no, a bit more than a little too much.

It was enough for the shots to break through the wall of violas and graze Levis's cheek, enough for her to slow her sprint, *to prevent her from carelessly approaching them.*

The force behind the magic was intense, more intense than it should have been given that it was a short cast.

They've been firing off their magic. Why haven't they hit their limits?

The elves had advanced through Knossos, reaching the depths of the Dungeon.

It didn't matter if they worked in recovery with items. With their output and number of spells, they should have reached the limits of their mental strength. And yet, they continued to bombard the enemy without stopping.

By coordinating the front and back lines, the magic blades expelled their rapid-fire attacks to fill the gap between the blasts from the first row and those preparing their next round in the second row.

The stone slabs of the passage burst apart. The wall and the floor crumbled, and the chunks were blasted away.

They weaved together their chants in rapid succession, tens of spells overlapping, before destroying the wall of violas down to just a single monster.

The moment the wall between her and them disappeared, Levis saw *it*.

"_____"

She saw the jade magic circle that all the elves were inside, illuminating the area beautifully, absorbing all the remnants of magic drifting around the hallway and returning them to the elves.

It was increasing their magical strength, bestowing royal protection.

——*A rare skill.* Levis went bug-eyed. That was all she could determine.

"Just as Finn underestimated you—"

Using the time bought by the elves' fusillade, the high elf had finished her chant, her voice ringing out sweetly through the passage.

"—You looked down on us too much." Riveria mercilessly spoke to the creature—one that hadn't put in any effort or devised any sort of plan, trying to approach its prey head-on.

"*Blow with the power of the third harsh winter, advent of the end—my name is Alf!*"

As she lined up with Lefiya, who'd chanted Summon Burst, Riveria readied her long staff. The jade magic circle gleamed as the voices of the two elves, master and disciple, overlapped with each other.

""*Wynn Fimbulvetr!*""

Levis recoiled at the simultaneous frozen cannons—six blizzards in total.

"Tch?!"

Kicking off the floor of the main passage, she flew into a side path by a hairbreadth.

Her left arm and the cursed sword couldn't escape the firing line in time, swallowed up in the jaws of the blizzard. The eyes of the creature distorted as she made the instantaneous decision to *abandon it*, snapping off the frozen arm and narrowly avoiding getting dragged away by the explosion.

Less than a second later, the loud boom of an avalanche resounded behind her.

The twin cannons of ice froze everything, leaving a track of blue covering the entire main passage. The interior of the labyrinth was consumed unbelievably by an enormous cold wave.

Levis persisted, even as her skin was getting frostbitten, managing to escape onto a side path...When she lowered her right arm from her face, the scene of a frozen passage unfolded before her eyes.

The area was covered in frost, filled by a giant block of ice and icicles.

There was no path through the ice cavern, defying all who tried to get past.

"Insects...you've got some nerve!"

When she pummeled the frosty pillar before her eyes in a rage, the surface cracked under the impact, but the enormous chunk of ice would not break. She was unable to proceed down the large passage. It was impossible to follow Riveria's squad from there.

The labyrinth was made with stones of the obsidian soldiers that diminished the effect of magic, and it was absolutely terrifying to see it entirely frozen over, albeit it was one section of the maze.

It should have been impossible. It was a tremendous firepower, accounting for the Summon Burst and simultaneously firing identical magic.

"As if I've got time to sit around recovering!"

She'd lost an arm. With her left arm below the elbow severed and the wound frozen over, her prided healing skill was having trouble getting going.

Done in by the elf master and disciple, Levis trembled in humiliation.

"L-Lady Levis?! Wh-what happened...?!"

"You guys do something about this ice. I'm chasing those elves by a different route."

After demanding that the Evils who'd gathered at the crash deal with the frozen passage, Levis went in the opposite direction.

That high elf is a nuisance. If I'm not careful, this will happen again. Should I prioritize regenerating my arm?...Damn it. This is gonna take time.

The recovery hadn't started when she bitterly cursed to herself.

The door slammed open with a loud *bang!* as if in response to her anger.

"She left."

Riveria's ears twitched when the violent door-slamming sound reached them.

They *hadn't* changed locations. They hadn't thoughtlessly moved away, either. Instead, they'd hid themselves behind a bend in the passage and waited for Levis to leave. Lefiya and the others breathed a sigh of relief when their bold move paid off, gazing out at the hall covered in ice.

"Don't leave my magic circle. I'm retrieving the magic energy."

"Yes, Lady Riveria!"

With Riveria at its center, the jade-green magic circle swept together the remnants of magic filling the passage, allowing them to absorb back into her and the other elves. That was the true nature of the skill that had astonished Levis.

Alf Regina—a rare skill that none save Riveria had ever developed.

The effect was an enhancement of her own abilities and the amplification of the effectiveness of magic wielded by fellow elves inside her magic circle by recovering the magic energy in the surroundings and converting it back to Mind.

In other words, along with Riveria, all elves inside the magic circle would increase in magical strength and recover their deleted Mind.

In particular, the latter effect was peerless. Even if it paled in comparison to the nonsensical recharge of the demi-spirit on the fifty-ninth floor, its recovery effect was significantly more pronounced than the Mind auto-recovery effect from Spirit Healing.

Finn had ordered the surprise attack on Knossos because he knew of that skill. Alf Regina would allow them to enhance their magical abilities and recover their Mind as they ran around in a giant labyrinth of an unknown size.

When she'd developed the skill, Loki had danced wildly, excited to create an elf-only squad centered around Riveria. Seizing the opportunity, Loki had even tried to give it a gaudy name like "Fairy Force," but Riveria hated decorations and embellishments, and she'd rejected it.

That said, the name had been surprisingly popular among the elves in the squad, who called themselves that behind closed doors.

It was an incredibly valuable party skill befitting the image of Riveria, the city's strongest mage.

"Lady Riveria, what should we do from here?"

"First, resupply. My skill isn't all-powerful. It can't heal you in full. Treat the wounded."

"Yes!"

The squad had certainly been taxed, particularly Lefiya, who'd been firing off heavy blasts and even using Summon Burst. Alicia started the work of resupplying.

As Riveria let them continue their work, she turned to a single girl.

"Rakuta, the mapping?"

"Y-yes, it's coming along," squeaked a single person, a girl of a different species amid a squad composed of elves.

It was the hume bunny Rakuta. There was a reason why Finn had sent her along with Lefiya for their romp in the deep levels: her genius at mapping.

"B-but it's full of holes...! It's not even a map...!"

"That's fine. It will serve us well when we challenge Knossos in the future."

Riveria took the map-in-progress as Rakuta's rabbit ears twitched.

True to her word, it was a fragmentary map, covering only the areas they'd passed through. That said, the number of doors and other openings were all noted in detail. Considering it'd been created in her spare time as Riveria and the elves were fighting around her, it was worthy of praise. In the Dungeon, they couldn't use compasses due to a special ore running through the structure, but in Knossos, there was no such limitation. It was extremely valuable to deduce that their present location was to the south of Daedalus Street.

It was more than enough to avoid needlessly wandering in circles.

"Rakuta, I think we've gone down around ten floors' worth of stairs. What is your judgment?"

"I—I had the same feeling! Compared to the Dungeon, I think we're around ten floors deep..." responded the mapper with her superior depth perception.

Riveria started to think.

That creature won't fall for the same maneuver again...Next time we run into her, she'll destroy the entire squad. If we're to find an escape route, this is the time...

Riveria had no intention of underestimating Levis. There was no way she could.

They'd handled her well because she'd looked down on them. If the creature attacked them as seriously as she'd done to Finn, Riveria's squad of mages would be wiped out as soon as she could get close enough to attack.

And it wasn't as if they could keep fighting the remnants of the Evils forever.

In the end, the enemy could overwhelm them with their strength.

*It's possible to...devise a means of escape...If the god in Aiz's legend was a patron god of the Evils, one of the evil gods, then...*Riveria thought for the briefest of moments before deciding on a course of action.

"We're going to find a path connecting to the Dungeon and move from the south to the southwest."

"Yes!" With Rakuta, the elves stood up and immediately began to mobilize.

To avoid running into Levis, they distanced themselves from their battleground as much as possible. Following Riveria's instructions, they quickly located a staircase leading down from the tenth floor and proceeded to it.

And from the eleventh floor, they went down one more to the twelfth floor.

They moved carefully—and quickly.

When the monster attacks started, they had a lucky break with the help of Rakuta's surveying techniques.

"The Dungeon...!"

"We did it!"

A crash resounded, and the labyrinth wall gave off smoke, and there emerged Lefiya and the others. The group cheered as they saw the mist—it was unmistakably the twelfth floor of the Dungeon.

"It seems the god used Knossos to set that wyvern after Aiz nine years ago..."

Upon opening the connecting door and breaking through the wall of the labyrinth, Riveria looked back at the stone path leading perfectly into the Dungeon before turning away.

She wasn't sure whether all the floors were connected to Knossos. But Riveria had a clue. She knew the story of how Aiz had encountered a deity with the appearance of an evil god on the twelfth floor not long after she'd joined the familia. The god had disappeared from the Dungeon, even though he shouldn't have had a path to escape. In other words, he'd used Knossos to leave, meaning there was a connecting path on the twelfth floor.

Riveria finally caught her breath, but her thoughts were focused on how to fight.

We retrieved a second key. It's full of holes, but we have the makings of a map of the labyrinth. We found an escape route, too...But it's not enough.

Entrusted with the invasion, she felt she hadn't produced adequate results.

Find the location of the demi-spirit or strike the enemy facilities... **That's what I want.**

Now that the enemy fortress was thrown into chaos, it was a once-in-a-lifetime opportunity.

Riveria could tell that the efforts of *Loki Familia* to cut off the enemy's flow of supplies and monsters hadn't been wasted, now that they'd raided this far into Knossos. Finn's surprise attack plan was part of their success, but the enemies hadn't been prepared for the battle at all. They would never get this chance again, and she wanted to obtain information about Knossos to render the hellscape as powerless as possible.

I'm guessing the plant producing the inexhaustible supply of water spider monsters...is somewhere in Knossos. We've seen too many of them for it to make sense otherwise. If we can find and destroy it...

If she was to point out an issue with that plan, it would be Levis.

That creature is wounded...My magic and Lefiya's took one of its arms.

When they'd hit Levis with Wynn Fimbulvetr, Riveria was sure she'd seen her arm and the cursed sword plucked from her body and buried in ice. Levis would avoid an imprudent second assault and focus on recovery—or rather, if Levis actually wanted to come at them with half strength, Riveria would gladly perform her last rites.

If the creature happens to approach, I can keep the second-tier attack spell Rea Laevateinn deployed and sense her before she comes near us. That would buy us enough time to retreat...Now that we've secured a path out, it's not a bad gamble.

Upon weighing the risks and returns, Riveria made a decision, raising her head to look at the elves.

They were exhausted, but the light of battle in their eyes was still there. They remained in high spirits to avenge their comrades and crush the den of the demons. Riveria nodded at their morale.

"We've obtained our escape route. Use this as a starting point. Let's lay waste to Knossos once more. If time permits, of course."

She gathered the elves on the Dungeon side, announcing her intention to commence the assault again. As expected, no one voiced any opposition. From Alicia down, the elves renewed their desire to rampage.

"Fortunately, we took possession of a second key. I want someone to take this, go through the Dungeon and Babel to Daedalus Street, and bring reinforcements."

Dropping to one knee, Riveria looked around at the girls sitting in a circle, scanning the group for someone to get back to the surface as quickly as possible. Considering the condition of their Mind consumption, her eyes stopped at a brilliant burst of beautiful yellow hair.

"Lefiya, you go."

"!"

Riveria chose their irreplaceable lance, the girl who'd put in so much effort in the labyrinth. Because she was the newest member of the Fairy Force, she'd shouldered the biggest burden.

It was unfortunate to lose Lefiya's firepower and Summon Burst, but Riveria judged she was the best choice.

"This is a critical role. It will be imperative that we have support when we withdraw...Bring them as soon as possible, okay?"

"Yes! I shall be back in three—no, one hour!"

"I'm counting on you," Riveria said, smiling slightly as Lefiya put her right hand on her chest and stood up.

While the elves prepped for the second attack, Lefiya turned her back on them, dashing to the entrance of the room. After glancing at her once, Riveria looked back at the path leading into Knossos.

"Let's go!"

"Yes!"

The battle wasn't over yet.

Aiz sunk into despair.

The clouds rolled through the sky, and she stood there alone, bathed in moonlight.

As expected, the difference between her and the one she'd tried to believe in was like that between the foot of a mountain and the summit. As she'd feared, the boy had made her misgivings manifest. She shouldered an unbearable sadness.

"...And the vouivre is alive," Aiz whispered in the northwest of Daedalus Street, in a back alley that should have been empty.

Agitation filled the air when she spoke the word *vouivre* before it settled into complete silence. Aiz stood in the center of the street, staring dejectedly at the empty space before her.

"Come out..." she said.

And all of a sudden, the empty space quivered, casting off its veil to reveal a single boy's figure beneath the moonlight in the next second.

His white hair shimmered like virgin snow beneath the light. The black undershirt and the plain iron-gray armor gave off a faint luster, piercing Aiz's eyes.

Bell...

White hair, red eyes.

He stood in the middle of the street.

Aiz painfully murmured his name in her heart, as if whispering the name of a lover.

And when she saw the monster—the vouivre—clinging close to him, her gold eyes looked down.

"I've been thinking about...why you asked me that question... ever since."

Aiz had quickly started chasing Bell again after getting stalled by the masked adventurer.

And when she caught up to the presence of the invisible boy, she saw what she'd pretended not to notice while chasing him. It was an unbelievable scene.

Together with a renart girl, he'd been hugging the vouivre, a human and a monster sharing a moment of joy with teary eyes.

Upon witnessing that scene, seeing the monster's tear-filled smile, Aiz felt as though time had frozen in place, and she hadn't been able to stand before the boy until now.

She was faced with the reality that she'd been desperately trying to avoid for five days.

Let's say a monster could smile, like a human.

Or be consumed by worry, like a human.

Or shed tears, like a human.

Or was self-aware, like a human.

She'd been uncertain about the true meaning of his questions, which now stood before her eyes.

"So this is what you meant......"

The vouivre he'd protected to the point of standing against them wasn't dead.

The impetus behind this whole incident, the cause of her and Bell walking down separate paths, was still here—

Aiz slowly lifted her head.

Her body quivered as her eyes met those of the vouivre standing stock-still and holding on to the boy's hand.

Its amber eyes reflected Aiz's face and housed an undeniable intelligence.

They mirrored the Sword Princess's cold, dark, emotionless gaze.

"Miss Aiz!! This girl is—" Bell started, turning in place and trying to protect the vouivre from Aiz's gaze, pleading with her.

"My answer," she cut him off, speaking with a razor-sharp tone, "will not change."

And she put her hand on the hilt of Desperate.

"If anyone cries because of a monster—I'd *kill it*."

The boy froze at the Sword Princess's answer—at her drawn sword.

As she held back the grief in her heart, Aiz took a step forward.

"Wait...Please wait, Miss Aiz! This girl hasn't harmed anyone or anything! She would never do something like that! This girl—Wiene—is different!"

She had no more desire to lend an ear to his nonsense.

"Will you be able to say the same thing if that vouivre goes on another rampage?"

"_____"

"I won't allow it."

He didn't have a response.

The vouivre trembled, and the crimson stone in its forehead glimmered like a garnet. With the knowledge that her expression had become coldhearted, Aiz thrust peremptorily with her response.

The boy didn't know why Aiz was being this unsympathetic, and he probably didn't want to know.

But one thing was clear—there was no room to negotiate. She hammered home the grave reality that they were already in opposition.

"U...ah..." he moaned.

Get out of the way.

Approaching the deathly pale boy step by step, Aiz desperately wanted him to move. But at the same time, she already knew that her wish wouldn't be granted.

For no other reason than that he'd already given his answer.

On that day, the fool who had stood against Aiz and *Loki Familia* would not go back on his resolve. He'd arrived at the opposite answer from theirs, as if a reflection in a mirror.

Aiz's eyes narrowed with sorrow when he took the hilt in his hand and drew his pitch-black knife.

"—Gh…" The vouivre faintly whispered something.

"…" Aiz wore a coolheaded mask.

"…Why?" Bell's lips quivered.

"…*Why?*"

In the face of the boy who was consumed by emotions, Aiz resolutely kicked the ground.

"—Damn it!"

A sorrowful clash of blades rang out.

THE
WHEREABOUTS
OF A
SCHEME

Гэта казка іншага сям'і,

месцазнаходжанне проста

"Cruz, the attacks from Knossos have stopped!"

"Good—use this time to finish recovering!"

A familia member's voice resounded in the large stone passage.

The underground passage beneath Daedalus Street in the northwest. *Loki Familia*'s squad was exalted by the fact that the violas had stopped pouring out.

"This is thanks to Riveria, isn't it? This means…!"

Cruz had been deployed to lead the squad and recognized this as evidence of the chaos in the enemy's hideout. Knossos was being devoured by the unexpected invasion of the elf squad, and they couldn't divide their soldiers or even their monsters to deal with Cruz's group. He suspected that on the other side of that one door, the northwest of the labyrinth had been deserted.

They'd been forced to fall back by an intense attack by the monsters, but now they had the passage to themselves again.

Is there any value in having the northwest passage under control? It might be better for us to move to the southeast…But we still don't know the location of the armed monsters. I can't mess up the captain's formation on a whim…

They'd sent a messenger to the main base to report in and ask Finn for instructions.

"How do you do? Ladies and gentlemen of *Loki Familia*."

"!"

A single god appeared in the hidden passage.

"You…Lord Hermes?!"

The figure donned a winged traveling hat and loose clothes for travel.

Cruz was shocked as Hermes walked up.

He didn't even have guards from his familia. His lack of vigilance was incomprehensible. It was unnatural for a god to be on a battle-field alone.

Even though they were on the same side after forming an alliance, that didn't exempt *Hermes Familia* from their shady behavior. Not to mention that there was a good chance they were on *Hestia Familia*'s side in the struggle going on around the Labyrinth District, based on Finn's analysis earlier.

More than anything, it was ominous.

His orange eyes were hatching a plan.

Everyone was confused, but Cruz alone stayed on his guard.

In response to his attentive gaze, Hermes let a suave grin play on his lips.

"To tell you the truth, I just wrapped up a contract with Loki. I came to report on it—and look, it's the magic item you guys were searching for."

"!!"

He pulled a silver sphere—the Daedalus Orb—from his breast pocket, transfixing Cruz and the others. It was the item that Hermes had received from a certain Goddess of Beauty. He made a show of it, as though he'd just fulfilled the commission from Loki during the skirmish with Rakia three weeks before.

It was a key to Knossos—and the thing they currently wanted more than anything else.

While the other members of the familia stared, entranced by the jewel and unable to peel their eyes from the magic item and its ominous radiance, Cruz managed to wrench a response from his mouth.

"…Thank you very much, Lord Hermes. Could you please hand it over?"

Cruz's face remained tense as he held out a hand.

Why did he go out of his way to come to us instead of Loki? Why is he on the front lines?

He received his answer in no time.

"Sure, no problem. But before that, I'd like to receive my reward."

"What?"

"Could you please *take your squad here and leave*, my good man?" the god requested with a hint of sarcasm, smiling as his eyebrows arched.

"Wh—?...Do what?!"

"In exchange for handing over the key, I would like all of you to disappear from here. What? That's all I want. Honest. That's a cheap price to pay, right?"

"Why would you want that?!"

"Because as the god who rules over negotiations and contracts, I believe it would be sufficiently valuable, my boy Cruz."

Cruz couldn't put his finger on it, but he had goose bumps when the god spoke his name.

He couldn't understand—neither Hermes's demand nor the words he was speaking. None of it.

It's a trap. Or rather, he's planning something.

He could feel the other members behind him shrinking back as a drop of sweat ran down his cheek.

"...Our mission is to maintain control of this underground passage. That isn't something I can decide with my own discretion. If the captain gave directions to—"

"That's no good."

The corners of Hermes's mouth rose as he challenged Cruz, not letting him finish.

"Here. Now. You decide."

Cruz gulped at the god's pronouncement.

It contained an absolute will that wouldn't allow him to dodge the question.

It was an unnatural negotiation table. It was obvious that he couldn't take the offer. But they had to get their hands on the key, no matter what. Would it be better to capture him and take the key by force? It would be a simple feat to force a god to hand it over if their strength were equivalent to that of a normal person. But, but, but, doing something disrespectful to an unarmed god—

Cruz's expression twisted over and over as he struggled with a choice that was far above his pay grade.

Hermes sighed.

"If you say you can't take the deal, then I guess it can't be helped. There are lots of other people who want this key, after all, so maybe I'll give it to one of them…"

"Please wait!" Cruz shouted as Hermes started to turn away.

If he let him go now, they would never get that key. He was the kind of god who would really do that. At least, that was the feeling Cruz got from him.

In his anguish, Cruz remembered Finn's words.

Our number one priority is to obtain a key. The destruction of the monsters and the Evils is secondary.

Forced into making a choice, the chienthrope…followed the captain's instructions.

"…Understood. We'll withdraw from here."

"Thank you. Negotiations are complete. Please take this."

With a cordial smile, Hermes held out the key, which Cruz took without a word. As everyone else remained quiet, he quickly led the squad out of the underground passage.

The sound of boots hitting the ground reverberated for a while before silence fell once again.

A voice called out from the empty space in front of Hermes.

"It appears they've pulled back. There is no one from *Loki Familia* in the surrounding area," announced an alluring woman with blue hair as she let down her invisibility.

Asfi Al Andromeda reported in, holding a jet-black helmet in one hand.

Hermes nodded in response.

"I see—then, bring them here."

A group of armed monsters appeared from the opposite direction of Cruz and the others.

"Calling this sort of thing a secret path…"

"It's all the same, right? The only difference is that this one was just now created."

The black robe of the mage standing at the front of the group swayed in apparent disdain, but Hermes responded nonchalantly.

Hermes Familia was more precisely acting as a smuggler now.

They had made *a secret deal* with the armed monsters *Loki Familia* was hunting, moving them through the underground tunnels to prevent others from finding them and delivering the group of monsters to that point.

The passage contained an entrance into Knossos.

"With this, you can bid farewell to the world aboveground. After you enter Knossos, I'll have to ask you to take care of yourselves. I'm afraid I can't afford to go that far. I pray you safely make it back to the Dungeon."

The entire group of armed monsters was silent, nonviolent. Their faces were clearly those of beasts but contained hints of gloominess.

The handful of *Hermes Familia* members, Lulune and the others, made a point of not meeting the armed monsters' eyes—to focus on fulfilling their mission or to avert their eyes from the uncomfortable feeling of standing next to monsters without trying to kill each other.

By her patron god's side, Asfi furrowed her brow, a complicated emotion washing over her face.

"Lord Hermes...let me confirm one last time. Is it okay to let them go?"

"Yes. Gros's sacrifice is a proper recompense. That was the deal, after all."

Sacrifice. The monsters' faces strained when they heard that word. Their faces should have been hideous but looked akin to that of a person trying to endure pain.

Advancing like a funeral procession, they moved in front of the door.

The orichalcum door opened without a hitch, thanks to the key in the hands of the mage in black. By chance, the inside was exactly as Cruz had imagined: entirely deserted.

There were no defenses on the Evils' side.

The only things were darkness and the cool air.

"Lord Hermes...what is your aim...?"

"I said, didn't I? The world wants a hero."

After the last monster had entered the labyrinth, the mage turned back, and Hermes coldly responded.

In the next instant, the door closed with a violent crash.

The monsters disappeared from *Hermes Familia*'s eyes.

"All right—time for the return of a hero."

While Asfi and the others remained silent, the god turned to leave, lowering the brim of his hat as the corners of his mouth turned up.

CHAPTER
6

THE HERO'S SELF-DENIAL

Гэта казка іншага сям і.

адважны Катсумі

"Captain, I'm sorry…We've lost track of the monsters."

Aboveground, one of the familia member's voices melted into the still night air.

They were in the central area of Daedalus Street, in *Loki Familia*'s encampment.

Listening to the report as he chewed his lip, Finn retreated quietly into thought.

When Gareth got pinned down, should I have moved Riveria? That black fog made it harder to communicate…No use thinking about that now.

The clash in the west of the Labyrinth District had been the crux of the battle aboveground.

If they'd gotten control there, they probably would've caught the armed monsters. But they managed to escape their grasp as a result of Finn looking down on their strength—and the power of their supporters, *Hestia Familia*—and lack of dedicating forces to that front.

Moving Riveria aboveground would have been a big risk…especially when we had no way of knowing when we'd manage to get our hands on a key.

If he'd moved Riveria aboveground, the Evils would have gained control of the underground passage. Which meant they wouldn't have been able to pull off a quick one on their unprepared enemy. The two fronts had been at odds with each other.

If they had been greedy and managed to get everything, that would be one thing, but if they lost everything because of it…As a commander, Finn had to weigh the risk of that.

The black minotaur hasn't been found, either. Did someone kill it…? No, someone must intend to do something with it.

He was most concerned about the Irregular that hadn't been

caught yet. The minotaur hadn't roared out. The Labyrinth District was too quiet. It was ominous.

Plus, I can't read the enemy's movements...

It was the armed monsters' route. They'd totally betrayed his expectations. The moves were irregular, as if they were being guided *in the wrong direction*.

"The monsters were last seen in the area around Twentieth Street, right?"

"Y-yes, sir."

Finn furrowed his brow upon confirming with the familia member.

Twentieth Street... We investigated it, but...Impossible. That's...

Something was off. As if two gears were out of sync.

Finn's thumb wasn't aching at all.

"...What the hell are they after?" Finn's whisper was erased in the wind.

Raul was acting as his aide and seemed to misinterpret this as pained silence.

"I'm sorry, Captain...It's my fault. If I hadn't gotten tricked, if I hadn't broken the formation..."

"Raul, I'm not blaming you. Besides, your mistakes are my mistakes. I'm responsible for taking *Hestia Familia* too lightly."

Finn wasn't going to allow Raul, who was busy hanging his head in disappointment at himself, to think that.

"We were able to strike back at Knossos, but we let the armed monsters get away..."

That murmur described the current state of affairs.

They'd lost the battle but won the war—he couldn't placate himself with that. Finn had greedily and insatiably intended to win it all. He intended to destroy the armed monsters after using them, calm the chaos in the city, get his hands on the key from the beasts, and beat *Hestia Familia* and that boy who had rebelled.

And he hadn't been able to because he'd misread the situation and made light of *Hestia Familia*. He was the one who had split his forces between them and the remnants of the Evils, and he couldn't use that as an excuse any longer.

It was his blunder.

"It won't go according to plan, huh…? Good grief." Finn sighed slightly, crumpling up the completed plan in his head and throwing it away.

Switching gears.

They hadn't achieved the outward goal of eliminating the armed monsters, but the main plan—the surprise attack on Knossos—had succeeded. He should just accept that as good enough for now.

And besides, the fight wasn't over yet.

There were more things left to do.

"Send trackers to Twentieth Street. Have them search every nook and cranny, including any underground passages connecting to dead ends. I want to know how they got away."

"Yes, sir!"

"Twenty-seventh Street. Where Rox and the others were hit. That's probably the location of the black minotaur. Call Bete, Tiona, and Tione to the east…no, to the north to search for it. If they find the target, they are to shoot a signal into the air immediately."

"Understood!"

"Raul, has Aki reported in yet?"

"Yes, they're currently fighting underground, pushing at the southeastern door while it's open, but…the Evils are fighting back hard…"

"Got it. Tell them that depending on the enemy's resistance, they are to pull back. If a creature appears, they should retreat at once. Now that we have a key in hand, it's pointless to get hung up on one door."

"All right!"

As Finn handed out orders left and right, the familia members responded.

Because his plan had two different fronts, the squads were divided above- and belowground.

Aboveground, the team was a younger generation of first-tier adventurers, while the underground was important enough to be left to the most dependable forces, Gareth and Riveria. Partway through, he'd had to change the deployment, playing it by ear, but they'd managed to produce results, albeit minimally.

To Finn, the battle had already been decided. All that was left was to determine the route and escape path of the incomprehensible armed monsters and locate the whereabouts of the black minotaur. With that, the skirmish aboveground could be wrapped up.

"If Riveria is moving according to plan, they should be securing an escape route. A report should be coming from the Dungeon anytime now. We wait for that."

"Understood!"

"Reassemble all forces aboveground. Surround the north and corner the black minotaur—"

Finn had already assumed there would be no more disturbances.

At least until that moment. That was when his thumb suddenly started to ache.

"Wh—…?"

"H-hey! That's—!"

Even before he heard the familia members' voices, Finn's blue eyes saw it—grotesque shadows rising into the air above 20th Street, not far from the encampment, just on the western edge of the central area.

The winged beasts bat their wings, roaring as if unveiling their true monstrous nature.

"OOOOOOOOOOOOOOOOOOOOOOOOOOOO—!"

The thunderous roar of a gargoyle shook the night sky.

The swarm of monsters flew to the north of Daedalus Street, howling as if to draw attention to themselves.

It was at odds with their previous actions. Finn couldn't understand their intentions. The prum was bewildered but quickly narrowed his eyes.

"C-Captain?!"

"I know."

Finn didn't even glance at Raul, who'd rushed in, looking at the northwest outer edge where the monsters had touched down.

"This is just like the Dungeon…" He let out a long sigh at the series of extraordinary events.

Finn had judged from their previous movements that they wouldn't attack in the north where the residents were evacuating, trusting the instincts of Bell Cranell, who hadn't been worried about the armed monsters.

Because of that, he hadn't deployed any familia members to the outer edge of the district. The defenses were light.

The inconsistent movements of the monsters were so out of place that he felt the presence of a third party in them.

Can I attribute their mysterious route to that third party? Someone trying to use this situation… This doesn't sit well with me.

Finn understood that it had come to this, that *Loki Familia* had to send out a squad, too.

At that, his eyes dropped to his right hand.

It was slight, but there was an ache in his thumb.

Is there something there?… Or is something going to happen?

As he licked his thumb, Finn remembered the words of his patron goddess.

"See through it with my own two eyes, eh…? Sheesh," he grumbled, sighing once before he made his decision.

"Huh? What is it, Captain?"

"Raul, I'm taking a squad and heading over there."

"What?! You're going yourself?! Wh-who will give orders here?!"

Riveria will be back eventually, he indicated as he left it in Raul's hands, intending to clear his name. In response, a pitiful wail rose up, which Finn ignored, moving out quickly.

He gave the lower-tier members and even the first-tier adventurers a standby order as he headed to the northwest with a unit.

"…It's no good, Thanatos. We lost one of the varg plants."

In the base inside Knossos, the labyrinth master's room, Barca spoke flatly, standing before the pedestal to observe the inside of the maze.

"Argh…Was it Nine Hell's team?"

"Yes. They found the plant on the twelfth floor, following the path of the swarm of monsters that was drawn to its magic…"

Barca looked down at a screen of water that reflected the image of the high elf's side portrait as she moved. As the remnants rushed around, struggling to move heaven and earth, Thanatos looked up at the ceiling, taking in Barca's report.

"Not just Braver…but Nine Hell is after us, too…I guess I really shouldn't have let Valletta die this easily."

Even though he was the God of Death, he still regretted allowing a single soul to return to heaven.

That said, the god couldn't wipe the smile from his face, even though he'd been duped. It was as if he was enjoying the mystery of the unknown, continuing to move pieces on the board, amusing himself with the lost battle with no thoughts of surrendering.

"There's another…no, two more groups of invaders besides *Loki Familia*. Well, they aren't people…"

On the surface of the water, an image of a monstrous shadow flashed across the screen instead of Riveria's group. Barca's visible eye, which was inscribed with a *D*, narrowed.

"Ahhh, one of Ikelos's toys, huh…? Our hands are full enough with *Loki Familia*. To tell you the truth, I wish I could let them be, but both sides have keys. Can we bring them down?"

"We won't be able to get the small group…the one with the vouivre. They came in through the abandoned door connecting straight to the seventeenth floor. Did they break through the collapsed hidden passage…?" Barca postulated as Thanatos sketched out the battle situation in his head from his position atop the steps.

The Evils had lost one of their plants, leaving them with half their battle power—well, half might be overselling it, but it was a painful blow. It wouldn't be fun to get their asses handed to them and let *Loki Familia* go.

They'd ascertained that the current location of Riveria's group was on the tenth floor. Even if they pressed in force, the monsters weren't enough to stop them. The actual members of the Evils' Remnants were split between fighting *Loki Familia* on the first floor and tracking down Riveria's squad. The latter group was still moving through the ninth floor.

"And Levis?"

"Healing her wounds. Which seems like…it'll take a while."

Upon hearing the status of his last dependable bodyguard, Thanatos drummed his fingers against his temple.

They had enough firepower to crush Riveria's group—though it wasn't as if he could send out the demi-spirit. And if the situation repeated itself, Levis would get killed this time.

But, like, based on Nine Hell's movements, I'm guessing they've found the connecting path to the twelfth floor…

Even if Thanatos got his forces together with the intention of wiping them out, Riveria could easily retreat from Knossos. It was possible. Very possible. The only reason they were still rampaging around the labyrinth was because they had a means of escape.

Thanatos wanted time to ready his forces and to create a situation that wouldn't allow the enemy to run away even if they tried.

A lure to keep the fairies in place.

"…Barca, where are the other invaders?"

"The tenth floor. Far away from our troops."

Thanatos pondered in silence for a moment.

"Open *all* the doors to the routes that I'm about to specify."

"…What?"

"Manipulate the doors around the loitering vargs to prevent them from getting in the way of the intruders."

He wouldn't stop them. Instead, he instructed that they be drawn deeper into the labyrinth.

The enemy had a key to freely move inside the maze themselves. If he was unlucky, they might stumble across an important facility or a spirit room.

Barca swung around, doubting his ears, as Thanatos's eyes narrowed coldly.

"We'll collide with 'em."

"Are we really doing the right thing, Fels?!"

The black-robed mage Fels paused upon hearing that voice.

They were inside Knossos.

With their deal with Hermes, Fels made use of this escape path, breaking into the Evils' hideout with their team. This area was connected to the Dungeon.

"This is a good option if we're thinking about Bell and his gang! But abandoning Gros and the others? It...feels wrong for us to return without them, right?!"

"You're wrong, Lido. I believe in him."

They had somehow managed to make it through *Loki Familia's* counterattack. They had been in the process of trudging toward the Dungeon when one voice rose in opposition. The mage clenched their jet-black gloves, robe trembling, despite being one who wouldn't lose their composure even before the old god Ouranos.

"To think that foolish boy would overcome a deity's divine will—"

Fels ran, filled with trust for a certain boy. As the mage moved forward, the others pushed on to continue along the path, too.

They rushed down the stairs. Fels was looking for a path back to the Dungeon. To let those behind them escape, the mage continued deeper and deeper underground, farther from the traces of the battle above.

With the key, Fels opened the orichalcum doors. One of their party used high-frequency echolocation to accurately pinpoint the best route in the winding maze that they could steadily and confidently proceed through without getting lost.

"If you make it into Knossos, it's your victory, he said...but it won't be that simple in a hideout for the Evils—now will it?"

When a swarm of monsters appeared before them in the winding passage, the black gloves of the mage released a shock wave that blew away the swarms of vargs and detonated parts of the larger violas' bodies. This team's counterattack cleaned up the enemy in no time at all.

But we've only encountered monsters—not the actual members of the Evils...Is something happening in here?

Fels suspected something abnormal was occurring in Knossos, since the remnants of the Evils weren't resisting with as much force as expected.

The mage guessed correctly. In an unknown location, *Loki Familia* had robbed the Evils of all their leeway to deal with intruders, especially when they were also dealing with Anakity's group in the hidden passage underneath the Labyrinth District near the open door. They were all out of forces to split off to deal with the newest intruders.

"If it's like this..."

We can make it, Fels was about to say.

Bam. A deep sound echoed through the passage.

"...?"

Followed by: *bam. Bam.* A series of the same noise.

Fels quickly realized it was the sound of doors opening—but they hadn't done anything to unlock them, and the mage couldn't fathom the reason behind this sudden change.

Are the Evils operating the doors...? Is it to lure in the monsters? No, but...this open route is...

Following the echolocation despite Fels's misgivings, they arrived at the stairway to the next floor.

"Fels! I can faintly smell Mother—the Dungeon! It's connected down here!"

"..." Fels fell silent amid their excited shouts.

There was a connecting path to the Dungeon on the floor below. If they got there, they could escape Knossos.

But this timing...Is this a trap?

Are the Evils intentionally leading us to the next floor?

"Hey, Fels? What are you doing? Those bizarrely colored monsters will come after us!"

"...No, it's nothing. Let's go!"

Either way, Fels's group had no information about the structure of Knossos, which meant there was no real choice to make. If there was a path before them, they could run through it as fast as possible to avoid the enemy's traps, and that was it. They couldn't let this opportunity slip away.

"Full speed ahead! We can get out soon!"

Fels and the others accelerated down the stairs.

Their decision was correct. The mage guessed they could crush any enemy in hiding with their battle strength. Fels was confident they could deal with any man-made Dungeon gimmicks using insight and magic items. All of it was correct.

But if there was a flaw in their calculations, it would be the fact that they'd crossed into the twelfth floor; that the enemy was leading them not to a trap but to another group; that they would encounter the vicious fairies rampaging through the labyrinth.

"_____"

The first person to notice their presence was Fels.

"This is…"

"The thing that emerges when adventurers…use magic…?"

They stopped moving *inside the jade crest* spread across the ground. Only Fels guessed the true nature of the crest extending out from the door thrown open by the Evils.

It was part of a magic circle, spreading across an extremely large range. This ability materialized with an enormous magic power polished through a combination of once-in-a-lifetime talent and extreme effort.

Someone on the same floor had cast a net of magic power.

The magic circle crawled across the ground and arrived at them, moving past their feet.

It can't be…searching—

The jade brilliance shone up from their feet, a magic response almost screaming that it had locked onto its target.

—Have we been caught?!

In other words, they were already in range of the onslaught.

"Get out of the circle!" warned the mage with too much talent.

"—*My name is Alf.*"

The mage heard an incantation that they shouldn't have been able to hear.

"*Rea Laevateinn!*"

A multitude of giant pillars of flame surged out of the ground in front of them, out of the magic circle.

"Uuuu—*ooooooooooooooooooooo*—?!" They screamed and leaped backward as bursts of infernal fire exploded before their eyes.

Just as they were about to be burned by the blazing pillars rising from their feet, they managed to scramble out of the magic circle, avoiding being turned to ashes.

With a tremendous wave of heat and sparks, the labyrinth was scorched in an instant.

"Fels?!"

"…This is a special robe made to protect against magic and curses, but…that really nailed me good," Fels admitted in tattered clothing, standing at the head of the group and last to escape.

Smoke rose as the mage looked down at the charred black robe, letting out a groan that resembled a wry laugh behind the hood ensconced in darkness. Supported by one of the team members, Fels had managed to stand up.

Thud.

"To think we'd run into you in a place like this."

The sound of boots rang out from the smoke in the passage, which parted to reveal long jade locks of hair. It was Riveria, holding her long staff and leading her group of elves.

"*Loki Familia*…!" Fels groaned at the unlikely encounter.

Riveria had been in Knossos on the twelfth floor, using Rea Laevateinn to distinguish between humans and monsters. In the words of her patron goddess, she had been using radar—expanding the magic circle to search the floor.

Riveria had been looking for enemy forces. But when she encountered a response that wasn't Levis, the remnants of the Evils, or their accomplices, the vividly colored monsters, she'd decided to unleash a preemptive attack.

Fels couldn't have predicted an attack spell triggered through walls.

"Those armed monsters…managed to slip through Finn's attacks and made it all the way here, huh?" Riveria's eyes narrowed sharply at the scene before her.

Those cowering behind Fels were a group of armed beasts, eleven of them in total.

With teamwork and divine plans, the monsters had gotten past the city's strongest faction and managed to make it into Knossos— against all odds.

This reaffirmed to Riveria that the monsters were a threat. It didn't matter how they managed it—their existence posed a danger. Faced with a prearranged encounter, Riveria immediately moved to eliminate the force standing before her.

"—Riveria Ljos Alf—no, *Loki Familia*, I would like to negotiate with you."

Fels was a step ahead of the high elf preparing to cut them down, opening their mouth and stealing the initiative before Riveria could move. The mage understood they were in the wicked hunting grounds of Knossos and wanted to avoid turning it into a battlefield. To make it out alive, Fels opted for a negotiating table.

"…You're the mage leading the monsters. You're Lord Ouranos's messenger, right?" asked Riveria as she gazed grimly at the mage.

"That's correct. I'm here obeying the divine will of the creator god of Orario," Fels readily confirmed upon deciding that it wouldn't serve any good to hide the truth.

The mage knew it would be better to persuade her, to draw out every card possible, to use anything with the potential to help them in their cause. But when the younger elves, plus Rakuta, heard about the divine will of the founding god, it shook them up.

Riveria mentally chided herself. Her subordinates' will to fight was dampening, and they'd lost much of their determination. The proud elves would hesitate to attack the mage now, much less the monsters.

She discerned from this short exchange that the mage was extremely wise and extraordinarily dangerous.

"You let them rampage aboveground. And now that you're in a predicament, you're suggesting we negotiate? How convenient. Did you think we'd accept this nonsense?"

"When we were aboveground, everyone was directing their malicious intent toward monsters. Even if we'd tried to force contact with you, it wouldn't have been possible for us to engage in a level-headed conversation. It has nothing to do with logic and everything to do with emotion."

"..."

"And in the one-in-a-million chance that a third party happened to observe our negotiation, *Loki Familia* would have had no choice but to exterminate the monsters. We would never have been able to propose negotiations under those conditions, but then this opportunity fell into our laps by chance...Do you understand where we're coming from?"

I see. They have a point. And they are familiar with the war of words.

Riveria could recognize the mage's wisdom was coming from an age even greater than her own, as a high elf who boasted a life span longer even than normal elves. The mage before her eyes was wiser than she was. It would be impossible to try to win the argument.

"...As someone who's argumentative, I'm sure my words are insufficient. I'd like you to hear it in their own voices," Fels suggested, stepping aside to allow a single lizardman to move forward.

Riveria couldn't tell the expressions on the ugly faces of monsters apart from one another. But she could see the strain in its orpiment eyes that harbored the light of reason.

"...We just wanted to help Wiene...to help our vouivre comrade. That's all," the monster said.

The faces of Alicia and the others paled.

"Did it just speak?!"

"A monster...?!"

"How...repulsive...!"

The elves moaned. Each reacted in her own way, but they were all as one would expect: recoiling in disgust, or swaying, or gazing in agitation with eyes filled with fury. The elves had a reputation for being fastidious for a reason, but the reality of a monster speaking was shocking. They were all extraordinarily bewildered. All save Riveria, who'd already heard Finn's speculations.

"We came out aboveground because we wanted to get back our comrade. Not because we wanted to attack people and not because we wanted to kill them!"

They were taken aback, unable to respond immediately to its sincere and earnest pleas. Without giving them any time to recover, the black robes quivered again in encouragement, and a single beautiful siren walked out—displaying golden feathers, golden wings, and beauty in no way inferior to an elf. It closely resembled a person.

"Above all…we want to talk with you. We don't want to trade blows but words…" She spoke awkwardly.

The elves' uncertainty increased at her words. Even without looking back, Riveria could tell that the elves were disturbed.

The mage is good at this. And crafty. Riveria acknowledged their skill from an objective perspective.

Fels was sending out the monsters that most resembled people at the perfect time. The elves' confusion had already reached a fever pitch.

"What are the monsters…?!"

"But, Alicia, if they're telling the truth…"

"If we can't respond to discussion…that would make us more barbaric than they are."

"Thinking back on the times when we fought them aboveground, it seemed like self-defense on their part…"

"Gh…!"

Wavering. The elves' determination was wavering.

This was what Finn had been afraid of. If they acknowledged that they could reach a mutual understanding with the monsters, the adventurers would begin to doubt their blades.

They would no longer be able to strike down monsters.

"Self-aware monsters...We call them Xenos," Fels explained, looking at the confusion growing in the elves, Alicia, and Rakuta.

"They're our only hope."

"'Hope'...?"

"Yes—my patron god, Ouranos, wishes for people and monsters to live together peacefully."

Without missing a beat, Fels dropped another bomb.

A shock ran through Alicia and the other elves unlike any other.

"Wh—?!"

"Are you crazy?!"

"Our history has been fruitless. Always hating each other. Always killing each other...We want to bring an end to all that. The Xenos are our last hope."

Don't listen. Ignore it. Riveria could have given that order as the girls shouted back at the mage, their faces changing color. But she couldn't go against her own feelings. If she didn't know the desires of the mage and monsters or their aim, if she didn't know everything, she couldn't come to an answer. If she just cut them down without question, that itself might make her a barbarian.

After all, she was a trueborn elf.

"The existence of Xenos has the potential to be a bridge connecting monsters and humans. Instead of brandishing fangs and claws, they want to use thought and words to get to know us people, to live together with us...That's what they have been looking for."

"—?!"

"They raised a prayer in the Dungeon, and the almighty Ouranos acknowledged it. The Xenos are an Irregular that even the Dungeon couldn't have foreseen. A new possibility that the mortal realm gave birth to after all this time."

Alicia and the others gaped as Fels spoke of the monsters, including the lizardman.

The power of Ouranos's name was extraordinary. After all, his achievements had him praised as the ultimate god, even in Orario. It was enough for the elves to start to think about hypotheticals and the underlying truth.

Their outlook was shaking. Their grasp on common knowledge was collapsing.

Standing in the space between shock and hatred, the elven girls were pushed to the verge of mental shutdown.

Above all, their greatest source of confusion was that they didn't feel fierce hatred when faced with these monsters as they did when standing off against the normal ones. Fels's case was all the more persuasive because these monsters didn't evoke those feelings.

If they'd felt hatred, they wouldn't be struggling, choosing to cut them down.

Riveria herself would've been the same.

"It doesn't have to be immediate. But to bridge the gap between the world above and below, to put an end to this chain of loss...we would like you to understand them."

The mage held out one hand.

Please overlook them just this once, he was pleading. The eyes of the monsters behind the mage were boring into them.

Their wish. Their yearning. *We want to get to know you.*

The lizardman, the siren, the lamia, the unicorn, the troll, and many other monsters gazed at them without a roar.

It was an impossible scene between people and monsters.

It was heretical.

The monsters before their eyes.

That was Ouranos's secret: the Xenos, different from people and from monsters.

"..."

Riveria closed her eyes as scenes flashed across the backs of her eyelids: setting off from her home forest, encountering the goddess and prum in the worst way possible, joined by the dwarf she found absolutely incompatible, journeying together until today.

The image of her obstinate, audacious, tactless prum friend.

And a glimpse into his worries and resolve as he sat on the bed and clenched his fist the other day—

"..."

Finally, Riveria opened her eyes.

"*Loki Familia*, if you could somehow take this—"
Interrupting the mage's words, she rejected him.

"Are ya stupid?"

Everyone froze as Riveria spat out a refusal.
"—our patron goddess would say."
Riveria shocked the other elves, glaring back at Fels in their quivering black robe, ignoring the resignation written on the Xenos's faces as if they had lost count of *how often they'd encountered something similar.*

"Can you prove it? Is there anything substantiating your claims? Do you have any plans? Any explanation that could convince people who've lost their families to monsters? Any way of showing their sincerity?"

As Fels spoke of ideals, Riveria parried back with reality.

Arching her brow, slightly raising her chin, Riveria narrowed her eyes coldheartedly.

"Right now, I don't want to hear your ideals or delusions; it's a purely realistic discussion. Don't appeal to our emotions with underhanded tears. Use logic."

"..."

Riveria didn't let up on her rebuttal tinged with denunciation, silencing the mage.

"Unless and until you can do that, I can't accept your argument."

"...Cap...tain?" Alicia murmured in shock at the sight of Riveria elaborating cogently.

She couldn't believe her eyes. The beloved and revered queen of her race was overlapping with the figure of a certain prum. Based on her speech and that unwavering determination, Riveria bore a strong resemblance to Braver.

No, it was exactly like him. A mirror image.

"Mage, let's test your resolve. Forget all this hypothetical talk about 'someday' and show me a resolve convincing enough to move me at this time, right now...Do you actually have that in those black robes of yours?"

Riveria was *Finn Deimne* without a doubt.

Out of respect for his determination, she channeled him, speaking on behalf of her friend who wasn't there. She knocked away the monsters' hands, word for word in the way of the revered Braver.

"If there isn't, then…" Riveria ruthlessly declared, "your story is a pipe dream more meaningless than the fantasies of a child longing to be a hero."

She put an end to their negotiations, slicing them down and spitting out her words almost venomously to prevent the morale of her team members from deteriorating further. At the unwavering pronouncement of the high elf, Alicia and the others swallowed hard and then cast aside their doubt.

"…Riveria Ljos Alf. Or rather, Finn Deimne."

Both stood at the head of their respective groups. Fels looked closely, crestfallen, at Riveria, their black robes shaking.

"You're both wise. And you have the necessary elements of a hero…And a faith that doesn't balk even when confronted with sacrifices that must be made."

Upon seeing the character of a hero in the high elf standing in the Xenos's way, Fels responded in frustration.

"I can't help thinking…what would have happened if you'd been our ally."

"A meaningless hypothetical. Even if we were to talk with you, our position would not change."

"I suppose so. Then…to survive, we've no choice but to resist." Fels reluctantly assumed a ready stance, jet-black glove shining.

The faces of the Xenos behind Fels showed anguish, as if detesting the idea of people fighting against one another.

Loki Familia and the Xenos were about to clash.

"Get them—!"

"" ǁ ""

The followers of the God of Death rushed in at top speed.

"The remnants of the Evils!"

"Now of all times?!"

Alicia and Rakuta screamed as a large force of the remnants

rushed them from the open doors and the ones that'd been closed. Riveria's brow furrowed deeply.

"It would take time to gather this many of them...I'm guessing they were stalling from the start, huh?!"

Before Riveria could regret it more, Fels groaned.

"This must be why they led us together...! To push both our forces to fight!"

This had been Thanatos's aim all along, the two leaders realized.

With a firm grasp on the battle that had unfolded on Daedalus Street, the God of Death predicted that if *Loki Familia* and the Xenos encountered each other, a fight would inevitably break out. At the very least, they would both stop, which gave Thanatos time to pin *Loki Familia* down in Knossos and make them unable to retreat. With that in mind, he'd gathered his own forces on the twelfth floor.

He was looking to profit from their conflict by turning it into a three-way battle.

That was the situation Thanatos had wanted.

"I can't tell how many enemies there are!"

"W-we're being surrounded! There are monsters in the passages to the right, left, and behind us!"

"...Gh!" Riveria tightened her grip on her staff as the elves cried out.

She was confronted with the fact that she hadn't been able to maintain her composure when faced with the extreme Irregular, the Xenos. Her guard had slipped in Knossos once and only once, and that had brought her to this predicament. The vision of a smiling God of Death, someone she'd never met, passed through the back of her mind.

As she shelved the regret filling her breast, Riveria howled. "Break through one part of their formation! Ensure our path out!"

"Lido, Rei! Intercept them! *Loki Familia* and the Evils, too!"

Fels shouted again as the monsters reluctantly readied their weapons. The Evils' forces surged into the passage with *Loki Familia* and the Xenos.

"Kill! Kill theeeeeeeeem! Kill *Loki Familia* and the monsters, too! For Lord Thanatos and for our wish! Kill all of them!"

"OOOOOOOOOOOOOOOOOOO!" They let out a fiendish battle cry as their enthusiasm went off the rails all of a sudden.

As the adventurers, monsters, and Thanatos's followers mixed together, they commenced the three-sided struggle.

"What's the situation?" Finn asked the familia members who'd come first as he arrived from northwest of where the monsters had descended to the outer edge of the Labyrinth District.

They were on the roof of a building that could look out over the whole area surrounding the plaza.

"The evacuation of the residents hasn't finished yet! Adventurers from other factions are fighting the monsters. And Little Rookie is…"

As he heard the report, he saw the boy and gargoyle struggling against each other.

You again, huh…Bell Cranell? Finn's pupils narrowed as he watched the boy's face lose composure from the side.

As he thought, he tried to get a grasp on the situation: the swarm of monsters attacking, the residents of Daedalus Street falling into fear and scrambling to escape, the Guild members and other lower-tier adventurers trying to direct the evacuation. *Ganesha Familia* was prioritizing the lives of people as they made their way through the city. The top-tier adventurers were desperately fighting against the monsters and struggling to combat the strength of their enemy. There'd already been several casualties.

And Little Rookie was clashing with a gargoyle while protecting a half-elf Guild member.

"…Take your positions. Those on the ground, check them while we snipe at them from here so that they can't escape into the sky."

"Yes, sir!"

He handed out instructions as the leader of his faction, making snap judgments.

The familia members dashed off to share his orders with the group on the ground while the remaining members readied their bows. Finn looked down at the prepared stage. It could hardly be called a battlefield.

They don't really seem to be Irregular...For monsters hidden away from people for this long to intentionally attack evacuees...They exposed themselves for the masses to see. The other monsters are keeping the other adventurers back; the gargoyle is ostentatiously fighting with Little Rookie...It's too much.

His strange feeling from before turned to certainty when he saw the scene unfold before his eyes. He could sense the intent of a third party—a divine will that had created the scenario, even manipulated the monsters to bring about this performance.

Hermes Familia...?

If it was a group with deep knowledge of the armed monsters and the ability to bend them to their will, there was no one else save those who'd sided with Ouranos as his faction had done. Had *Hermes Familia* been moving around behind the scenes as they were fighting *Hestia Familia*?

The odds were that this was an action that went against Ouranos's divine will.

And Bell Cranell didn't seem as though he was acting as he desperately tried to defend himself.

An independent action. Hermes's face came to mind. He was a god who Finn couldn't quite grasp.

Is that gargoyle...being manipulated? It's only aiming for the Guild member Bell Cranell is protecting. Considering Perseus's crazy magical items, I guess that's believable?

The half-elf girl was wearing a bracelet giving off a mysterious purple light. Utilizing to its fullest the enhanced kinetic vision of a prum, Finn easily saw through the events.

A god was toying with the mortal realm, rewriting the plot to achieve his desired ends.

"The plaza is a stage, the residents are the audience, and the monsters and adventurers are the extras to excite the crowd. And the star is...a single boy crossing blades with a reactive gargoyle," Finn murmured to himself softly, so that the members readying their bows didn't hear him.

Below his eyes, a stir rose from the residents who still couldn't manage to escape the plaza, from the "crowd." And it wasn't out of fear.

"Little Rookie…"

"—Little Rookie? That one? Bell Cranell?"

"He's fighting…for our sake…"

They were talking about the adventurer putting himself on the line to protect the half-elf under attack, the brave boy who'd gallantly appeared in their moment of need.

How would it look in the eyes of the people who'd criticized Bell Cranell?

"Bell…" murmured the orphans who Finn had met the other day in the crowd.

Among a group of human, chienthrope, and half-elf orphans, Ossian the prum boy was there, watching Bell's battle in shock. The disappointment in his eyes gradually faded as he struggled to understand what was going on.

The crowd's disapproval of Bell Cranell was dissipating.

A farce…

The crowd had been attacked, the heroine was in peril, and the hero protected them from the monsters.

It was all drama.

It was all absurd.

Anyone would be drawn in by the performative manipulations of a god.

Should he praise Hermes for his talent? Or should he be disappointed that the residents of the mortal plane were made to dance for him? Upon understanding the god pulling the strings behind the scenes, Finn alone looked at the "stage" with clear eyes.

Other than him, the only ones who saw through the creation of the stage were gods.

As he saw *Hestia Familia* arrive in the plaza with their patron goddess and stand there when they realized they were unable to do anything, Finn thought to himself.

If his actions five days ago were a folly…this is a purification ceremony.
A ritual to earn back the title of hero as a coda.

The reaffirmation of a hero as arranged by a god.

Did Hermes intend to force Bell into the role of a hero? Finn didn't know his divine will, but that was his best guess.

If I were in his position…

If it were Finn, what would he do?

Would he dance if he knew everything would turn out as he desired? Or would he brush it off, saying he couldn't possibly stomach it?

But in the end—Finn suspected he would prioritize his ambition.

He'd go along with the ulterior motives of the god. For the sake of his people, he would throw away his pride. He would return to take the role of a hero.

After all, he was a created hero, a hypocritical hero who'd weighed everything in the balance as he moved.

"Loki…sorry, but there's nothing to see through here."

This was a stage brought forward by a god. Everything was moving according to the script. There was nothing left to discover.

And this was Finn's response to the goddess's advice.

The monsters are pathetic, too…They were setting out to return to the Dungeon but became manipulated by a god.

Finn didn't feel any pity for the monsters, but just this once, he looked on with compassion at the gargoyle rampaging wildly on the ground.

"Captain, everything is in order!"

"All right, give the signal."

The familia member had reported that everyone was in position.

With a brief order, Finn readied himself to throw his Fortia Spear.

He wouldn't try to destroy Hermes's stage. It was quite the opposite. Finn would use it against him to suppress the monsters. And the vindication of the boy was incidental, a bonus. It wasn't as if he had no desire to knock down the Little Rookie. As he'd told the orphans, Finn acknowledged the boy himself.

—Or it was because he wanted to see what conclusion Bell Cranell would reach.

Would he be unable to decide anything and be torn to shreds by the monster's claws, committing the worst possible folly?

Or would he go along with the divine will, kill the monster, and reclaim the title of hero?

Which of those two choices would he pick?

Finn's blue eyes observed the boy, along with those of the people in the crowd, to see his decision.

"*Loki Familia* has come!!"

The squad on the ground broke into the plaza.

The adventurers and residents cheered, and the winged monsters roared, ready to die.

"—*Hng!*" The fiendish gargoyle spread its wings wide, flapping, making a suicidal charge along the ground.

It was a desperate attack that didn't give the half-elf in shock or Bell Cranell any opportunity to avoid or defend.

The finale was fast approaching.

"Get ready." Finn equipped himself with his own spear, ordering the familia members to prepare to pierce the winged monsters with their arrows.

As he steadied his long spear, Finn looked at the monster and the boy and nothing else.

People screamed.

Monsters howled.

Everything was being yanked around by the strings of divine will held by a smiling puppeteer.

While his surroundings closed in around him, the whole world condensing into an instant, the boy's eyes flashed.

The claws of the monster were about to skewer him.

In the face of them, Bell took action.

To believe.

"———" Finn froze.

The boy had spread his arms, waiting, as the monster's stone eyes filled with shock at his defenseless stance.

In the next instant, the gargoyle stopped his charge, dodging out of the way.

"—Wait!" Above the plaza, Finn reacted faster than anyone, shouting for his familia to halt, shocking them all.

His bugged-out blue eyes were glued to the gargoyle that'd stopped its attack.

Did it stop? Could it stop? Did a monster stop its attack? And not just by breaking free of brainwashing—but of its own will?!

Finn didn't miss the monster's behavior, recognizing that it hadn't stopped its attack because it'd returned to its senses. When it was confronted by Bell, it'd stopped its charge of its own volition.

At the same time, Finn realized his deduction had been wrong.

——*Wasn't the monster controlled from the start?*

——*Then did it choose to sacrifice itself for Bell Cranell from the beginning?*

——*Did it make a deal with a god to repay the boy who'd protected the vouivre with his own body?*

——*Was a monster acting...for the sake of a person...?!*

In the span of a second, these questions and answers swirled in his mind. Finn was rocked by the shock with as much impact as a lightning strike.

Say it was an intelligent creature. A genuine monster had protected a person without any ulterior motives or calculations.

It had responded to the trust of a boy.

More than that—Bell Cranell!

He'd chosen the most foolish of alternatives, a third choice where he neither killed the monster nor sacrificed the half-elf.

A third choice that surpassed Finn's predictions. He'd believed there were only two options available.

But the boy had destroyed the scales.

He'd shredded the absolute will of the gods.

He'd kicked aside the seat of a hero set before him and roared in rebellion against the world. It was an unprecedented foolishness, but Finn saw it as dazzling—almost blinding.

"———"

At that moment, as Finn was caught in a dizzying swirl of emotions, his thumb ached with a pain sharp enough to shut off his thoughts.

The strongest warning bell that something was approaching.

Finn was the only one who looked up.

"OOOOOOOOOOOOOOOOOOOOOOOOOOOOOOOOOOOO OOOOOOOOOOOOOOOOOOOOOOOOOOOOOOOO!"

A loud roar resounded, crushing all doubts, conflicts, and plots.

"Thousand Elf?! What are you doing out of the Dungeon?!"

"I'm sorry! I'll explain later!" she shouted, breaking away from the *Ganesha Familia* guards in shock as she flew out of Babel.

Lefiya was running.

With her declaration that she'd return in an hour, she'd broken through the Dungeon at a blinding speed, dashed up Babel's underground stairway, and arrived aboveground.

"Quickly...to the captain and the others...!"

For the sake of those still in Knossos, Lefiya set out to cross Central Park for Daedalus Street. She leaped over five meders to the roof of a shop, jumping from building to building in a straight line to the city's southwest region.

Even as she struggled for breath, Lefiya resolutely sprinted to call for reinforcements.

"OOOOOOOOOOOOOOOOOOOOOOOOOOOOOOOOOOOO OOOOOOOOOOOOOOOOOOOOOOOOOOOOOO!"

"—Gh?!"

Her sprint lost its momentum as that bellowing roar rocketed into the night sky.

"That roar...Is that the black minotaur?!"

Lefiya was sure that fearsome bellow on par with the howl of a floor boss belonged to the black minotaur for which they were on their utmost guard.

It was a cry with enough strength that she could tell she wasn't the only one who cowed upon hearing it, that people all throughout the city quivered at it.

Lefiya had stopped moving in shock. As she nervously ignored the residents of the city and subconsciously opened the windows on the upper floors of the building to gaze to the city's southeast, she steeled herself.

She kicked off with enough force that a piece of the roof broke away when she flew, and she accelerated toward the Labyrinth District.

Where are they in Daedalus Street?! Are they rushing to the minotaur?!

Lefiya tried to narrow down where the black minotaur had emerged in the giant labyrinthine district, but in the end, it would prove unnecessary.

Because after she crossed Central Park and set foot in Daedalus Street, she saw the battlefield at the northwestern edge of the district unfold before her.

"Ahhhhhhhhhhhhhhhhhhh!"

"OOOOOOOOOOOOOOOOOOO!"

Bell Cranell and the black minotaur were fighting one-on-one.

"Wh-whaaaaaaaaaaaaaaaaat?!" Lefiya let out a bloodcurdling scream at the sight when she landed in the plaza.

It was a *howl of rage.*

—Weren't you protecting an armed monster, that vouivre?!

——Then why are you trying to kill another one now?!

Lefiya was on the verge of exploding.

I pressed him hard to explain himself, and he refused to give me the slightest answer—only to take a contradictory action now of all times, resulting in this mortal combat. I don't get it at all. What was the fighting with the monsters on Daedalus Street for then?!

Lefiya could only imagine that the boy who seemed to do incomprehensible things was either an egotistical piece of trash or an insane rabbit.

She completely forgot her mission as her face turned bright red, ready to start ranting and raving at a moment's notice.

"—Ah."

That was when she realized something.

That it wasn't contradictory at all.

The boy was fighting to respond to the minotaur that wished for a battle to the death—for a rematch.

He was fulfilling the wish of the monsters that desired to return to the Dungeon, accepting its determination to fight.

It was a setup to draw the attention of the adventurers and *Loki Familia* and to stall for time to let the main group of armed monsters escape. If she thought about it, she would have found plenty of meaning in the fight. But all of that was trivial.

Lefiya realized something frustrating when she saw the face of the adventurer taking on a terrifying enemy with nothing but a knife. Even without understanding the situation, there was something she could understand.

That the boy was on an adventure at that very moment.

"That's..."

There was no calculation in it at all—and no desire, either.

It was determination. That and nothing else. It was a lust for victory.

The other adventurers in the plaza and the residents could understand that.

That boy was betting his all at this moment.

"That's...what Miss Aiz and the others said..."

A battered plaza for a stage.

And in the center of it all, surrounded by a throng of people, a minotaur and a single boy engaged in a seesawing struggle. A battle between one beast and one person who'd destroyed the script of divine will and shone all the brighter for it.

It was a battle as they were in fairy tales, one that held everyone's eyes, that took everyone's breath away.

Lefiya realized something.

"This is...the one who fought the minotaur...Bell Cranell's adventure."

It'd been a battle that had even stirred the first-tier adventurers in *Loki Familia*.

"*Uuuuuuoooooooooooooooooooooooooooo*—!"

Look.

Gaze at the single ferocious strike from the minotaur that split the air and shattered the ground.

Stare at the gallant figure of the boy avoiding it and decisively stepping in.

Feast your eyes on the dazzling sparks following the clashes of the Labrys and knife.

"Go for it, Bell!"

"Bell!"

"Fight...!"

Listen.

Hear the voices of one, then two children, their cries rising into the sky.

Concentrate on the praise for the boy soaring upward.

Lend your ears to the voices of the people enthralled by his adventure, erasing all their malice and hostility.

Lefiya's chest trembled. Her navy-blue eyes were on the verge of tears.

Before they realized it, a handful of adventurers opened their mouths at the shock of the battle igniting in the depths of their heart.

"Go..."

"Do it—"

Someone murmured, coming from the crowd rooted in place and from the adventurers.

Lefiya forgot everything and screamed, "Don't lose!"

That was the trigger. Lefiya's voice catalyzed in a loud roar.

At the center of the plaza, voices called out to the boy fighting the terrifying and ferocious beast.

A single word turned into countless shouts before transforming into a billowing wave that came crashing down.

"———————————————————————*Gh!*"

In response to the mortal combat, the wild roar and scream intertwining, the frightened residents shouted until their voices cracked. A Guild member was at a loss for words, and that turned into cheers of support as adventurers raised their fists above their heads.

Everyone raised their voices for the boy.

Everyone quivered as he embarked on his adventure.

Everyone saw a hero.

"…You did it, Ottar."

Finn sighed for appearances' sake, glancing sidelong at the tremendous stage.

"…" The boaz warrior standing before him said nothing.

All members of the *Loki Familia* squad had gathered in the northwest area, where they'd run into *Freya Familia*. Finn's group was held back by Warlord and their other first-tier adventurers, preventing them from interfering with the battle between the boy and the minotaur.

Finn realized that they hadn't been able to catch the black minotaur on Daedalus Street because of these adventurers. Everything Ottar and his allies had done was for the sake of setting up this battle. They had beaten back other adventurers just to guide the black minotaur to this place.

"As my lady wishes," Ottar commented, shifting his body weight to throw his great sword.

The large hunk of metal split the wind as it rotated, landing in the middle of the central plaza, right between Bell and the minotaur.

The boy sprinted, grabbing the hilt and drawing the sword.

The beast's body shook, as if it was rejoicing.

"Hu——!"

"*UOOOOOOOOOOOOOOOOOOOOO!*"

The great sword and Labrys flashed, sparks flying.

As their battle accelerated, the throng of people roared again.

*I was wrong about this, too…*Upon witnessing the fight, Finn realized his error.

He'd judged that the black minotaur was an Irregular, that it randomly sowed destruction with its violence unlike the other self-aware monsters. That was why he'd told the familia members to be the wariest of it as the thing that needed to be dealt with above all else.

But he'd been wrong.

The minotaur was self-aware—it had a goal.

It desired single mortal combat, a battle with the boy. That was all.

"..."

Finn watched the scene that birthed a maelstrom of wild enthusiasm, the battle that ignited the hearts of all—young and old, man and woman, even gods.

"...Argonaut."

Tiona had called him that once. Or perhaps she meant to bring up one who was a heretical hero, like Bell Cranell. Everyone had pointed and ridiculed his foolish behavior. And everyone was in awe when he finally achieved great work in the end.

There had been interesting scholarly research on it that said the age of heroes in the Ancient Times had begun with Argonaut. A weak, pitiful, flourishing kingdom at the center of the world had roared as the next generation of heroes was born one after the other, guided by the back of that pseudo-hero. The ferryman of heroes. The one who pulled a multitude of heroes—the Argonaut.

"Ottar..." Finn had begun to speak somewhere in the middle of all this.

"...What?"

"You know, I'd set out to match Phiana. For the glory that had brought my race hope."

"I know...that's the only reason you're fighting."

"Yeah. But I'm going to stop that now."

Ottar's eyes opened wide at Finn's declaration. It was genuine shock, which he usually never showed.

Phiana's knights. In the Ancient Times, she'd killed multitudes of monsters and rescued countless people, demonstrating the bravery and embodying the first and last symbol of glory of the prums.

Deified in posterity and worshipped as a goddess, she was the hero of his race and the person Finn held in highest regard, the one who'd stood tall before even Argonaut.

Finn had been struggling to become the next Phiana, to become the light of the prums in the stead of their great ancestor.

However, Phiana wasn't enough. His race had lost its foundation, fallen further than it had been in Ancient Times.

That was why—

"I have to surpass her."

Ottar's expression changed from one of surprise to understanding.

"Watching him…even has an effect on me," Finn noted.

As the battle continued to unfold, he thought about having to transcend the part of him that had come to just accept casting things aside.

That he had to become a hero who obliterated the scales, too.

"'Or is following in the steps of Bell Cranell too much for you to handle?'…Heh, ha-ha-ha-ha-ha-ha-ha!"

Finn laughed out loud as his own motivational speech boomeranged back at himself, giggling like a child, causing the familia members nearby to get flustered and Ottar to look at him dubiously.

Bell Cranell had continued on the path of the fool to the very end, eventually finding his way back to the path of the hero in the process. He'd struggled and strived without casting aside anything. Even if it was a miraculous walk on a tightrope, a paper-thin margin, it was something he had reached with his own strength—without yielding to the world to cast aside divine will.

This is the type of hero the gods…and the world wants to see, I think.

In that case, Finn would remove his facade, start anew in a way that wouldn't lose to the heretical hero.

He was being shaped. He was changing. He knew it. And that was fine.

Someone who could stand still after being enthralled by this boy's adventure wasn't a true adventurer.

I…should bury Deimne.

Bury the hatred for monsters in the depths of his heart for the time being.

Loki's advice had been good. He'd made his decision when he saw that gargoyle.

Whether for the sake of its comrades or the boy.

Because the monster offering up its life either way—that was the bravery Finn had been seeking all along.

"...Arcus. Pull back the squad."

"What?!"

"As long as Ottar and the others are here, we won't be able to do anything. It's a waste of time. We should start on another matter."

Finn shifted his gaze. He saw Lefiya reluctantly turning away from Bell's battle with the minotaur and heading back toward the rest of her familia.

"...Not going to watch it to the end?"

"I already know what Bell Cranell will accomplish. Now that the monsters are gone, I've no use for this place."

As Finn made to leave, Ottar looked a bit surprised, though only those who'd known him the longest would recognize this expression.

It was a day filled with odd expressions for him.

Finn smiled like a child again, satisfied and exhilarated.

Yes, he already knew in his bones the result of this battle.

Just like that time before, the boy would ignite a fire in people's hearts and demonstrate his way of life—drawing in, fascinating, and urging everyone.

Like a page in an epic.

"I should take a risk...no, go on an adventure, too."

"And so you've gone, Finn..." Loki whispered when she heard the report from the messenger.

The encampment was devoid of the main members of the familia.

Raul had lost his cool and shouted "Whaaaaaat?!" at the report that Finn was taking Lefiya and the other familia members to the Dungeon. When Gareth had gotten the order to withdraw from the underground passage and meet at the Dungeon, he dashed away, grumbling, "Oy! You're really dwarf-handling me here!"

Watching it all from the spire, Loki raised her head and looked out over the northwest of the Labyrinth District as she sat cross-legged in front of the window.

Now that Dionysus had met up again with Filvis and left, Loki was alone, thinking back on what had happened a few hours before.

"—Hey, old man."

Before the battle had started in the Labyrinth District, Loki had gone to Guild Headquarters, meeting the old god alone at the underground altar.

"I heard it all from Hestia. About the monsters yer callin' Xenos."

"...Is that so?" Ouranos's expression didn't change in the slightest as he lounged on his seat, almost as if he'd anticipated the information would get to Loki from Hestia. He didn't panic or welcome it.

"You got yerself a real bomb there, with what y'all are hidin'. It might even be a bigger deal than the city destruction scenario that we're chasin' right now."

"..."

"Dionysus's instinct was right, in a way."

It was a world-class Irregular that wouldn't stop with just Orario.

With his secret exposed, Ouranos closed his eyes, almost as if in resignation.

The old god was presumably about to ask, *What do you intend to do now?*

"But right now, I don't give a shit about that one way or the other." Loki spoke first. "If Finn happens to come to the answer that y'all are hopin' for—when that time comes, you damn well better not get in his way," she warned with a straight face, to Ouranos's surprise.

"Right now, that child is tryin' to change. He's been moved by the uproar y'all brought, he's worryin', and he's tryin' to reach a different answer than he had up until now!"

Loki saw the wavering heart he'd hidden when he heard Ikelos's answer.

Loki had watched over it, as he was shaken by Bell Cranell's actions, as the hero had constantly questioned himself in anguish.

She had not intervened.

She left Riveria and Gareth to get close to him, watching over him as a parent while he tried to come to his own answer. She knew better than anyone that he didn't want the advice or guidance of a god.

"I don't know which path he'll choose, either! No one can predict it, and he might run down a rugged, high path! But that's his story and his choice!"

Because Finn wanted to weave the ballad of his own heroism.

"If you try to take advantage of that, I'll kick yer ass in the blink of an eye! If you try to extort him, I'll damn sure beat yer ass!" She berated Ouranos vehemently as he opened his eyes wide.

Finn had crushed the fear he'd let slip in front of Riveria and Gareth, the seed of destruction on the path of Braver, the collar that would force him into Ouranos's camp by extorting him into making a deal with the monsters.

Loki was telling the old god not to get in Finn's way.

"Tell that playboy, too! If you get in his way, the rules of the mortal realm be damned: I'll be comin' to murder ya! Try to run to heaven—see if I care. I'll chase ya until I destroy you and there ain't even a speck of dust left! And that goes for you, too, old man!"

That shout, verging on bluster, contained all of Loki, all of her love for Finn.

Or perhaps it was the scream of a goddess trying to protect her child.

"If you try to get in the way of his goal, I won't forgive you."

It was the one and only time Loki would interfere, a divine will stepping in to ensure that Finn would be able to walk his chosen path without any gods getting in his way.

"If you can abide by that, then…I'll keep quiet about your bomb, the Xenos."

"…Very well." Ouranos accepted after a few moments of silence, judging the deal to be sufficiently of value.

The four large torches on the altar crackled.

After the two gods made their deal in secrecy, Ouranos asked, "Loki...why are you going so far to support Braver?"

"Huh? That's easy. Like that playboy might put it—"

Almost contemptuously, almost boastfully, she couldn't help responding to the old god.

"—because I'm that hero's first fan."

The cool night air brushed Loki's cheeks as she descended into thought, warm wind blowing from the northwest.

The pulse of the hero who had returned.

"Finn, don't get left behind."

Remembering her response to Ouranos's question, Loki narrowed her eyes.

"Carrying out your initial goal is a great thing. I love that unwavering side of you. But ya know...if you get too caught up in that, you'll be overtaken in a flash."

She sent good wishes to her follower who was continuing to worry, struggling to come to an answer even then.

"But you're best when you're sticking to your resolve and duty, carrying all of that even as you move forward. You won't lose to anyone, not even that shrimp's kid. Win for me."

Loki opened her vermilion eyes and smiled.

"Win this hero's race."

"For our dreeeeeam—!"

Another one of Thanatos's followers blew themselves up, shaking the passage with more explosions.

Inside Knossos. The twelfth floor.

The three-sided battle among *Loki Familia*, the Xenos, and the Evils raged on.

It was a melee in a passage the size of a room in the Dungeon.

Under Riveria's command, the elves sang as beads of sweat scattered and they fired off magic. The intelligent monsters desperately pushed their battered bodies, rampaging with the aid of the black-robed mage.

The Evils' Remnants and the richly colored monsters tried to crush both forces at once. The followers of the God of Death charged with beastly howls as the violas' feelers and the vargs' fangs danced without restraint.

The sheer number of enemies encircling them was more than enough to make the elves, including Alicia, uneasy.

A raiding unit that normally used Concurrent Casting to attack with long-distance hit-and-runs couldn't unleash its true strength in a giant free-for-all with no real way to move around. That was what happened when they stripped the Fairy Force of its advantage of high-speed combat.

Taking wounds to her cheeks and arms as she endured the fierce attacks of the Evils, Alicia was struggling to breathe.

"—! Don't get close to me, you heretical monsters!"

"Kuh?!"

She swung around, lashing out at the siren that had unintentionally drifted close to her in the shock wave from the explosion.

The Xenos fell to the ground, its beautiful golden feathers severed.

"Repulsive! Know some shame! Trying to pass yourself off with the words of people!"

"—Gh...!"

"Do not...deceive us!"

The siren's face warped in sadness, stung by the high-minded elf's sharp rebuttal.

Loki Familia was attacking the Evils, of course, and striking back at any Xenos that approached them. The lizardman and troll had no intention of attacking, trying to defend themselves as best they could.

But even as both sides recognized this as the intent of the Evils, even in this precarious situation, the adventurers refused to join hands with the monsters.

It was a profound testament to the relations between monsters and people.

As the God of Death chuckled, watching the scene unfold from his seat beyond the board, he grinned at the predetermined performance he'd arranged.

"Kuh—?!"

"Lady Riveria?!"

Amid a melee that didn't allow time for predictions, Riveria was exposed to the intense suicide attacks conducted by the Evils' Remnants.

They turned themselves into weapons, blowing themselves up in an attempt to stop the artillery fire of the city's strongest mage. With them weaving in close by using the chaos of the brawl to their advantage, their sacrificial attacks forced Riveria to stop Concurrent Casting. They didn't even balk at engulfing their allies in their attacks, creating an absurd chain of explosions.

"They intend to take care of us by any means possible, huh?!"

More detonations went off, violas' giant bodies collapsed, and elves screamed. Fels's black robes trembled as the battlefield turned to pure chaos.

A huge free-for-all among the three forces mashed up together in the enclosed space.

And as if to announce their death sentences, a door slammed open.

"This is where you were—pest."

"—?!"

There was crimson hair, the color of blood. Deep amid the battle, Riveria shuddered, recognizing the green eyes that locked onto her.

It was Levis. She'd finished healing her wound and missing arm, raising her ominous, cursed weapon now that she had reached the feast that Thanatos had prepared for her.

Visible unease lit Riveria's face.

Now that they no longer had a path to retreat, total destruction was inevitable.

"Die."

Levis didn't give Riveria an opportunity to respond. Cocking one of her twin blades behind her back, she threw it with inhuman strength.

The wind roared and a dull clap of thunder boomed as Levis's blade split the air. The violas and vargs in its path exploded into fragments of meat like burst balloons. The indiscriminate attack sent the heads and arms of Evils flying like toys.

A spray of blood rained down in its wake as the blade cut through the battlefield, rushing full speed toward Riveria.

But before it could reach her—a single elf was destined to become its prey first.

"—Alicia!" There was only enough time for Riveria to call her name.

As she knocked away one of the remnants, Alicia looked up and immediately froze as the assassin's missile approached her at sonic speed. The pitch-black cursed sword reflected in her eyes, silently, mercilessly handing down her death sentence.

It was going to crush her head without even allowing her enough time to let out a dying scream.

"Guh. Aaa—"

"—Huh?"

Right before it hit, a golden wing spread across Alicia's field of vision, moving into the path of the cursed sword. The siren had crossed her arms and wings, absorbing the impact of the blow.

It pierced her folded wings, burrowing all the way into her right shoulder.

The siren put all her strength and awareness into her torso muscles, keeping the sword from tunneling through her body any farther.

"Rei?!" yelped the lizardman, along with the other Xenos, as the siren was knocked back, tumbling into Alicia, who was right behind her.

"...Why?"

Alicia had landed hard on her back. Sluggishly pushing herself up to a sitting position on the floor, she barely managed to whisper that much.

The siren lay powerlessly on her chest, shoulder and face stained crimson. Her long lashes quivering, she opened her eyes and smiled.

"Your hair is prettier than my wings. I just thought that...I didn't want it...to get dirty."

"—Wha...?!"

"I had a dream...that if you could ever...somehow forgive me...I wanted to be friends with you..."

Alicia's face cracked as she looked down at the siren whose breathing was ragged even as she flashed a peaceful smile on her face.

The elf could no longer control the whirlwind of emotions that appeared on her face: an infant on the brink of tears, an enraged fairy, a lost child who didn't know where to go.

There was no proof. No evidence. No plan. No sincerity or logic to convince those who despised monsters.

There was earnest love—one-sided, but it was a precious *philia*. Friendship.

This was a monster: a noble being, starved for affection, who put herself on the line and willingly threw away her own life for the sake of others.

Was this a beast?

If it was, then what would that make Alicia, the one who wouldn't lend that noble woman an ear and swung a sword at her instead? Did it make her a far more depraved monster?

This shocking revelation summoned a storm of emotions that overflowed from her heart. Her value system was shattered at its core: The idea of monsters as a symbol of absolute evil was gone. Alicia's eyes darted around. She was unable to hold the siren's body close, even as she looked down at her chest, where death was approaching the being by the second.

Loki Familia's elves saw that, too, and Riveria's face warped, displaying the agony in her heart as she stood still in shock.

The Xenos were on the verge of tears as they watched the actions of their comrade.

"Missed, huh...? Well, whatever," Levis commented, watching their drama play out without a trace of emotion.

"I'll just hunt down those defective monsters, too."

She swung her blackened sword, signaling the tragedy about to begin.

The real monster was the woman who had been given free rein over the whole of the battlefield. A moment of silence fell as everyone, even the monsters, stopped moving, sensing the icy chill and intense bloodlust of the overwhelmingly powerful creature.

The elves paled, the Xenos recoiled, and even the Evils gulped.

Riveria moved faster than anyone else to resist, beginning to sing a spell. Fels's robe quivered as if to say *I can't die yet* when the mage moved to break the deadlock. And Levis coldly narrowed her eyes, ready to kick off the ground.

"Sorry, but I've no interest in watching a tragedy."

Bam! A door slammed open on the opposite side from the one through which Levis had entered the room.

A hero with billowing golden hair stood at the entrance to the large passage.

"Especially not after seeing the real-life epic of a hero."

It was Finn, holding out the key in his right hand and his long spear in his left.

"Finn!" Riveria shrieked upon spinning around and recognizing him and the other members of their familia.

Her jade eyes filled with light. The high elf had never given up hope or lost faith in her old friend.

On the other hand, Levis kicked the ground with a sharpened gaze, leaping out to cut Riveria's neck before she could resist.

"Like I'll let ya!"

"—Gh!"

She was stopped by the battle-ax of a dwarf flying in at a right angle from behind Finn. Gareth had dashed to the scene upon being summoned by Finn at the main base, and he crossed blades with Levis now.

Upon impact, a massive shock wave rippled out, causing the air to tremble as the dwarf warrior clashed head-on with the creature who'd defeated both the Sword Princess and Braver. Levis scoffed as Elgarm grinned ferociously.

"Everyone, support Alicia and the others. Secure a path for retreat!" Finn barked his orders as he dashed.

When Levis relied on speed over power to swipe at Gareth, Finn butted in from the side with his Fortia Spear, challenging her even though he'd been cut down once before. He weakened the momentum behind Levis's sword, supporting Gareth through teamwork.

""Riveria!"" They called for the high elf, seizing the advantage in this fight.

"Heh!!"

"Tch…Three Level Sixes!"

Wielding her long staff, Riveria joined the front lines with Finn and Gareth, adding to the raging battle.

The teamwork among *Loki Familia*'s three leaders was divine, assaulting Levis from three different sides to create a storm of continuous attacks. The Xenos, who'd been swept aside in the flow of events, were filled with awe.

Even though she was a mage, Riveria was keeping up in speed and working in perfect unison with the prum and dwarf in close-range combat. She'd always had more skills and tact than anyone else, working with Finn to nip Levis's counterattacks in the bud while Gareth's top-tier strength made up for their lack of power.

These three had fought together longer than any other team. That was the reason they were called the strongest fighting force in *Loki Familia*.

"*—Harbinger of the end, white snow!*"

"—Rg?!" Levis's shoulders trembled as Riveria decisively started Concurrent Casting while attacking with her staff.

As the creature acted cautiously, wary of the blast that had stolen her arm, Gareth stepped in, seizing the advantage.

"Yer full o' openings!"

"Guh?!"

His battle-ax swung up, hitting the side of her cursed sword, just barely managing to block it. Levis's body was knocked back in an arc as her sword shattered, landing some distance away from them.

Riveria cut off her spell mid-chant.

By drawing the attention of their enemy to her chants, Finn and Gareth had attacked. Their original plan to ambush a decoy.

"It's my first time doin' it with a creature, but...it's certainly dangerous. That woman is full of energy!"

"That's what I told you, isn't it? Fighting her head-on's not a good plan."

Gareth's tone was rougher than usual—perhaps because it was the first time in a long while that the three of them were fighting together. Finn responded with a complaint reminiscent of old times. Riveria finally got her taste of relief since this battle had started.

"Sorry...Finn, Gareth. Thanks for the help."

"It ain't over yet! Did ye forget?! The adventure lasts until you make it back!"

"Yeah, don't get sloppy on me, Riveria."

Riveria let herself smile as the others glared at Levis without letting their guard down. Her face quickly tensed, matching theirs.

"Narfi, we'll be the rear guard! Heal Alicia and them, then go back down the path we came on!"

The other familia members had moved in from the surroundings in a surprise attack to rescue the Fairy Force. Breaking through the Evils who'd clumped together in panic, they had returned to that path with the elves in tow.

"You think I'll let them go that easily, prum?" The creature's green eyes burned as she swayed, trying to stand.

Without words, she proclaimed her intent to exterminate them all, unleashing an overwhelming bloodlust. Even with Finn, Gareth, and Riveria teaming up together, they were still fighting on the Evils' home base. Even if they somehow managed to hold off Levis, the others would be crushed by the Evils, who held an advantage in their numbers.

And on their side, Riveria was exhausted, so she would be the first to run out of stamina. Without their teamwork, that would be the end. They were not a match for Levis individually. It would be a defeat in detail.

Finn responded to Levis's statement. "Sorry, but we've got no intention of fighting you straight-up."

He didn't rise to her challenge, raising his voice the moment Rakuta and the elves had all been evacuated.

"Lefiya—do it!"

The next instant, a magic circle spread from their feet.

"——" Levis froze as the jade circle expanded through the large passage, past where she'd been standing.

From inside the path that Finn's group had entered, a golden-haired elf had been left behind.

It was Lefiya.

"Ahhhh, how annoying, annoying, annoying—"

Wielding Forest's Teardrop in both hands, she unleashed a tremendous magical light.

"—Because of that human, my body is burning!"

Enthralled by Bell's battle with the minotaur, Leafa felt as though her heart and body were burning.

Just like Finn, Lefiya had been fascinated by the boy's adventure, and it renewed her determination.

She converted the strength of her thoughts into a heightened magical power.

The blast had been on standby with the use of her Summon Burst. It had reached critical mass while Finn's group had stalled for time—the magic of the city's strongest mage.

The monsters took notice of the source of magic power overflowing like a cup brimming with water, but it was too late.

"I can do it, too!!"

Unleashing her white-hot feelings, she turned her body into a blazing inferno to save her comrades, giving birth to an unprecedented firepower.

It was an extermination blast that could pass through walls, stealing her master's thunder. Having led Finn all the way there, the elf had bided her time, waiting to drop her own supersize support.

"Rea Laevateinn!!"

A pillar of hellfire shot up from the floor, rising to the ceiling.
"OOOOOOOOOOOOOOOOOOOOOOOOOOOOOOOOOOOOOO?!"
A hellish inferno emerged. In an instant, the web of passages was overwhelmed by the columns of flame, which blasted everything inside its field of magic with a blistering heat wave. The first to rise were the screams of the vibrantly colored monsters, followed by the fearful cries of the Evils. Though the Xenos weren't targeted by this attack, they screeched, enveloped by the aftermath and dashing away from it.

"Tch—?!" Levis covered her face with her arms, retreating at an inhuman speed as the inferno shot up at her.

Finn didn't miss a beat, immediately realizing the Evils had fallen into complete chaos as he barked out his orders. "Retreat! Full speed! Get out of here!"

Just as they had arranged it beforehand, the familia members in the rescue squad moved in perfect concert. Riveria and Gareth departed in haste, darting one after the other to their escape route down the path where Lefiya was waiting.

"C-Captain...I..."

"..."

At the entrance to the path, Alicia was the last to leave, looking up at Finn with a full range of emotions on her face. Hauled there by the others, including Narfi, she felt her legs give out as she sat down on the ground.

Alicia was holding on to and couldn't let go of a siren at death's door whose shoulder was pierced by the cursed sword, covered in blood, just like she was. Alicia tried to say something, but nothing would come out.

Upon seeing her troubled expression, Finn understood everything. And with that, he spoke. "Carry this monster, too!"

"!"

For a few moments, Narfi and the others were stunned, struggling to move, but they eventually pulled it together to obey his order. As they supported the inhuman body with wings instead of arms, they lifted it out like they would have a human. After reaching the escape path, the members of the Fairy Force supported them. Alicia was among those helping.

"Finn Deimne...!"

Fels witnessed the scene of the humans carrying out one of the Xenos and saw the prum looking back at them and gesturing with his jaw. That gesture sent a jolt down the mage, who froze in place before finally calling out in a voice filled with faith.

"Lido, follow *Loki Familia*!"

"Got it!"

The monsters went along, rushing down the labyrinth drowning in the remaining vestiges of fire, and escaped out of the large passage, charging at full speed as the cries of the Evils' Remnants continued to ring out behind them.

"As if I'd let you get away..."

Inside the large passage-turned-crimson-hellscape, Levis stared at the backs of the adventurers and Xenos disappearing beyond the rampaging fire, about to mercilessly hound them down.

"Don't chase them."

"!" A masked figure appeared from behind her, putting the brakes on her plan.

It was wearing a hooded purple robe and metal gloves on both hands. It was another creature that Finn's team was aware of—the one called Ein.

"Don't chase them? Is there any purpose in letting them escape from here?"

"..."

"You had one job. And you can't even get that right? Why is *that guy* still alive?" Levis spat with animosity and annoyance, baring her fangs like an untamable wild animal and ratcheting up her bloodlust to full.

"If all you can do is get in my way...I should just kill you. What do you think of that?" Levis suggested cruelly to the fellow creature.

It fanned the flames with its robe and responded, "This is *Enyo's* order."

"!!" Levis's green eyes snapped open wide.

In the words of the gods, the *city destroyer*. The being behind everything.

There was a short silence.

Upon staring at the masked creature, Levis scoffed and turned away. "You tell Enyo that if this plan fails...I'm coming to kill you."

And with that, Levis left, moving with her back to the large passage and the remnants who still hadn't quelled the chaos. The masked creature watched her disappear into the darkness, casting a glance down the path that *Loki Familia* and the Xenos had taken before melting into the darkness without leaving any trace behind.

"They aren't following us..." Finn murmured in the rear guard as he looked over his shoulder.

Though they were faced with intermittent attacks from the remnants of the Evils and their monsters, his biggest fear, Levis, never made it to the scene. Finn was suspicious, but nevertheless, he dashed out of Knossos along with the other familia members. Opening the door to the connecting passage and breaking through the wall of the labyrinth, they arrived at the twelfth floor of the Dungeon.

"They...probably won't be coming. Seems like we finally shook them, eh?"

"Yes..."

As they moved from the area connecting to the passage to Knossos, leaving a fair distance between them, Finn finally took a breather with his comrades. They stopped in a room shrouded in fog.

But many of the familia members didn't let their guard down—namely because the heretical monsters had come to the same place, concerned about their comrade that *Loki Familia* had carried with them.

"Everyone, lower your arms."

"Finn..."

The familia members had separated themselves from the monsters, glaring across the room at them, when Finn raised his hand and gave an order.

While Gareth murmured, marveling, the prum moved toward the high elf.

"Riveria, you have the medicine?"

"Yes..."

"Use it."

"...Is that okay?"

"Yeah. It's fine."

While Lefiya and the others were dumbstruck by the exchange that only Gareth could understand, Riveria looked into his clear blue eyes and nodded, kneeling beside the siren who'd been laid on her back. From her breast pocket, she took out the medicine—a magic item for dealing with cursed weapons that Amid had made. Finn had requested it beforehand in preparation for the surprise attack on Knossos. She used it on the siren who'd been pierced by the cursed sword, which had afflicted her with a curse that prevented the wound from healing.

A murmur rose among the familia members.

The Xenos stiffened.

By the siren's side, Alicia was stunned when Riveria used recovery magic, conducting a full healing. This action was equivalent to Finn ordering them to not fight the Xenos.

"Finn Deimne, you..." Fels murmured in amazement.

Finn walked over to the mage leading the Xenos.

"Unorthodox monsters, I'd like to negotiate with you," he began to say, holding his long spear and looking out at the monsters with a clear gaze.

Loki Familia and the Xenos were paralyzed. Lefiya's eyes opened wide, Rakuta gulped, and Alicia spun around in surprise.

Riveria and Gareth were the only two watching Finn's actions in silence.

"Negotiate? You of all people, Braver...? That's more than a little hard to believe..."

Fels was bewildered by the unexpected proposal but didn't lower their guard. The black-robed mage knew enough about Finn's ambition to understand just how strong his resolve could be. Fels made clear their suspicions that there might be something hidden in this suggestion to catch the Xenos unaware.

"It's simple, really. I've decided I want to use you."

"Use us...?"

"For the assault on Knossos."

That made everyone gulp.

"Now that we have our hands on a key, we're going to embark on a campaign to clear Knossos in the not-too-distant future and drag the Guild, who wishes for peace in Orario, into this mess."

"..."

"When that happens, I want you all to participate in the attack. Under the strictest secrecy, of course."

They still didn't have a full grasp of that hellish labyrinth or nearly enough manpower to clear it out.

Which was why they needed to borrow the aid of the monsters. As Finn explained this plan, Fels maintained their silence.

"...Braver, I don't know your real intentions. Put bluntly, we thought you were one of the only ones who would never consider a deal. I'm sorry, but I can't trust you—"

"It's already been shown that the armed monsters won't attack people. At least, I've come to that conclusion. I've also confirmed that the Evils are clearly our mutual enemy." Finn interrupted Fels mid-sentence.

"And above all...there are people in my familia who can't point their swords at you."

A handful of the elves twitched, including Alicia, which Finn noted out of the corner of his eye.

There was no longer any way to sweep the existence of self-aware monsters under the carpet. Even if Finn exterminated them here and now, the knowledge of them would spread through the familia from someone present who'd seen them.

In which case, he would change course and use them as much as he could.

And that was the choice Finn had come to just a little while prior.

"If…and when it comes out that we're connected…that you had dealings with us, you know your reputation will plunge. That would be the end of your ambition to reinvigorate your race. You must know that, right?"

People would talk. And eventually, ruin would befall Finn—just as Bell Cranell had experienced. That was Fels's point.

"Then, after losing everything, I'll come back as a hero again. This time, not an artificial one. Yeah. Maybe I'll be an unprecedented leader who reconciles with the monsters…or something like that," Finn responded nonchalantly, half sarcastically, shrugging with an annoyingly shameless grin.

Fels stiffened.

Lefiya and the others stared openmouthed.

The Xenos's eyes tensed.

Gareth's shoulders trembled as he started to chuckle, and Riveria clutched her head as if suppressing a coming headache, but even she couldn't help breaking into a smile.

Finn's expression was clear and untroubled, like someone who'd broken free of all ties, but then he quickly assumed a serious look.

Finn continued. "With the potential destruction of Orario impending…I'm casting aside my personal feelings and my hatred toward monsters."

He was prioritizing the fate of the city.

As Fels maintained their silence, Finn added, "Don't misunder-stand me. This deal is a one-time thing, for the duration of a joint battle. I've no intention of trying to get along after that. And I'm not signing up to help you achieve your goal. If you appear before me again after the battle, I might annihilate you, depending on the situation."

His expression was cool. The Xenos sensed that the adventurers were looking at them differently. Finn's eyes were only on Fels.

"…Let me ask one thing. What changed you, Braver?"

Finn's face softened. "I regained my childlike mind. That's all there is to it. I stopped fixating on the idea that there's only one possible answer."

Fels stopped trying to probe for his true intentions upon seeing another shift in Braver's expression and turned around to acknowledge a nod from the lizardman—representative for all the Xenos.

"Very well, Braver. We'll make a deal with you. Not that we have much of a choice in the first place."

Finn responded with a nod and cleared the way. Fels and the Xenos cut past *Loki Familia* and their lowered weapons. The troll lifted the siren, whose wounds had closed, struggling for a moment on what to do before sluggishly lowering its head in thanks.

The siren faintly opened her eyes, smiling at Alicia. As she stood up, Alicia's eyes were wavering.

Then the monsters vanished into the depths of the mist-shrouded labyrinth.

"…In the near future, I'm going to formally report on this incident to the familia. Until then, the events of this day stay among us. Obviously, it should never leak outside our faction," Finn instructed in the middle of a silent room.

Upon receiving orders to return to the surface once the wounded were treated, the familia members stiffly started to move out. There were some who seemed anxious, others looking like something was lodged in their throat, and still others who seemed to be deep in thought. There was a range of expressions, but there was no one who could fully accept his judgment—because Finn himself had voiced his valid misgivings before.

But upon seeing the monster protect Alicia, several people were starting to have a change of heart.

"…Will this be all right, Finn?"

"If I had to pick between good or bad, well, this is bad. But there's no helping this outcome. We can't erase the memory of the

intelligent monsters from the others, and it'll be a waste to exterminate them. If we can make use of the strength of that black minotaur,
that right there is more than enough compensation."

Gareth had questioned Finn away from the other familia members.
Finn indicated that he'd already made the necessary calculations as
he shrugged with almost too much flexibility.

"The problem is whether our team will hesitate to attack other
monsters...We have to find a way to nip this in the bud. Especially
Alicia. She'll require careful consideration. Riveria, you should stay
with her for a while."

"I don't mind, but..."

"That's not what I mean...Like you said, Ouranos might just put
a leash on you, now that he and his lackeys have got a firm grasp on
your weakness. You really okay with that?" Gareth asked Riveria,
who'd made a difficult face at Finn for approaching this situation
from a completely different attitude than hers.

In between two of Loki's most immeasurable, unknowable followers, Finn appeared carefree as he said, "Ah, that's what you meant.

"I'll burn that bridge when I reach it. Like I said, if I lose my fame,
I'll start again from scratch."

"Is your head on straight?"

"Yeah. I'll be a hero who surpasses divine will...I was thinking
that might actually be the fastest route to my goal."

Gareth had opened his eyes wide, but upon hearing Finn's confident response, he softened them to a fatherly gaze with a smile.

After answering Gareth, Finn looked to Riveria. "Sorry for worrying you."

"That's all right. It's good to have this kind of problem from time
to time."

Finn had no choice but to smile wryly when the high elf fired back
light sarcasm, making no attempt to accept his apology.

Riveria met his eyes again. "Finn, one question. What changed
your mind?...Was it Bell Cranell?"

Finn was visibly surprised. "How did you know?"

"That's what you said. If things were to occur, it would be because of that boy."

"…Now that you mention it, yeah."

If anything was going to provoke Irregulars, it would be him, Finn had said before the fight began, in front of everyone.

That adventurer had far exceeded Finn's expectations, enough to redetermine him.

"Sheesh. We've been with you for so long, but a mere adventurer was the one to move you…I'm jealous of that boy."

"Ga-ha-ha-ha, he's a prum who does as he pleases. There's no helping him."

Their comments took the form of reproach and complaints. But Finn felt bashful and awkward upon seeing Riveria's smile despite her verbal prod, and Gareth's teasing tone added to it.

It was as if his friends had seen him get childishly enraptured by a heroic epic for the first time ever. It was comparable to that sort of embarrassment.

However, the high elf and dwarf seemed to welcome the change in the prum.

Closing his eyes and clearing his throat, Finn forcibly switched gears.

"It will probably take some time to reach an understanding with the members of the familia."

"It seems that way. Even if we can't get them to understand, we have to give them a clear explanation."

"Mm-hmm. If not, we won't be able to line up an attack on Knossos."

The three of them spoke as they watched the other familia members from a small distance away. Finn had discarded his doubt and gone with his principles, but the others had not come to a clean decision, as he'd been unable to until recently.

The depth of the antagonism between people and monsters was still following them around.

"Starting with Bete, the voices of opposition will get louder, but—"

Finn cut himself off there, raising his head. "First things first…how do we explain this to Aiz?"

Riveria and Gareth both fell silent.

Finn quietly took a deep breath, thinking about his greatest concern.

To start with the end, it would turn out that their anxiety was misplaced. Because even before Finn closed his deal with the heretical monsters, the dark side of the girl had run out of places to go.

EPILOGUE

THE
RESOLUTION
OF A
GIRL

Гэта казка іншага сям'і.

◆

вынік дзяўчыны

A determined assault swiped the boy's body, hitting him with the back of a blade.

Even then, he could tell it was the moves of the Sword Princess without a doubt. Each and every hit was powerful enough to be a finishing blow. It was a flurry of attacks that a Level-3 adventurer had no hope of enduring.

But he was not defeated.

Even as he vomited and his eyes lost focus, nearly blacked out, he still stood back up.

And he refused to move away from the door.

Not only did he refuse to move away, but he came out swinging.

"...?!" Aiz's eyes darted around.

Her chest trembled as Bell Cranell fought back.

At first, she hadn't wanted to fight, but then she'd sunk into despair when she found the boy protecting the vouivre.

Crossing blades with him was difficult, and painful, and something she never, ever wanted to do. She tried to ignore him and chase after the vouivre, but the boy hadn't allowed that.

He brandished everything Aiz had taught him atop the city walls, returning it to her, and at some point, Aiz stopped trying to hold back, callously beating him down.

As she averted her eyes, she crushed his resolve, pummeling the boy whose strength didn't match his determination.

Or that's how it's supposed to be, but—

The situation was changing.

Aiz was in the superior position from start to finish, but the one forced to give ground was—

—Me?

The boy had used a hidden passage to let the vouivre escape.

If she opened the hidden door he was guarding, if she could just somehow get him to move aside, Aiz would be able to kill the monster.

And yet, and yet, and yet.

It didn't matter how bloody his armor got or how battered he ended up—the boy would not stop, clenching his jet-black knife in his fist, swinging again and again.

It sent sparks flying as it clashed with Aiz's Desperate, and his rubellite eyes pierced through Aiz's golden ones all the while. Her blade quivered from an extraordinary strike.

Why...why am I getting pushed back?!

He'd gotten strong. She'd praised him for it once before: The boy had become powerful.

But it wasn't something Aiz had taught him; it was a strength born of protecting someone.

"—!"

Why?!

Why—?!

Why are you going this far?!

I'm not in the wrong!

These monsters have to be killed!

And yet! And yet!

Why are you looking at me like I'm in the wrong?!

—Why?!

As her heart screeched, she unleashed a brutal diagonal slash, clipping the boy's shoulder.

Choking on blood, his body slumping over, the boy with the rubellite eyes that looked ready to roll back into oblivion—didn't fall to the ground.

As he held on, the boy howled with all his might. "Miss Aiz...Miss Aiiiiiiz!!!"

He called Aiz's name over and over, assailing her with shouts, trying desperately to convey the feelings hidden away in his heart.

No!!

No, I won't forgive you.

She would lose if she opened up to accept his attacks, let his feelings reach her.

Aiz wouldn't acknowledge anyone's resolve if they didn't have the strength to back it up. Conversely, that meant if the boy could ever demonstrate a strength that matched his will, she would have to pay attention to him.

She would have to listen to the discussion she'd been rejecting all along.

To the reality she'd been avoiding.

No! Impossible!

Behind the mask of the Sword Princess, she was shaking her head as if a child throwing a tantrum as she parried his knife.

She was losing the mental battle. *Reject it. Don't lose.*

Is this okay to hurt Bell, to hurt me? Is this what you want to do?

Her thoughts spun chaotically as the confused voice in her heart gave birth to swordsmanship full of doubt.

Deep in her heart, someone was whispering to Aiz.

The younger Aiz was looking at her, a heartrending sadness in her eyes.

She pretended not to notice, tried to shake free from the confusion and bewilderment, to clear it away with a blade whose purpose was to kill monsters.

A high-speed diagonal slash. There was no way he could block it.

She swiped up. It was knocked away from the side.

A full swing to mow him down, not letting him evade her attacks.

She thrust forward. He saw through it.

A roundhouse kick. A direct hit.

They engaged and broke off. They overlapped and separated, using the techniques she'd taught him and the tactics he'd stolen. Of all the times to do it, he was wielding them to their utmost effect now.

Until this moment, she'd never encountered such a stout opponent.

It didn't matter what technique she broke out. She couldn't cut through, or break, or crush his resolve. Aiz's eyes wavered.

It didn't stop.

It couldn't be stopped.

His growth was unrestrained.

Using his feelings as sustenance and screaming his maddening wish, he tried to cross the hopeless gap between them. Every minute, second, and instant, he repeatedly accelerated, only to be stopped by his limits. Then he would try to accelerate again. He was improving.

All for the sake of protecting a single monster. A singular desire.

You're embracing that emotion to the point of foolishness!

"—aaAAAAAAAAAAAAAAAAAAAAAAAAAH!" Bell howled.

His howl shook Aiz's arm. His irredeemable desire whittled down the force of the Sword Princess's blade. His two knives with their miniscule power accelerated, finally threatening Aiz for the first time.

"—?!" Aiz unleashed a slash in shock.

Taking aim at Bell, who'd missed with his crimson knife, she unleashed a second attack without a moment's delay. In response, Bell protected himself with the gauntlet on his left arm. The Sword Princess's blow slid off the dir adamantite armor. Bright sparks scattered between them, accompanied by the sound of metal scraping against metal. He pressed in with all his might to enter her reach.

Aiz stood frozen in time.

It lasted an instant, but it certainly happened: His technique had surpassed hers.

And then at extreme close range, their faces practically touching— at the range that was her specialty, Bell swung the goddess's blade up.

"Ahhhhhhhh!"

A purplish arc slashed into the air. Long golden locks of hair billowed in the wind.

Aiz chose to retreat for the first time in this fight—suddenly touching her hand to her chest.

"…!" Her silver breastplate had been grazed, as if something very sharp had cut into it.

It was proof that his howls had reached her—and that he had the strength to back up his resolve.

For an instant, Aiz was at a loss for words.

Defeat. It was now time to confront the reality from which she'd averted her eyes.

Looking at Bell covered in lacerations, her brow furrowed in anguish, and she came out swinging again.

"Ugh—?!" He caught the silver sword that swung down at him with his black knife.

As their swords locked in place, she asked, "Why are you going this far?"

Bell was visibly surprised at Aiz's first question. "I want to help that girl!"

"Are you seriously saying that? Even though it's not a person but a monster?"

"She's different from ordinary monsters! She can talk! We laugh together! We've held hands—with the same emotions that you and I do!"

"You're wrong. It's not the same at all. Not everyone can do that."

At the very least, not all humans could walk hand in hand with monsters.

A confused providence. An awful paradox. A menacing body with claws and fangs that brought to mind the image of blood, a flame that brought death, a voice steeped in brutality. They were all symbolic of things that violated people. They were all signs of the death and destruction that people had borne. They were all objects of hatred.

How could someone take that monstrous hand? How could someone hug that body?

With her sword in a tight grip, Aiz slammed her weapon into Bell's knife in a rebuttal.

"Guh—?!"

"Monsters kill people. They can take so many lives...and make people shed tears..."

A few memories flashed through her mind: a broken-down village. A paradise without peace. A wintery scene of everything destroyed.

There were people wailing, people bleeding—and eventually, people who could move.

There was an adventurer who'd used up all his strength. There was a warrior who'd died nobly protecting his comrades. There was an important person who'd left behind only an empty smile.

Aiz took all these visions, these emotions, and put them into her sword.

"But...don't we as adventurers do the same thing?"

"...—!"

"Your sword—and my knife!"

Aiz's sword dulled at the truth behind his words.

There were people who killed their own and the Evils trying to destroy the city and take untold lives. There were certainly people more repulsive than monsters.

When asked what separated people and monsters, Aiz could not answer.

"I..." As he knocked away her sword and took his distance, the boy hesitated when he opened his mouth.

But with resolve, he swallowed all his doubt and conflict.

Warning bells rang in Aiz's head.

"...I want a place where we can live together with them."

Time stopped moving as he faced her and stated his intentions clearly.

"I want a world where everyone can smile, including Wiene!"

A world where people and monsters can smile together, he'd said.

"What are you talking about...?"

I don't understand.

I don't want to understand.

But she was sure she was already too late and Bell was on a separate path from her. She felt that the white rabbit had come in her dreams and gone to a place she could no longer reach, where she could no longer chase after him.

They were separated by the moonlight shining on her and the dark shade covering him.

Aiz shook her head limply. "Enough...Move."

Aiz couldn't accept it. She could not acknowledge this foolish wish. But Bell would not budge.

Pushed past its limits, his body slipped to its knees. He looked up at Aiz from below, anguish filling his face. He still refused to yield, protecting the door behind him.

"I don't want to…"

"Stop it."

"I don't want to…"

"I'm asking you, please."

"—I can't!"

"—Move!"

They screamed at each other like never before.

I don't want to say any of this. I don't want to do this sort of thing.

What went wrong?

How did we end up on different paths?

I…really wanted to be…with you…more…

Leaving aside the thoughts in her mind, Aiz leveled her sword at Bell's eyes.

"You know I'll cut you down, right?"

"…!"

"It'll hurt a lot. So…" She let out a series of clumsy words, laughable, barely even a threat.

It was Aiz's final warning, all the strength she could muster.

Even then, Bell did not move.

Aiz's eyes filled with sadness. Bell's face twisted in distress.

The next instant, the corners of her eyes flared in determination, and she put her strength into the sword's blade as her hand trembled, creating a silver flash glinting in the moonlight.

"—No!"

The door behind him flung open, and a shadow rushed into Aiz's field of vision.

With a fluttering robe, a slipping hood, a monster leaped out before their eyes, arms spread wide.

"Leave Bell alone!" it shouted in a high voice no different from a human's.

Time stopped. Aiz saw the pale inhuman figure with azure and silver hair. Bell saw her winged back.

"Wiene...? Goddess, why?!" Bell called out in confusion while Aiz stared in disbelief.

Upon seeing the vouivre protect the boy, the flood of emotions she'd just barely managed to hold back threatened to overwhelm her once again.

"Please...don't hurt Bell."

"—!"

Don't look at me like that. Don't look at me with that un-monsterlike gaze, those eyes of a person protecting someone dear to them. It's wrong. This is wrong. It's a lie.

It was nothing like the monsters that Aiz hunted.

As the boy had pleaded before, if there were such a monster, Aiz would—

"Stop...Please don't talk."

Aiz's mask crumbled. Her heart flooded with emotions. The sword she pointed at the girl trembled in agitation. Aiz's head hung like an abandoned doll. Her bangs covered her eyes, erasing everything from her sight, letting herself sink into the darkness gathered at the bottom of her heart.

And then Aiz's back was shrouded in a dark-black blaze as she howled.

"...Why does something like you exist?" she asked in a quiet, desolate whisper that didn't sound like her.

Slowly raising her head, she saw Bell and the beast deathly pale and at a loss for words. A monster in the shape of a human before her eyes, that repulsive monster was all Aiz could see.

"What do you and your kind want?"

"I—I want...to stay with Bell."

"—I won't let you do that."

Aiz's eyes narrowed, sharp as blades. She didn't notice that Bell was frozen as she pierced the petrified monster with her gaze.

"I'll never allow you to roam aboveground like those monsters."

Her back was hot. Her back was burning. Her back was crying out with a maddening hatred.

Abominable. How detestable. I knew it. That endless urge to kill. This is why they have to be killed. Monsters must be destroyed—along with this wish.

"Your claws will hurt someone.

"Your wings will scare people.

"That stone of yours will kill so many of us."

She hammered blame, hatred, and rejection into the monster, listing the world's undeniable truths. She spun her words, led by the black blaze bursting from her back.

Aiz's back was whispering. The strength carved into her back flickered, reminding her, calling to her.

Yes. The crumbling earth. The monsters flowing out. The falling snow, stained red. The trampling, the shouts, the destruction. The screams, the lamentations, the loss.

And that sinister pitch-black demise—

———!

The place I loved was destroyed! Those fond days shattered! My loved ones were stolen from me! First my mother! Then my father!

"Sorry...I'm sorry, Aiz."

And then: "*—Live! You have to live on!*"

And then that kind hand pushed me away, me, the weak one, and then—! Everything. Everything! Everything!! It's all your fault!

The nerves in her eyes burned out. Her back howled with unceasing hatred. The wild black inferno raised a tearful laugh, wrapped in the intense blaze of her cold winter memories, turning the world to a crimson plane of flames and conflict.

Aiz did not scream or go wild or cry.

She put all her rage and hatred, all her sadness and the darkness in her heart into her sword.

Staring down the dragon in front of her, she thrust her weapon.

"I can't turn a blind eye to you," she declared with a sharp, sword-like conviction—a honed, weapon-like resolve.

In the face of Aiz and her eyes filled with a smoldering black flame, the monster was frozen stiff, overwhelmed.

Quietly, it lowered its hands, gazing at the sharp claws that Aiz despised. It grabbed all of the claws on its left hand.

"Huh?"

Was that Aiz or Bell who spoke out?

The monster's breath was ragged as it snapped its nails off.

Crack. With a painful sound, the claws fell to the ground along with chunks of flesh, as drops of blood welled from the fingers like tears.

The hand was bathed in its own blood.

Next its right hand. Then its wings.

As the boy screamed, the monster's clawless hands tore off the dragon wings from its back, letting them fall to the ground with a *thud.*

Aiz froze as its humanlike blood splattered across her cheek.

"Wiene?!" Bell cried out, hugging the monster that collapsed to the ground.

Aiz was speechless as the despicable claws and wings fell at her feet.

Having offered up pieces of its body, almost as reparations, the monster leaned against the boy's chest, struggling to breathe as it looked up.

"If I...if I ever stop being myself again," it started, placing a hand on the red stone in its forehead, "I'll disappear for good this time..."

Her hand moved from her forehead to her chest and her magic stone.

Aiz's mask cracked at the actions that should have been impossible for a monster.

"...I was alone for a long time." The monster slowly moved its lips. "It was cold and dark...and I...Before I became myself...I was alone. Nobody came to save me. Nobody ever held me close..."

She spoke hoarsely, drowning in a sea of dark memories, and that sadness, that loneliness ate away at Aiz.

The blazing black inferno, the fury emanating from her back dissipated.

The outline of the monster melted.

"I was cut; I was hurt…It was scary. And lonely."

Its eyes became dim as a single tear cascaded down its cheek.

What are you doing?! her back cried out.

Don't lose yourself, Aiz's skills shouted.

But she couldn't stop anymore or peel her eyes away from that tear.

The fog of the black flame cleared. The monster completely vanished.

In the end, what she saw standing there was a crying dragon girl and—

"_____"

The younger version of her, a young Aiz hugging the dragon and protecting her, just like Bell, pleading for Aiz to stop with tears in her eyes.

Standing there with her sword thrust out, Aiz could hear her heart cracking. She didn't know how to put these feeling into words.

Should I call you a liar? Give you hell and say I won't forgive you? Tearfully beg you to stop?

Hey. I want to ask you—over there looking at me like you're about to cry:

Was I wrong when I thought we understood each other? Was it all an illusion? What are you doing? Why are you over there?

Why are you protecting that monster?!

You're cruel! Heartless! Inhuman!

You're a ruthless traitor!

We should be one and the same!

On that day, we had everything stolen from us and realized that we had lost everything! We swore to kill monsters together!

Her legs trembled. Deep in her heart, the other Aiz was sobbing.

"But when I was all alone, Bell saved me."

"!"

"When everything was hopeless…when no one would help me, Bell saved me!" cried the girl.

Aiz had come to a realization. When she heard the dragon girl shouting, it all fell into place. The past and present overlapped. The moonlit scene before her eyes and the desolate winter scenery sleeping deep in her memories—the dragon girl and the other, younger version of her melted together. They blended and merged into one person.

Reflecting in her eyes was…*Me…*A crying Aiz.

It's me…

Aiz's composure melted away.

——*She's the same as me!*

The one who had lost everything, who was always alone in the cold and dark, who no one would save.

But—

The boy had appeared for the dragon.

And no one had come for Aiz.

The boy had held out a hand for the dragon.

And no one had taken Aiz's hand.

"Wouldn't it be nice if you met a wonderful partner, too?"

"I hope that, someday, you find a hero—your hero."

She remembered the mother's and father's words.

You both lied to me!! her heart cried out.

A hero never came for me!

It didn't matter how much and how long she cried; no one appeared, until she finally realized that no one would come save her. That was why Aiz had taken up the sword herself!

The dragon before her, that other her, had her hero appear before her!

No fair! No fair! No fair!

No one came for me! I had no choice but to choose the sword!

Inside her crumbling heart, the young Aiz's whines echoed. The girl was crying, the sobs of the weaker version of her she'd left behind.

Aiz looked at Bell, at the dragon girl's one and only hero holding her tight.

Anguish filled her. Sorrow enveloped her. Her golden eyes trembled in envy.

"............"

As she sealed away the remnants of her past with her last scraps of willpower...Aiz slumped over, like a doll whose strings had snapped. The sword she'd thrust out clattered to the floor.

"...I can't kill this vouivre anymore," she admitted in a hoarse voice, all she could wring out of her worn-down mind and body.

"Miss...Aiz..."

"I...I can't help feeling you two were right...That's why I can't do it."

"..."

"I can't fight you anymore."

She was bathed in moonlight, not raising her head.

She couldn't bring herself to look at the dragon girl or the boy's face, because she was afraid she might start hurling absurdities at them.

Upon losing her composure as the Sword Princess and the armor of an adventurer, Aiz was just a girl. A ground-down, empty shell of longing that had always waited for a hero.

"...—Gh."

Left frozen by that shape, Bell pulled back the hand he'd started to extend, averting his eyes. He hugged the dragon girl close so her slender shoulders wouldn't leave his hands.

Aiz didn't say anything.

No self-deprecating laugh, no mournful voice, no falling tears. As she resigned herself, she mustered the last conscious thought of her rational mind and clumsily took an elixir out of her pouch.

"I can't help you...I'll be here."

"Miss Aiz..."

She placed it on the stone pavement and stepped back, turning away.

"Go."

"...Thank you."

Bell took the elixir and left with the girl. Aiz didn't turn around. Her golden hair fluttered in the wind. Forgetting to sheathe her sword, she let her gaze fall to the ground as the white moonlight bathed her in its glow.

On this day, Aiz broke her vow, the precious promise she'd made with herself: that monsters were to be killed.

"Aiz."

"…"

"Is this okay?"

"…Yes."

"…"

"…"

"I'll head back."

"…Thank…you."

"What do you have to thank me for?"

The young man who'd appeared, the werewolf who'd seen it all from start to finish, left without saying anything.

Tranquility set in again. She was left behind.

The girl moved her lips as she looked up at the night sky.

"Someone…help me."

Status Lv.6

STRENGTH:	H 100	DEFENSE:	H 117
DEXTERITY:	H 131	AGILITY:	H 112
MAGIC:	H 154		
HUNTER:	G	IMMUNITY:	G
KNIGHT:	H	SPIRIT HEALING:	I

MAGIC: Airiel

- Enchantment
- Wind Element
- Chant: "Awaken, Tempest"

SKILL: Avenger

- Active Trigger.
- Enhances attack power against monsters.
- Greatly enhances attack power against dragon-type enemies.
- Effect becomes more powerful as the user's feelings of hatred increase.

FAVORITE WEAPON: Desperate

- Unbreakable, a superior Durandal.
- The only weapon that has endured the full force of Avenger, which is the strongest skill currently known among all races and familias. The only other exception was Sword Yell, which discouraged Aiz from breaking her bond with Riveria and the others during her youth.
- In the past, Aiz cracked this unbreakable blade when she combined her magic with a storming black wind.

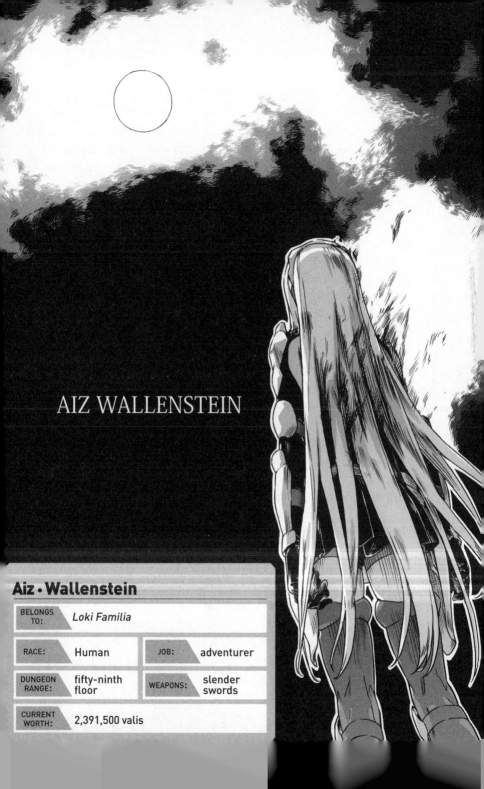

AIZ WALLENSTEIN

Aiz · Wallenstein

BELONGS TO:	*Loki Familia*

RACE:	Human	**JOB:**	adventurer
DUNGEON RANGE:	fifty-ninth floor	**WEAPONS:**	slender swords
CURRENT WORTH:	2,391,500 valis		

Afterword

I'm sure that some people may have noticed, but the sequence of events in this book was shifted from the main series to make it easier to follow. It might be interesting to compare the two stories.

On that note, this is the tenth book of the side story.

I often wonder what I should show in this offshoot, but this time, I went with "the victims of Bell Cranell." That might not be the best way to put it. I may have been affected by the main character of the main series.

The protagonist of the main series is weaker than the team in the side story, and his relationship to them isn't that straightforward. I couldn't use the standard literary technique of having him arrive to help them in a pinch. If he went to help, he would end up getting saved himself. Then what to do? Was there some other way to show his attitude toward life?

As we grow up, there are moments when we're jealous of children. When I wrote the phrase "man-made hero" in this book, I thought it was mean, even though I was the one writing it. I suspect there are a lot of people who think that something they're doing is superficial and they have no choice but to keep going at it. The truth is, I wanted to do a plot where Thousand Elf betrayed them and joined the side of the hero in the main series, leading a clash between her and her elven teacher à la the color insert in the eleventh book of the main series with master and disciple squaring off. But in the process of writing, I ended up wanting to see a certain character's true feelings, which is why I changed course. I'm sorry, Miss Fairy Heroine. Please keep up all your hard work, Mr. Hero, for her sake.

I'd like to move to giving my thanks, albeit sooner than usual.

To my editors Takahashi and Matsumoto, I'm incredibly sorry for turning in my manuscript late as always. To chief editor Kitamura, I'm sorry for making you worry about this indecisive author. To Kiyotaka Haimura, who provided these wonderful illustrations, your drawings are always an incredible help. Thank you. And to everyone who helped make this book happen, I extend my thanks.

There will be a drama CD going on sale with this tenth volume of the side story. To all those who helped with that endeavor, you have my sincere gratitude. And to the cast who managed to overcome a terrible script, thank you. I thought I would die of embarrassment listening to it. I'm sorry (particularly to —nishi and —moto).

With this book, the side series has reached its third arc, and it's about time to put a period on the plot that's been continuing since the first book. It would be wonderful if you could keep watching over the characters as they reach their respective fates.

To all the readers, thank you for reading this far.

Let's meet again in the next volume.

Fujino Omori